BELOVED
IN THE ATL
OUT IN THE LIGHT

SHAUN HECKSTALL

Paperback ISBN: 979-8-9927963-0-8
Hardcover ISBN: 979-8-9927963-1-5
eBook (EPUB) ISBN: 979-8-9927963-2-2
eBook (PDF) ISBN: 979-8-9927963-3-9

This book is dedicated to…

John 1:14

Sharon, my forever person—

I love the way you call me "Shaunie Shaun!"

You a*re my heartbeat.*

Donnay, my ride-or-die family.

Curtis, my friend who believed in me when no one else would. This is for the New York Co-op City block that produced you—and for the foundation your words still give me. I carry them every day.

To every student I've taught over the years—

You are etched into this work.

Especially to the scholars of **Mays High School** and **Tri-Cities High School**:

You grew me as a teacher, received me as a mentor, and taught me what ATL swag *really* is. That rhythm, that pride, that brilliance—I carry it in my bones.

This one is especially for the **Classes of 1999 and 2000.** Y'all didn't just rep Atlanta. **You are Atlanta.** Truly *"a legacy to keep and an image to uphold."*

To **Kandi** and **Big Boi**— I knew what was creatively possible before the world caught on, because I taught y'all. And y'all been showing your teacher the way ever since. I hope this book makes you proud.

PROLOGUE

"You can't talk about Southern hip-hop without talking about that night. It was one of the biggest moments in ATL history."
— *Shanti Das, on André 3000 and the 1995 Source Awards, The Atlanta Journal-Constitution*, November 2, 2023.

I, the ATL, got something to say—a story to tell

I swear to tell the truth, the whole truth, and nothing but the truth—so help me MLK.

And oh yeah—thank you, Shaun, for letting me take the stage. It's only right. After all, I've been speaking through your pen all along.

You and I? We know how we move.

"The party don't start 'til I walk in, and I probably won't leave until the thang ends. But in the meantime, and in between time—"

But I ain't just here to party.

I'm here to bear witness.

To tell the story of love, of loss, of blood in the red clay.

To tell the truth about what it really means to be beloved in the ATL.

You know who I am.

I'm the ATL. But I wasn't always.

I was born in 1837, just another Southern city fighting to find my place. Burned to the ground. Rebuilt. Scarred but standing. For years, I was Atlanta—polite, buttoned-up, striving to prove myself.

Then one night, on a stage in Los Angeles, the pastor, the prophet, stepped up to the mic and said what needed to be said.

It was 1995. The Source Awards. Andre 3000 looked out at a room that never respected us and said:

The South got something to say.

In that moment, I was baptized.

At 158 years old, I went from Atlanta to the ATL. Andre spoke it into existence, and ever since, I've been telling the world—

I got something to say.

I'm more than just peach trees and politeness. Morehouse men gonna get my Spelman girls across the way to let their hair down. If not, the Clark girls got them covered. You gotta know this in these ATL streets- ass gonna get got-These girls? Country-fed, hot, seasoned just right—ages 21 to 81. Please believe it.

I'm trap beats and church choirs. My Varsity can heal your blues after a concert at the Fox or a curbside pickup at Emory Hospital. I'm Peachtree Street corners that seem never-ending and boardrooms eager to let beautiful, educated Black people ascend.

I'm love and struggle. History and hope.

But here's the thing.

For centuries, I poured out love like a Centennial Park fountain. Too often, love ain't poured back.

Grandma always says,

"You gotta bring some to get some."

Out of the mouth of a teenage mother, the words would sound like fighting words. But from Grandma—the wisdom of many years on a job that gave her nothing—gave pause. I, the ATL, was grounded in the solid concrete of urban wisdom.

I've tried to take Grandma's wisdom - and, I ain't snitching—but I've had to fight my own. And I got some Black eyes to prove it.

Does anyone know how we lost the fight to have my airport hold just one last name? Jackson—the first Black mayor—would have been enough. But we had to be too busy to hate, giving credence to a one-time segregationist. But I digress.

I've been claimed, codified, and sometimes over-commercialized. The dream of Black excellence I hold so dear? It's threatened.

Threatened by crime that scars my streets. By gentrification that locks my people out. By a world that takes my culture, my music, my soul—but never truly sees me.

But stay tuned. Through this love story—this thriller—I got something to say.

Now that you're listening like a tourist on vacation, curious about my prose, you ask:

What do I want?

My motivation ain't complex. As Deion—our number 21—recently said:

I ain't hard to find.

So, along similar lines, I want to be truly loved. Not just by the ones passing through my airport, snapping selfies with my murals, claiming they're from here when they're not.

I want the kind of love Damien and Sheena feel whenever they hear Xscape or Lil Jon. The kind of love that comes from knowing me—all of me.

From Bankhead to Buckhead. From Grady Babies to Spelman grads.

I'm telling this story because I need you to see me. To love me the way Damien Kirkland Deburg and Sheena Elise Colucci love me.

Damien knows my streets. Sheena feels my heartbeat in every song, every sermon, every protest. Together, they're part of my redemption story.

Because this isn't just their journey.

It's mine, too.

But before this becomes all about me, let me tell you about the two souls who carry my heartbeat in their veins.

Because my story isn't just mine.

It lives in two soon-to-be lovers who walk my streets, embody my songs, and crave my love—

Swag my spirit, rep my name, embody my love.

My heart and my soul—Damien and Sheena—are here.

Here is our story.

BeLoved in the ATL: Out in the Light.

INTRODUCTION

Atlanta. It's a romantic thriller. A love story—yeah, I know… another love story.

You're already thinking, *Not me. I don't need that.*

But wait—before you brush it off, before you roll your eyes—

Let's get something straight.

This ain't just love and butterflies.

This is *the* A-T-L.

And no, my name ain't "Atlanta."

That's what outsiders call me.

Round here? I'm the ATL.

The city with too much soul to sleep. Too much history to fake.

So before I tell you about Sheena and Damien—before I spill a single secret—

Let me check myself.

Better yet—

Let me check you.

Because this ain't just a story.

It's a reckoning.

And yeah… it starts with love. But it doesn't end there.

So remember this. Tuck it in your spirit as you lend me your imagination:

In the A-T-L, everybody wanna be loved…

until the city calls you out in the light.

And Sheena and Damien? Love ain't the only thing waiting in the dark.

"Oh, hell no! Y'all done up and done it!"

And now, right when I'm trying to roll out this love story—BOOM—ATL don't let me.

As I speak (cuz I got something to say), somebody's car is creeping slow, bass knocking, shaking the block like it got something to prove—

and they blasting—you guessed it—Usher Raymond.

It's driving me crazy (driving me crazy)
Because I'm missing my baby (missing my baby)
I'm going out of my mind and I'm running out of time...

Damn.

Usher—interrupting me. Shit, I know it's worth it—but.

Just like that, the story ain't just beginning—it's rolling.

This might be the part that doesn't just throw us into the book... but straight into the movie.

Survival.

And the story.

In the ATL, everybody wanna be loved... until the streets call you out.

So, before I start to digress—what's Our Story?

In a city where dreams rise with the red clay-stained heated streets and southern secrets simmer like J.R. Crickets wing grease—slow and low down under the surface—

one man's search for intimacy becomes a journey through love, loss, and redemption.

Detective Damien Kirkland DeBerg, a Benjamin Elijah Mays High School graduate, knows Atlanta like the back of his hand.

Washington Road goes to Campbellton Road, and Cascade goes to Southwest Atlanta.

For him, the ATL's streets, stories, and soul collide in authentic ATL pride.

But when renowned Criminal Psychologist Sheena Elise Colucci, Ph.D.—specializing in Black body efficacy and African-American social justice reform—

herself a Mays High School graduate and his high school sweetheart,

the woman who's always seen through his armor,

steps back into his life—

he's forced to confront the truths he's buried deep:

his longing for connection, his fear of vulnerability, and his desperate need to be truly seen.

As Damien navigates Atlanta's vibrant culture—from the trap beats of the city's music scene to the boardrooms of its most influential players—

he's faced with the ultimate question:

Can love bring him out of the shadows, or will his past keep him hidden forever?

But before we go forward,

let's look back.

Before the headlines, before the crime, before we lost our way. Let's take it back.
We need a flashback.
To when it was just us—young, reckless, in love with the city, in love with the dream.
When we were just beginning to learn what it meant to be—
Beloved in the ATL.

Mays High School 2000, Talent Show Sign-Ups

The lunch bell had barely settled before Damien was already at Sheena's desk again, leaning across her space like he had a right to be there. She barely had time to react before—
Splat.
Her Capri Sun tumbled over, splashing sticky juice all over Melloni's sleeve.
"Ugh! Damien!" Melloni yelped, jumping back like the juice was acid. "Would you stop already? We see you—I mean, Sheee-naaaaah sees you!"
Laughter rippled through the classroom, loud and knowing. Everybody at Mays knew Damien had been trying to get Sheena's attention since he transferred at the end of tenth grade. It was a

game at this point, a daily battle between Damien's persistence and Sheena's indifference—if that's what you wanted to call it.

Melloni, the beautiful, over-confident, plus-size mutual friend, loud and awkward, was built for Therrell, but her mama taught math there and wasn't about to spend her life juggling a full-time job and keeping her daughter in line. "Ah, no, thank you," she had said when picking a school. So, Melloni landed at Mays, and with a genius for both numbers and matchmaking, she was in the perfect position to stir the pot.

"So... do y'all go together yet?" she blurted, her words bouncing between them like a pinball.

"'Cause, like, what are y'all waiting for? She likes you, and you know he's all lovey-lovie for you, Sheena. Or should I be the first to say it—Shee and Day from the A."

She clapped her hands, eyes wide. "Whooooo! I like that. Shee and Day—the First Couple of the A!"

Then, with a grin:
"And really though, y'all need to do something together in the talent show. That would be so cute."

Damien raised a brow, grinning despite himself.

And then—*serendipitously*, in perfect unison, as if Babyface and Toni Braxton had whispered it into their souls...

As if Ryan Michelle Bathe and Sterling K. Brown had handed them a script soaked in forever...

Sheena and Damien spoke at the same time, voices wrapped in the kind of joy only Black love could carry.

"Shee and Day..."
"...That got a ring to it."
"That's got a ring."

Then, both stepped back into their individual roles.

Sheena sucked her teeth, " What talent does he have besides being cute and clumsy?"

Damien dropped his head like he'd been hit. But he came back quick. "So, you do think I'm cute?"

"She does!" Melloni jumped in before Sheena could deflect. "You cute and all—but Sheena right. You clumsy. So maybe the talent show was a bad idea. Y'all just trade numbers, get together, and walk around Greenbriar like y'all not broke."

Damien scoffed. " If I'm broke, it's 'cause every time we go somewhere, I'm the one paying. Right, broke friend? Straight-A math student, but still broke."

Melloni crossed her arms, unbothered. "Knowledge is power. And since I am an 'A student' and y'all are not—N.O.T.-not" she smirked, "I say y'all be a couple and get in the talent show."

Damien threw his hands up, "I rap. I got bars."

Sheena leaned back, eyebrows raised. "Oh, you got bars?"

He nodded. "Yeah, and you write poetry. So, let's put it together. A guy-girl rap duo. We gonna be legendary- hot fo life -fo sure - we will go down in Mays High History."

Sheena didn't brush him off for the first time in three months.

"Say less. We can get together after school- I skip the bus- can you drive me home?-live right off Cascade".

And before Melloni could dub them the next Jay-Z and Beyoncé, they were writing, performing, and winning before anybody could say a word.

The moment was forever sealed in the school yearbook, with their song reprinted in full and a photo of them holding their trophy, Damien cheesing and Sheena pretending it was no big deal.

But it was.

A song so legendary that this novel carries its name.

"Beloved in the ATL" (Reprinted with Permission from the Mays High Yearbook, Class of 1999)

Verse 1: Sheena
Yo, it's Sheena on the scene, reppin' B.E. Mays,
ATL fire, we were born to blaze.
From the West End streets to the skyline dreams,
Got the A-Town pride, yeah, you know what it means.
We got soul food rhythm, fried chicken beats,
Peach State vibes, bringing heat to the streets.
Classrooms to strip clubs, we all find a groove,
ATL life, yeah, we always improve.
Hook (Together)
BeLoved in the ATL, where the streets don't sleep,
From the boulevard grind to the passion we keep.
It's a vibe, it's a movement, it's the city we claim,
ATL, be-loved, in the heart, in the name.
Verse 2: Damien
This Damien, the protector, nightlight glow,
Security at the door, but my heart's on show.
From Bankhead to Buckhead, we hustle and strive,
ATL's our rhythm, it keeps the soul alive.
We got crunk with Lil Jon, but we did our own thing,
Made the beat knock harder, let the hood choir sing.
Talent show legends, yeah, the crowd got loud,
We built love in the A, and made our city proud.
Hook (Together)
Be-loved in the ATL, where the streets don't sleep,
From the boulevard grind to the passion we keep.
It's a vibe, it's a movement, it's the city we claim,
ATL, be-loved, in the heart, in the name.
Bridge (Sheena & Damien)
Sheena: The ATL breeze, the Varsity fries,
Damien: The rooftop views, the West End ties.
Sheena: From Piedmont Park to Cascade we roll,
Damien: ATL love, is where our stories unfolds.
Hook (Together)

BeLoved in the ATL, where the streets don't sleep,
From the boulevard grind to the passion we keep.
It's a vibe, it's a movement, it's the city we claim,
ATL, BeLoved, in the heart, in the name.

It was just a song. Just a performance. Just a night.

Sheena and Damien had no idea that night would become legend.

Years later, when everything fell apart, Atlanta wasn't just home—it was a battlefield.

Sheena would think back to this. Damien would pull strength from this moment.

Back to when being Beloved in the ATL wasn't just a song—

It was a bond of between high school sweethearts in the city they loved that loved them.

It was being in the spotlight.

Because like it's been said and they soon learned—in the ATL, everybody wanna be loved… until the city calls you out in the light.

CHAPTER 1

TWO LOVES ONE CITY

Moment I: Two Loves, One City

Damien Kirkland DeBurg had two loves.

And with them, his dreams slipped away—

Of being a great husband and the best father.
Of carrying the weight of a father he barely knew.
Of holding onto a girl who had already slipped through the holes in his life.
Of keeping the 'A' safe.

Not just from the filthy pilferers in the streets—
but from the ruthless criminals in the offices.

To Damien, love was what Black women in the South called "slow cooking time"—

You wait, you cook, you wait, you season, you wait, you cook.

And when you cook—there will be problems.

The city stretched out before him—alive, restless.

Atlanta never really slept, even when her streets emptied.
She hummed, pulsed—like a subwoofer under his skin.

Damien needed the ATL.

He needed Sheena Elise Colucci.

If he couldn't save them—
The city—haunted by a killer lurking in Atlanta's streets.
All the while, the conservative media's sycophants had already
branded him:
"The Wayne Williams 2.0 Conspiracy Theorist."
"The Woke Black, Not Blue Detective."
Breathing in pollen-laden vitriol,
Damien exhaled, poised vigilance at the weight of it all.
And her.
Dark brown, intelligent, intimate—the beauty he had always
known.
The boy became a man doing blue work to Black bodies—work
she would never agree with.
The things that kept him from coming for her.
And if he lost them—
Something inside him would wither.
And he wasn't sure if he'd ever get it back.
The rain hit the windshield in steady taps as he turned onto
Peachtree, passing the glowing marquee of the Fox Theatre.
Neon bled into the pavement, red and gold streaks reflecting
in the water pooled along the curbs.
ATL always shook her ass when it rained.

Something about the water made her shimmer, sensual, and violent in the same breath. A city dipped in gold, washed in blood.

He rolled the window down slightly.

Honeysuckle.

Asphalt.

Lemon pepper wings.

It always leaves my visitors and newbies stuttering—

"Is that—wait… is that the pretty brown girl—"

"With blonde hair—rockin' a drawstring split-hem cami dress—"

"With the new Jordan 5's… with—"

"Wait—wait, with the dude in the business suit?"

Classic ATL stuttering. Every time.

A little street, a little high fashion.

A little bougie, a little hood.

Luxury and hustle, all in one city, all in one moment.

Yep, only in the ATL could sophistication get a sprinkle of seasoning—then sold right back to the same people who once called its creators 'ghetto.'

Continuing along highways tangled in deep green plumes—sometimes too much green—too many urban billboards waved back:

"We in this thang!" – A declaration, a promise, a flex.

"Buy our perfume!" – Smelling like money is half the battle.

"We can make you fly, baby!" – Delta, private jets, or dreams too big for a small town.

"Oh, that ATL Kitchen Style Restaurant smell!" – Smoked turkey, mac 'n' cheese, collards, and peach cobbler—making even the freeway feel like Sunday dinner.

"Nigga—Big Daddy's."

"No, Nigga—This Is It!"

A scent that could only belong to the ATL- that no one can honestly agree on.

The ATL is a city that talks back—

Even through the billboards.

Then.

The music shifted on the radio.

Greg Street was trying to outdo Ryan Cameron by spinning T.I. on V-103.

The beat pounded, matching his pulse. A city built on ambition.

"Big things poppin', little things stoppin'."

Yeah. That was Atlanta.

Unapologetic.

Ambitious.

And a little ratchet.

His fingers tapped against the wheel.

But as he reached for the dial, he hesitated.

The station flipped.

Xscape. "Who Can I Run To."

The shift hit hard—

Like turning a corner and running straight into memory. Soft. Soulful. Painfully familiar.

On one station, T.I. roared Atlanta's grind. On the other, his wife Tiny crooned Atlanta's vulnerability.

The hard and the soft. The rapper and the singer. The hustle and the heart.

Keeping Peachtree Street hot—even when love ran cold.

Like him and Sheena.

Damien sighed, his thoughts circling back to her like they always did.

Sandy brown skin. A natural kind of fine. Sensual for no reason.

Sheena carried herself with a calm, steady focus.

No extra movement.

No wasted words.

She just was.

But now, he was looking back—through the eyes of a grown man, a Black man with a lonely heart. Was he being juvenile, chasing a memory? Longing for something that had never truly been?

Years go by. People change.

I'm engaged in a schoolboy crush.

We were just kids- I'm on some real Boys II Men shit 'bout now-way deep in my feelings.

The thought stung. Even now, he didn't know if it was love or a needful fantasy.

He had kissed her once.

The memory flickered against the rain-slick streets, warm and weightless.

Even if the softest kiss was all they had ever shared, her energy lingered.

Made it impossible to forget.

She had been his sanctuary once.

The one person who saw him.

Not as a detective. Not as a protector. As Damien.

But he lost her.

If I ever really had her.

And us now? I only need her professional help- that's why she came.

The city hummed beneath him.

The rain whispered across the windshield.

And her name still sat heavy in his chest.

It wasn't a fiery breakup.

No screaming match. No grand betrayal.

They were just kids at the end of high school.

She had just… left.

Accepted to Spelman—one of the best HBCUs in the country, undeniably the best for women.

But instead, she chose The Howard University—

Lived in the Quads—then Slow Hall.

Walked up and down Georgia Avenue—never stopped at Cook, where the football players stayed.

Took classes in Douglass Hall.

Ate French fries in the Punch Out.

Had the deep truth and meaning of 'HU—You Know!' etched in her soul—right beside the ATL.

And she never physically came back to the ATL.

Damien could still see that hot August morning.

The airport. The jet fuel. The sunbaked pavement. The political billboards.

The knot in his throat tightened as she stepped away— The same ache he'd felt as a boy, crumbling into his aunt's arms at his mother's funeral.

And just like his mother, Sheena left.

"Shee! Shee!" he had called out—

A last attempt to hold onto something sweet and familiar.

But she was already gone.

Disappearing into the crowd with a boarding pass in hand—

And the sky waiting to carry her far away.

And he let her go.

For eight years, he tried to fill the void.

Work.

Marriage.

Distractions.

None of it stuck.

Why didn't I reach out to her?

I heard she was happy and thriving at Howard.

A girl like that? She had to have moved on.

Howard had a lot of guys who she could love.

And even if—if I had—

the reflection responded with a head shake he was unaware of—

What would I have even said?

Would I have stuttered through small talk?

Would she have looked at me with soft nostalgia or distant pity?

Would she have even picked up?

I did the right thing…?

The thought sat heavy, settling deep in his chest.

Rhythmic.

Unshaken.

A silent, knowing beat inside him.

His marriage had been a slow bleed.

Tentative sex, performed like an obligation.

Conversations, filled with avoidance and disapproval—never quite finding the words that mattered.

Valentine's Day candy.

But no real sugar.

He craved intimacy.

He knew she was just faking it.

Because if it was real...

She would've let him make her scream—for real, real.

He craved real connection.

The kind that hit almost too deep.

Where her body answered before her lips did—

Where pleasure built, slow and undeniable—

Toes curling, back arching—tickling her in all the right places.

That kind of love—

The one that whispered in soft curves and slow steps,

that dared you to come closer.

More warmth.

More pull.

More of what you ain't had in too long.

So good.

So real.

The kind he'd only ever had with Sheena.

Or had he just convinced himself of that?

He knew from the tingle she said she felt—from their kiss.

The kind that only existed when you grew up together in the 'ATL.'

The Ritz-Carlton loomed ahead, its golden lights pooling against the wet pavement.

Damien pulled into the valet, handing over his keys without a word.

Deep breath. Steady hands.

Jacket straightened.

Mind focused.

He stepped inside.

His friend, Rory Davis—a Black gay man from an old-money Savannah family—had been his quiet finishing school, refining the raw edges of a life that began on Campbellton Road in the heart of SWATS. Rory had prepared him to move through wealthy worlds that once felt foreign, teaching him the subtle codes of power and presence without ever making him feel less than.

Their friendship was more than a trade-off—it was a quiet revolution, a sanctuary in a world that tried to make Black men choose between love and masculinity. In a society where their bodies were heinously labeled "punk" or "sissy" for expressing anything beyond hardened survival, their bond stood defiant.

"I love you, Rory Davis."

"I love you, Damien DeBurg."

No disclaimers. No justifications. Just boys—brothers—period.

A straight Black man and a gay Black man, standing in their own fullness, beyond the scripts of society. Their bond had nothing to prove, no hyper-masculine code to follow. Just brotherhood.

Because the world had already taught Black men to fear each other, to see difference as a threat, to stay in the boxes that white patriarchy had built for them.

Gay or straight, the world still called them boy.

But here, they had reclaimed something stolen. True, unguarded humanity.

The lobby buzzed with quiet elegance—soft murmurs, clinking glasses, the hum of wealth moving effortlessly through the room.

But Damien's focus was singular.

Her.

He moved through the restaurant, already claiming his reserved table in his mind.

Then—

The hostess greeted him, her tone polite but pointed.

"Right this way. Your party is already here."

Already here?

A slight, knowing smirk played at the corner of Damien's lips.

She was here. Waiting for him.

Every step closer to her did something he hadn't felt in years.

It grounded him even as it made him tremble—more than a high school reunion.

It steadied and stimulated something restless inside him—more than a swirling drink of smooth liqueur.

It reminded him who he was and that he had only ever been with her. A boy spiraling upward into a man.

Since she left, he had loved at, but never in love.

"Are you in love?"

"Not just sex?"

"Not just company?"

Strange and weak questions lingered on those freaks who only came out at night.

"Because you can't make a hoe a housewife, bruh."

But it was never real love—just the kind that unraveled him with every failed attempt to move on.

Moment II: Table for Two After All These Years

And then—

There she was.

Damien's breath slowed as his gaze locked onto her.

At the table-fashion runway-wedding alive.

She was impossible to miss.

Essence—sparkled.

Black excellence. Black beauty. Black power.

Her-"Shee!". Black womanhood does not tremble at the white gaze because, at the beginning of it all, it authored it.

Yet, she had never been anything but missed.

Sheena Elise Colucci.

The one who'd walked away.

The one he needed now more than ever.

"Shee!"

"Shay-Baby!"

Sheena sat with her back straight, her posture as poised as ever. Her Hershe chocolate dark brown skin glowed from spa oil under the dim lights, and her eyes—those damn pretty light brown eyes—locked onto him the moment he entered the room. The deep emerald green of her Cushnie slip dress shimmered softly, its simplicity a quiet declaration of confidence. Her Brother Vellies heels clicked softly on the floor as she rose to greet him—elegant, polished, and impossibly composed.

She was the same, yet ultimately changed.

Damien swallowed hard, suddenly unsure of himself.

But there was no turning back now.

"Damien."

Her voice was smooth and steady. But something else was

underneath—a softness, a vulnerability he hadn't heard in years. He missed all of her.

"She!"—covered in Christmas morning, boyish glee—squeaked out.

"I mean, Dr. Sheena Elise Colucci."

He inadvertently licked away her almost too-sweet chocolate milk from his full, perched lips and ivory teeth.

He sat across from her, his heart pounding like the bass line of an Outkast track.

I'm glad you asked me here," she said, her lips curving into a soft, Mac makeup-painted smile

"She," he murmured before he could stop himself, the name slipping from his lips like a habit he couldn't break.

"I am glad you came." "And you are here early because I'm not late," he said almost defensively, suggesting he would never have been late—no, not now.

She knew Damien; he meant nothing about it, offering a facial glow communicating acceptance.

They sat silently for a moment, the weight of the past pressing down between them. Their thoughts scrambled, circling back over missed opportunities to hold hands, hearing one another laugh at insider jokes, and not wanting to make excuses for birthdays missed and tender kisses never had.

Finally, Sheena broke the silence of their lost years.

"You said it was important."

"It is." Damien moved slowly, reaching for the glass of water before him. His fingers lingered on the condensation, his movements cautious and deliberate—buying himself time.

She tilted her head slightly, studying him the way she always had when she was about to pick apart a problem. There was no rush, no urgency in her voice. Just calm curiosity.

"Please, share."

Her confidence was calculated and honed by experience. But her face still held traces of the girlhood charm she refused to surrender—to a system, to a world that took from Black women daily, overpaid their lesser white counterparts, and still had the audacity to ask for more.

The kind of whiteness that overindulged mediocrity—ran for Congress in Georgia with a high school level emotional maturity where John Lewis served yet still demanded validation.

That necessitated the so-true reprimand:

"Bleach. Blond. Bad-built. Butch-body."

And when the scales tipped? Black women were left holding up the weight of the world—clocking the most hours, reaping the least return.

Damien exhaled, his gaze flickering around the room before landing back on her. The dim lights of the Ritz-Carlton dining room cast soft shadows across her face, but her eyes—those light brown eyes that had haunted him for years—never wavered.

"It's about the case. The murders."

His voice dropped, low and steady.

"Some in the media, especially on social media, are calling it Wayne Williams 2.0."

And just like that, the illusion cracked.

Damien discreetly interrupted what they had been pretending this was.

No—

Was it the case?

Or was it love?

The real reason he had contacted her blurred—duty and desire tangled so tight he couldn't tell where one ended and the other began.

The tablecloth rippled, elegant and effortless—like a designer skirt.

Then—

The government folder pulled up the skirt.

Nothing between them had ever been simple.

This moment was no different.

Case or love—Atlanta wouldn't let them separate the two.

Sheena's posture shifted ever so slightly, subtly tensing her shoulders.

"Wayne Williams?"

"Yeah."

Damien's lips pressed into a tight line.

"It's horrific. The pictures... they turn my stomach. God only knows how we call ourselves human. Let alone evolved."

He shook his head, his voice rough, strained.

"Four, maybe five Black males. If you count this last one."

Silence settled between them, thick as the humid night pressing against the windows.

And then—without warning—the image invaded his mind.

A charred, unrecognizable body.

The smell of burned flesh, suffocating even in memory.

The tablecloth rippled as his fist clenched, knuckles whitening against the pristine linen.

He left it behind to see her tonight.

And yet—

It was still here.

Sheena didn't speak immediately.

But he saw it—the shift.

The soft ease of their reunion slipping away.

The professional mask fell into place.

Dr. Colucci, criminologist, profiler—the one who made sense of chaos.

And for once?

He needed that version of her.

"You believe the cases are connected?" she asked, voice steady.

Damien nodded. "Yes. And now we've got a problem."

He ran a hand down his face, trying to dispel the tension coiling in his chest.

"The first three victims? Nobodies. Homeless. Day laborers.

But the last one?"

His gaze locked onto hers.

"I am not sure; one was connected. Wealthy. A frat guy and recently inducted into the 100 Black Men, a family man. Friends with people in the mayor's office."

Sheena leaned in, brow furrowed.

She was listening now.

"If it matters," she said, soft but edging, "tell me now. The 'streets' of Atlanta must be talking. They always do."

Her words settled between them.

She was right.

ATL never forgets.

Its past bled into its present, lingering like red clay that never washed off.

This case? A history scratching at old wounds, demanding to be acknowledged.

Damien exhaled.

Moment III: One of the First to Die- Jonathan

"Wayne Williams 2.0. Here it is."

Sheena bobbed her head slowly, tracing her fingernail across the table, making mental notes.

A name designed to make people remember.

"But it's more than that," she said. "This thing's ruffling feathers in high places—and I don't know why."

"I remember what it felt like when Black girls and boys went missing," Damien said. "And I remember how the money dried up. Deals stopped coming Atlanta's way. You know they've always pushed that narrative—'a city too busy to hate'—but then they get to the Georgia Dome and start compromising with the same folks who want us out of the city. Out of the state."

He paused, let the weight of the words settle.

"The first victim appeared not long after the pandemic started. His name was Jonathan Peters. A beautiful Black boy from Mobile, Alabama. He came to Atlanta believing two things: that being smart was an asset, and being gay was no longer a liability."

Sheena's eyes narrowed. Damien continued.

"His family was humble, proud. He wasn't a standout student, but he had heart. He enrolled at Georgia State—downtown— where the city never sleeps. Found his people: artists, dreamers, creatives. One of them told him he should've been at SCAD, not studying poli-sci. He started to believe them.

Then COVID hit.

Money dried up. He couch-surfed. Slept in the library when it got bad. Hustled to get by. Told himself it was part of the journey—all great artists suffer before they make it.

But even then, he kept going to church. Like most Black folks from the South—when life gets hard, you go to church."

Damien traced the condensation on his glass.

"But things got complicated. He started trading favors just to survive. A little money here. A place to stay there. He didn't feel exploited. He didn't feel like a victim. It was just life. The same way he had traded favors to pay his senior fees in high school. The same way he had to when his own father turned his back on him."

Damien's voice dipped.

"'I don't have a son if he's gay.' That's what the man said."

Sheena's eyes dimmed. She listened.

"Jonathan carried that rejection quietly. But he kept going. Kept believing.

Then—he disappeared.

They found his body by a creek, at the edge of a construction site. Wrists bound with an ironing cord. Signs of sexual assault. Strangled. Then burned. Left like trash.

At first, the police thought he was just another homeless case. Worn clothes. No ID. Didn't 'look' like a Georgia State student. Another tragic but forgettable Black boy in Atlanta.

But then—"

He looked directly at Sheena.

"The binding. The burning. The location."

"No billboard," she whispered. "Not important enough."

He nodded. "The site? It wasn't just any abandoned lot. It was being turned into a church. A second location for a fast-growing congregation. The land was sealed off. No one was supposed to be there.

"But Jonathan had gotten in.

Or someone had taken him there."

He paused, voice tightening again.

"Construction crew surveyed the area two weeks before. Nothing. Which means he was there for days. Alone. Forgotten. Until somebody finally decided he was worth finding."

Sheena tapped the table softly.

"Wow," she murmured. "There's a lot here. I'm glad you reached out. I'm glad I came. And I'm sorry… for this young brother."

Damien's voice darkened.

"He ran out of money. Wanted to be a fashion designer. Started bouncing from place to place..."

Sheena furrowed her brow. "Why wasn't it in the news?"
Damien let out a bitter laugh.
"Because they thought he was homeless. Gang-related. Just another Black boy in Atlanta nobody gave a damn about."

He looked at her.
"But he wasn't."

The words hung there, heavy and sacred.

Damien nodded silently as if inviting her insight—maybe even needing it. The question now was did he need professional or personal help?- His needs seemed to be running together under her confident beautiful dark brown gaze.

Moment IV: Plates and Unfinished Things

Sheena had always been perceptive of Damien since they were teens.
Now, as an intentional woman watching a vulnerable, tender man, she saw the muscle tension pulse sharp across Damien's jaw.
She tugged at her earlobe—subtle, unthinking—suddenly more concerned about him than the report.
"Damien," she said softly, lifting her wine glass, fingers delicate, effortless.
Her essence—Black woman soft and sure—slowed him down.
Made the pulse in his chest ease.
She charmed. She calmed.
Damn, Sheena... you all I ever wanted, he thought.
"I'm having the grilled prawns on the Caesar salad."

She had considered the lamb chops, but they'd demand her full attention.

Tonight, she wanted to be fully present.

To offer Damien comfort in the smallest, quietest ways.

He exhaled, grateful.

The waiter hovered nearby.

"What about me?" he asked, letting himself lean into her ease. "What do you recommend?"

Sheena smirked, a giggle escaping before she could stop it.

That sound. That warmth. It had been too long.

"Get the lamb chops," she said, her eyes soft, teasing. "And hopefully, you'll be a gentleman and give me your doggie bag."

Damien chuckled—a real, genuine sound.

For a moment, the city's burdens faded.

The streets of Atlanta could be loud, cruel, relentless.

But here?

Here was Sheena Elise Colucci.

The woman who had always been his sanctuary.

She lifted her glass, nails tapping lightly against the rim before taking a slow sip.

And he let himself watch her—just a second longer than he should have.

The waiter stepped forward. Damien glanced at Sheena once more before turning to order.

"Grilled lamb chops," he said. "Plate half. Caesar, no croutons. No potato."

A beat.

"And a Tequila Calirosa Extra Añejo. Tall pour."

The waiter nodded, disappearing toward the kitchen.

Damien wasn't a drinker.

Never had been.

But he had a taste for high-end tequila.

Calirosa Extra Añejo.

Fresh pastry.

Toasted almonds.

Something warm. Something smooth.

It reminded him of Sheena's skin.

Soft on the tongue. Lingering just long enough.

He let the thought settle.

Because he knew.

This wasn't just another case.

This wasn't just about the city.

It was about the kind of love Atlanta had always claimed to cherish—

but had never learned to protect.

The kind of love that left Black boys lost in the margins,

their stories buried beneath headlines that never came.

It was about them.

The last time he sat across from Sheena like this, his lips had been on her neck before the second glass of wine was poured.

That memory crept in now, uninvited.

Warming him more than the tequila ever could.

He shook it off—or tried to.

Too much was between them.

Too much had gone unsaid.

But that didn't mean the tension wasn't there.

It was.

It always had been.

Moment V: Cascade Bound

Dinner had been light and fun despite the weight of the conversation earlier. Sheena's laughter had filled the space, and for a moment, Damien had forgotten the city's burdens and the case and the darkness lurking just outside the walls of the Ritz-Carlton.

Now, with her doggie bag in tow, Sheena checked her phone, pulling up the Uber app.

"What are you doing, girl?" Damien asked, his tone half amused, half curious.

"I'm getting an Uber. An Uber to Cascade."

Her voice was a little slurred—not drunk, but relaxed. The combination of the wine, her attempt to enjoy Damien's tequila, and the long day of travel from Chicago to Atlanta left her feeling good but weary.

Damien frowned. "I thought you were staying here at the Ritz. If I'd known you were heading back to Cascade, I would've taken you to dinner somewhere more convenient. I don't want you out late if you don't have to be."

Sheena smiled, sensing his protectiveness, which had always been part of who he was. "I'm staying at my childhood home. Beth—well, 'Beat' now—had the house redone. She used some of the royalties she managed to get from Slim."

Damien nodded. "Oh, right. Slim."

"And by the way," Sheena continued, "thank you for getting that lawyer—' Roy- Roy' Davis? He really helped Beth get what she deserved."

Damien chuckled. "It's Rory. Not Roy-Roy. And yeah, Rory's one of the best entertainment lawyers in the business. He's as good as you at what he does. You two should meet sometime."

"Sure thing," Sheena said with a soft laugh. Then she held up the doggie bag. "Now, let's get these lamb chops to my hood- the SWATs, Cat-cade."

Damien smirked, shaking his head. She always had a way of shifting the mood.

But as she spoke, Damien caught the shift—the lighthearted tone that didn't quite mask the weight of their earlier conversation. Or her chosen nighttime destination.

He, more than anyone, knew what she had endured in that neighborhood.

The dark brown daughter of the "All-light-skinned Colucci Family"—Steven Colucci's oldest. The one who didn't quite fit.

After her mother's death, from whom Sheena received the blessing of her beautiful dark brown skin, and her father's spiral out of control, the streets didn't grant her a pass just because she came from something. No—she took the hits. A soft, sensitive, not-yet-confident teen girl, forced to harden before she had the choice.

And now, in the way she spoke about Cascade, about her childhood home—their shared history—he could hear it.

Was she still the same Sheena Elise Colucci?

The deep-melanin daughter of a high-yellow man—ashamed of himself and her?

He had courted Sheena's mother because she was Black and proud.

But in the end?

He didn't have the heart to love Sheena once her mother was gone.

Not because she wasn't light enough for his family.

But because he wasn't man enough for her mother.

Damien knew her story well.

He wanted to hold her beyond it.

Be part of the happy ending.

But—

We were just kids.

And Sheena?

She seemed to have healed.

She caught his lingering gaze, then smirked.

"I'm a big girl, Detective," she teased.

"A big girl from the SWATs, you know I stay—"

"Ah, hot-hot, Sheena—now that will go there nice—hot-sweet
pea-hot—
That tequila got you messing up that spit game."

Sheena rolled her eyes, smirking.
"I eat LT wings like I'll never get old,
Still rockin' that Mays Powder Blue and Gold.
Running backward down Campbellton Road,
With Dam-Dam in tow, making it known—full blown."

Damien couldn't help but laugh—but damn.
Even as he chuckled, he felt that familiar tightening in his
stomach.

She was rhyming.
She always did that when she was feeling playful—
But he could sense the weight beneath her words.

Still, he didn't want to press her.
Sheena guarded herself too well.
Instead, he leaned in, voice low, measured.

"Then I'm driving you home, Dr. Sheena Elise Colucci,
Ph.D.—the MC."

It wasn't a question.
It was a statement.
Respectful. Playful. But firm.

And Sheena?
She knew exactly what it meant.

Sheena tilted her head, considering him momentarily before offering a small, knowing smile. "Okay. But one last shot of that expensive tequila before we go."

"Deal."

Moment VI: Back in the SWATS

They smoothed onto I-75/85, the underpass alive with date-nighters, headlights bouncing off the pavement like fireflies in the city glow.

A familiar bump in the road.

"Damn," Damien kept his shoulder from bumping her's. "The ATL makes you close."

Sheena smirked. "We need to cut your salary, get rid of this nice 'whip,' and finally fix it."

Their laughter, light and easy, floated through the car. The unresolved bam-bam-buum-put of the pothole didn't matter. They knew it would always be there.

The streets whispered stories—

Some they knew too well.

Others were still waiting to unfold.

Then—Grady Baby Hospital—where notable celebrities started their life and infamous, less celestial beings lost theirs—purposefully had their red sign shout out:

"Welcome home, Sheena."

Notable billboards damn near waving—clapping their hands, spitting pimp game to get your attention—

"Fly, Delta."

"Fat...30 days."

"V-103. Kiss 104. Hot..."

"Injured in an Accident?"

Even the board BMF had back in the day now read—

"Our Pastor is Handsome—We Mega."

The pathway south welcomes all home, even churches rolling the dice in on the action.

The words landed soft on Sheena, familiar, but they carried weight. A weight only Grady Babies could understand.

Sheena smiled back. Home.

Now, the Grady Babies—high school sweethearts, familiar songs—had turned into a debate.

"Remember when Jellybean was the spot before Cascade?" Damien's voice was easy, like a song she still knew the lyrics to. "Every Friday night, the whole city showed up."

Sheena exhaled a laugh. "Yeah. I remember. The skating rink, the music, the outfits… it was a whole scene."

"And now?"

Sheena looked out the window. The city lights flickered, flashing across her dark brown skin like memories trying to resurface, grounding her in a past that felt both distant and close.

"Now it's all different." Sheena shook her and fixed a glazed gaze on the many colored lights. "Or maybe I'm just different."

Damien nodded, one hand on the wheel, the other drumming lightly against the gear shift. "Atlanta's still Atlanta. People change, sure. But this city? It's got a way of pulling you back in."

"Kind of like you?"

"Maybe."

Then—the music.

Usher, cascading through the speakers—

Spotlights (spotlights), big stage
Fifty thousand fans screamin' in a rage

Sheena reached over, her hand settling on his arm.

Damien felt it, that old spark still alive in her fingertips.

"Uncle Usher-the best-This the waaaay I see you in my dreams".

Sheena shook her head, smiling. "Oh, Lord. Day. We're back on this again after all this?"

"Absolutely. And don't act like you don't know. You've been

hanging out with Beth too much, talking about Chris Brown this, Chris Brown that."

" Boy, stop. Chris is versatile. And don't act like you didn't have Take You Down on repeat back in the day."

Usher's Superstar poured through the car, low but electric, shifting the air.

Sheena's lips moved, sparkling - she took Damien's hand in the air and kissed.

"Always, and A for effort".

Damien took his grade but wanted one of those back-in-the-day kisses.

Her gaze lingered on the old Krystal's hamburger spot, now shuttered and quiet.

Back in the day...

That wasn't just a burger joint.

That was Atlanta's heartbeat on a Friday night.

Letter jackets and cheerleading uniforms.

Private school kids would be freely accepted home, brought back into the fold as if they had always been classmates with those at Mays, Douglass, Therrell, Harper-Archer, Washington (the OG Blue Blood), and Northside.

Swing over to East Point and College Park—Headland, Briarwood, Woodland, Russell, Lakeshore, M.D. Collins—just a few years later, Tri-Cities joined the mix, rounding out the city's public-school pride.

And then there were the private schools—The Lovett School, Woodward Academy, Westminster, Marist, and St. Pius X—pushing their Black students home for the weekend, sending them back where they belonged, if only to get the boyfriend or girlfriend they weren't going to find in the halls of their elite campuses.

The schools that loved you—if you scored touchdowns, won track meets, or added a little flavor—but not too much. At some private schools, the Black students even dared to sit at the Black table—not because they had to, but because being from the ATL meant you could get a private school education in the city and still crave a connection that the sterile, well-intended "We're so glad you're here" couldn't entirely solve- "I'm Ivy League material but I'm ATL-HBCU made".

Pride and status riding shotgun in old-school Caprices, Crown Vics, and Monte Carlos.

Oh, and let's be clear—we didn't invent house parties 'cause we outgrew houses. We took over apartment clubhouses, skating rinks, and hotel ballrooms. Yep.

"Where the party at?"

"You got a ride?"

"That cute dude—what school he from?"

"Man, she like you—ask her friend on the drill team about me."

The ATL had been set trip'n for as long as Sheena and Damien could remember—back when Decatur still felt like outta town.

This was Atlanta—where the weekend blurred the lines between zip codes, school districts, and status. Where home was always waiting, no matter where you'd been Monday through Friday.

Really, it didn't matter what school you went to—as long as you knew you were from the ATL, hugged tight by I-285.

Sheena smiled. I-285. Wow. It connected them to everything—to them. Even when they didn't have much, it had always been there, looping them into the city's rhythm.

Shee and Damien had been part of that rhythm once—young, reckless, broke, but unbothered.

She could still feel his arm around her shoulder, his quiet claim on her in front of all the girls who envied her spot beside him.

Now, years later?

She glanced at the Ritz-Carlton doggie bag on her lap and smirked.

Time had a funny way of folding the past into the present.

She tilted her head toward Damien.

"Remember Crystals? Friday nights, four dollars, and nothing else in the world that mattered?"

Damien glanced her way, a small smile playing on his lips.

"Of course. I remember you always making me share my fries."

Sheena grinned. "You never complained."

"Because I had you."

Sheena shook her head, then smirked. "Oh, by the way, since we're this close to Greenbriar Parkway—whatever happened to Karen? You know, the one who stalked me all 11th grade, talking about you were her man even if you didn't go to Tri-Cities anymore?"

Damien's laughter cut off Karen- her outcome.

Sheena already knew—knew from the way he kissed her at the end of 11th grade—that it didn't matter what happened to Karen then, and it damn sure didn't matter now.

Even if it was still funny as hell.

This. This. This. Us. Day-you still -Not too sweet. Just right?

The car weaved and bobbed like only SWAT's potholes can make you roll.

J.J. Rib Shack held them old-school, closer than close— sweeter than sweet.

The scent of sauce and smoke, thick in the air, clung to them like history.

The warmth in his words settled—not in the air, not on the surface, but between them.

Unspoken memories moved like shadows across the dashboard lights—slow, heavy, and familiar.

The city stretched ahead. Almost home.

The past.

The present.

Sheena drifted back. *We all had a good place to grow up in the ATL.*

Damien caught the movement of her lips, reading the words before she even spoke them.

"The ATL wasn't perfect, God knows—but Sheena's lip gloss

and Friday nights at Lakewood went a long way to make it better. Yeah… overall, a good childhood. Especially our teen years."

The car dipped into a slow roll nearing Panther Trail, the street-lights casting long shadows across the pavement.

And then—

A sharp turn, the car slowed near Cascade, and Sheena's child-hood home appeared.

Moment VII: Am I Dreamin?

Streetlights washed over the driveway like memory—soft, golden, and heavy with the past.

Once a symbol of family, loss, and survival, the house felt like something else.

A mix of joy and stalking anticipation twisted her expression. Damien noticed.

He didn't say anything.

Because what was there to say?

He knew this place.

The house that saw her fall apart, then rebuild.

The neighborhood that chewed her up and spit her out—but never let her go.

The streets still whispered her name, his name, their names.

Now, in the driveway, the comfort of the luxury vehicle invited a last tender moment.

They sat there.

The hum of the engine.

The silence was heavy but not uncomfortable.

Then—

Spink-Spink-Spink.

Things are kind of hazy
And my head's …
… thought I'd have one to call mine".

Now the past was showing off.

Damien's fingers tapped to the beat.

He turned the volume up—just enough.

Am I dreamin'? (Well, well, well, well)...

Sheena sank into the moment like she used to.

She imagined him asking her to say, "Will this last for one night

Or do I have you for a lifetime?

A soundtrack for nostalgia proved they had always been making love, even with no touch.

Oh, the weight of everything unsaid.

Sing into each other—how they wished they had years ago.

"The ATL wants its time to speak," Damien murmured, voice low, reflective.

Damn. This boy has become a man. The ATL is sexy in his mouth.

Sheena chuckled, shaking her head. "ATL always wants to speak."

"And we've been listening our whole lives."

The city had always spoken through them.

Through their rhythm, their history, their heat.

And now, through their silence.

Then, she moved.

Sheena leaned over the console.

Her eyes caught Damien's in the dim light.

Her lips were glossed in soft pink—Jairus Candy Shop's finest.

Gloss tastings like honey dates and memory.

Sweet. Familiar. Unfinished.

Her lips brushed his—

A kiss that held questions neither of them dared ask aloud.

All at once.

What are we doing?

What if we never left this moment?

What if we were always meant to end up back here?

Sheena, inside herself, ahead of herself—

Damien came in—inside, deep, finally—

Atlantic Star is still daring her. *I need you; I need you to pinch me.*

But Sheena pushed Sheena back.

Get out of line to ride, girl. Now. First, take care of this past stuff—this coming cause.

Damien murmured, steady. "Hey. While you're in the city—if you get tired of staying here or in unfamiliar places—my directions and code."

Sheena understood. Appreciated. This was how he moved.

"No expectations. No questions."

She pocketed the code.

But later—would she use it?

Then—

The quiet click of the door.

Her heels tapped against the pavement, rhythmic, steady.

A goodbye—or maybe a promise.

Damien sat there for a moment longer—

With the taste of honey on his lips.

God, the cold ache grew again with each click-click away—a twin of that day she left.

He let the purr of the city wrap around him like a second skin.

Cascade flickered in the rearview mirror.

Day and Shee—well.

Some places, like some people, never really let you go.

And as *My head's all cloudy inside,* silky-filled voices lingered over the final chords of their first-last-next moment—

I need you to show me it's not a mirage.

Sheena—grown—second-guessed, and thought, By now, I should've been saying, 'Oh no, oh no, baby.'

Damien knew.

Sheena knew.

But again—they let go.

Like they always did.

If ATL had anything left to say,

Would it ever get through to them getting to each other?
Or was the city content to hum around them—
a witness with no loyalty,
a choir with no hymn?
Damien's car penetrated steadily into a purring, humidly moist,
and now tenderly dripping Atlanta night—
not rushing, not hesitating—
just sinking deep into everything they weren't ready to face.

CHAPTER 2

FAULT LINE

Moment 1: Cross the Line

Driving off into the dark, Damien shifted the moment. Sheena stood outside her childhood home, watching his taillights disappear.

Atlanta never stayed the same. The weather, the buildings, the people—up and down like an IG stripper. She giggled, even though coming back here—to this house, to the past—was no laughing matter.

She breathed, then punched in the magic code on the too-modern keypad. As the door swung open, a thought flickered in her mind—

It should've said, *"Open sesame—step across this threshold into more decadence than this house should have."* She smirked.

But what else would Beth—executive producer, designer of her own world—have produced? Of course, she hired Charles Wilson. Better known in Atlanta's Black elite as *"A Charles Production."* A man who turned average homes into movie sets.

Even when Beth wasn't there, Sheena could hear her sister's voice drifting through the halls— *"Lights, camera, action!"*

Inside, Beth's grandiose vision had escalated into something cinematic. Sheena took it all in, smirking like a fan stepping onto Hollywood Boulevard.

"Damn, Charles, you've come a long way since our days at Mays High. You did your thang."

Steven Colucci's house—once a declining mess—was now a gentrified prize. But for Sheena, the real question was: Would the ghosts of her past dance in harmony—or trip over each other awkwardly?

Her phone buzzed.

Text from Damien.

Just checking to see if you got inside okay. I hope I didn't keep you out too late. We both have events tomorrow.

Head spinning. Case—yes. *Kiss—I miss your kisses. See you later (strictly business with a smile emoji).*

Damien.

The message sent a small vibration through her chest, but as her gaze lifted toward the hallway, her focus shifted. At the end of the corridor, her old bedroom door stood waiting.

Suddenly, the giddiness of the evening gave way to something heavier.

We're not in Kansas anymore, Sheena.

She took a step forward. New crown molding... elegant light gray paint... *Beth, you outdid yourself.* The whole house was transformed.

But as Sheena moved through it, memories flickered like an old film reel. After their mother's death, Steven couldn't bear to stay in the master bedroom.

I can't sleep in that room now that Mamma's gone!

So instead, he had moved Sheena into it—like a relic, a living shrine. And yet, he had barely been a presence in her life. Except when he needed something.

Come out here and help your sister! Damn, you so damn selfish!

The new walls might have been painted over, but they still echoed old resentment.

She reached her old bedroom door. Unlike everything else, it hadn't been touched. No soft gray paint. No crown molding. Beth's masterpiece was everywhere—except here.

As much as things had changed, this door whispered that some things hadn't.

Sheena inhaled deeply, steeling herself.

"It's not the same." A mantra. An affirmation. A misguided attempt to pump herself up.

"But neither am I."

She stepped forward. She crossed the line. The fault line.

Like a magnet, Sheena's eyes landed on her old desk. She had spent countless nights there—studying, planning, dreaming. But mostly? Preserving the enormous moments of her life. The ones that mattered too much.

She had barely let herself breathe it in before her phone buzzed.

Tina Cummings. One of her closest sorority sisters. They had pledged together at Howard University's Alpha Chapter and never lost touch. Tina knew everything—the good, the bad, the diary-level truths.

And ever since Howard? Tina had been cheering for Sheena.

So it was no surprise that, having never met Damien, she still shouted *"Day"* after every shallow date Sheena went on.

She swiped to answer.

"Hey, girl."

"Hey! Just wanted to make sure you got in okay. How's everything?"

Tina's voice was bright, familiar—grounding her like a warm embrace. Sheena glanced around the room, the diary still in her hand.

"I got in fine. Everything's… as it was. You know how it is."

Tina laughed knowingly.

"Mm-hmm. Well, is it business, or is it gonna be pleasure?"

Sheena smirked, brushing her fingers over the diary's worn cover.

Funny you ask.

Damien's kiss. The memory of it brushed her lips again.

"Girl, I might cross the line. I hope it's both."

Tina's laughter rang through the phone. But it was only a precursor to sisterly wisdom.

"But, *Shee-girl,* I just gotta say—if you ever gonna be with 'Day'? You gonna have to face yourself. So you can let go and be his."

Sheena kept it light, breaking into song:

"Girl, I'm reaaaddddyyy!"

Tina, now full-out laughing:

"Then beeeee reaaadddy!"

And then, knowing her wisdom had landed—

"You better keep me posted. Love you, girl."

"Love you too."

Sheena's gaze returned to the diary. It was heavy now. Like a doorway to another time. The old desk, where it rested, seemed to push back against the echoes of the sisters' laughter.

As if it alone remembered the weight of all that had been written—and left unsaid.

In her mind, Tina's voice reemerged, carrying the same unwavering confidence she had during their pledge years:

Sheena, you got this. You gotta go through this night. Because if you don't... you'll never get to Day.

And just like that, Sheena knew—tonight, she wasn't just opening a diary. She was opening a reckoning.

Suddenly—still in the ethers of the room—Tina's tone shifted. Hollow. Yet profound. As though she had become Minerva herself, the Greek goddess of wisdom. Her voice reverberated—

Across the burning sands of fractured time. Through the cracks of memory, where truth had been buried. Into the fault line Sheena had long refused to cross.

And then—

Once upon a time.

The words landed like a spell. A summons. A reckoning.

And just like that—

Sheena crossed the fault line.

Her fingers pressed against the diary's surface—Sheena traced the edge of her diary, her fingers brushing against the worn leather cover. She hadn't read through it in a while, but she already knew what was inside. The words she chose to remember, the ones she had forced herself to forget.

She turned the page.

No more running. No more pretending. No more waiting.

It was time.

Moment II: It's Not Your Fault

Coletta Elise Colucci. She had been gone three years, but her presence still filled the room.

Atlanta had known her as unapologetically Black—a chocolate-skinned beauty who commanded attention wherever she went.

She had been Pam Grier's boldness with Angela Davis's fire—a Clark College alum, Ph.D. in political science, and the woman who had married into the Colucci family, Atlanta's bougie Black elite.

Mom was strong.

But she spent too much energy trying to make him a man.

Died trying.

Whose fault was he?

Stephen Colucci—mulatto-looking, privileged, and unaccomplished—had been the black sheep of his family. The Coluccis were political powerhouses, the so-called "talented tenth" of Atlanta. But Stephen had flunked out of Morehouse and rejected his family's legacy.

And he had resented Coletta for succeeding where he had failed.

Sheena exhaled sharply.

He couldn't handle Mom's death.

He couldn't handle us. Our beautiful Black skin.

After Coletta died of breast cancer, Stephen spiraled, drowning his anger in bourbon. His resentment targeted Sheena most of all.

I look like her.

Dark-skinned. Bold. Unwilling to cower like Beth.

Beth—the light-skinned "Cajun princess"—had never heard a harsh word from him. But for Sheena, there was venom in every interaction.

The "Dark one," he called her to his lecherous friends.

Laughing behind their drinks, amused at how proud a rejected girl could be.

And Stephen, in his drunken haze, had called her worse.

Then the window kiss.

It was the end of summer, just before senior year.

Sheena and Damien had been stealing soft moments together— his kiss, soft and electric, at her bedroom window—just inside.

She hadn't heard Stephen come in.

He didn't say a word.

Just stared.

Cold. Calculating.

Then he turned and walked away.

Left the door wide open—

The same way she had left the window open for Damien.

Her fingers tightened on the diary, the scene replaying in flashes.

Stephen retaliated against me—us—She and Day.

His name was *Shem.*

Like so many Black men carrying biblical names, it could have been a blessing.

Or a curse.

For Shem, it was the latter—a name that once carried the weight of promise but had long since become a bitter irony.

They called him "Shine" around the dimly lit bars near the now-demolished Omni Arena.

Not because he had any light to offer.

Because of the slick, greasy way he navigated life.

Shem was small-minded, a man who built his reputation on debts, desperation, and cheap favors. He didn't work for what he wanted; he negotiated, manipulated, or outright stole it.

And Stephen Colucci's drinking and depression made him an easy mark.

He was a snake in the Grass- the garden.

Shem had been circling the Colucci house for years.

In the early days, he wanted Coletta.

But Coletta would never have stooped lower than she already had with Stephen.

Even if she hadn't been married.

Shine was a snake. Always waiting to strike.

And when Stephen's bourbon-soaked bitterness left him blind to the wolves at his door—

Shine slithered in.

One debt at a time. One favor after another.

Until Stephen had nothing left to bargain with.

Nothing, that is—

Except Sheena.

Sheena stiffened as the memory of the evening Shem walked into her room.

"Not Mister," he had said with that slimy smirk.

"Your daddy said it's okay. Said it's time to make you a woman."

Sheena's stomach churned. The memory hit her like a blow.

Her fingers tightened on the diary as she breathed hard, but the moment wouldn't let her go.

It replayed in fragments—

Shem's weight pinning her down.

His breath was hot and vile against her neck.

His words—a dripping venom in her ear.

And then—

It was over.

"For what it's worth, your daddy don't owe me no more," Shem stuttered.

Now, he studied the words as if almost conscious of the grave harm he had just caused.

As though that could explain it.

He stumbled out as if crushed beneath the weight of his own brokenness—leaving behind a cap, its stench clinging to the room for two days until she found the courage to throw it away.

Sheena couldn't move for ten minutes.

Her panties hung by her shorts—tangled around her right leg.

She had often thought about giving herself to Damien—her Day.

But he had never asked.

Never pushed.

Never wanted anything more than a kiss.

To be loved by their shared innocence.

But this—this was darkness.

She never wanted it.

Not like this.

Never like this.

She didn't realize she was crying. The sound startled her.

Small. Choked. Sobs.

Like someone else was trapped inside her.

Mama— she remembered.

Her voice whispered inwardly.

Mama, come get me.

Sheena had gotten through therapy clinging to the imagined image of Coletta Colucci walking through the door—her mother's commanding presence filling the room, saving the day.

Ready to scoop her up.

Ready to make it all go away.

But instead—

She only remembered the empty room staring back at her.
Then, the cry for true love—
Sheena thought of Damien.
Wishing, for once, that he had come to the window.
Wishing, for once, that he had saved her.
Her therapist had told her:
Damien didn't need to save you.
Because Coletta's spirit in you kept you through it.
Took you to Howard.
Took you beyond.
That no man could give a Black woman what God Herself had already placed inside her—
Life. Strength. Wholeness. *Coletta Colucci.*
And all the Black women who had their physical agency compromised—
But never their spiritual agency.
I clearly remember Stephen's return.
An hour later, he stumbled in.
Bourbon on his breath.
Guilt nowhere to be found.
He didn't ask if she was okay.
Instead—
"That boy better not be in this house again!"
And then—
"Come help your sister get ready for school. Since you wanna be grown?"
"Fast ass! You grown yet?"
Sheena had swallowed it all, holding the weight of his words like a stone in her chest.
But before she left for school that morning, she had made her own reckoning.
She had sat at her desk, diary open, fingers trembling but steady.
And she had written.
Not a cry for help.

Not a confession.
Not even a plea.
But a truth—raw, unfiltered, unshaken.
Shem was gone—killed by some young guy who owed him money.
And Stephen Colucci was gone—died a failed husband and father, just like his father had predicted.
But Sheena?
She was still here.
She hadn't let the past write her.
She had written the past.

What happened- what happened to my voice?
They like him—oh, they like him.
They tried to steal my voice,
Shape my tone in lesser measures.
But they were too late.
Coletta, Mommie was in me.
She had been since day one.
It was my being—
A Way from the A, given to me by her in The A
Daring to search and find
That which was already mine.
Seeking what I thought I did not have,
I sought it in academic books; imagine "The Road Less Traveled."
In scripture that pointed inward;
"Remember beloved child:
Then Jesus, being filled with the Holy Spirit, returned from the Jordan and was led by the Spirit into the wilderness. The devil said, "If you are…"
And I found it—my voice on the road and in the wilderness.
My voice, my whole soul.
Yet still, another temptation-
To the future.

Now, like me,
Can you find your voice?

"I found my voice- my whole soul. And didn't and don't need anyone to save me."

Sheena shook her whole body as if to awaken herself from sleep—she didn't stretch—she took deep breaths. She wiped the tears from her eyes.

Not broken. Not afraid. Not undone.

Her gaze dropped to the poem she had just written.

What you take from me will never be as great as what she put in me. I miss you, mamma. I always have and always will. I'm trying.

The diary sat in her lap like an old sage—its pages filled with questions she hadn't been ready to face until now.

She put the history book back in its place, exhaling as her fingers traced the worn spine.

Her gaze swept the room—familiar, yet no longer suffocating. The past was here, but it didn't own her.

She reached for her bag, slung it onto the desk, and straightened her posture.

There was work to do.

The work. I gotta get to the work. This heart stuff?

The case file Damien had slipped her at dinner.

The keynote address was tomorrow at the Atlanta Concerned Black Clergy's Criminal Justice and Community Safety Symposium.

Activists, scholars, and ministers from all over the country had gathered—drawn by the call to action.

The Trump 2.0 administration was tightening its grip, using every legal loophole and political maneuver to leverage more Black bodies for profit.

Georgia's Republican leadership?

They were right there with him.

Sheena was here to remind them that Atlanta or her people *were* not for sale.

And just like that, her mind was clear, locked in.

Until—

A disruption.

A noise at the door.

She turned.

Louis Vuitton head to toe.

Dripping in status and armor.

Sheena had survived the diary and slipped into work.

But was she ready for who would cross the line next?

Moment III: Crossing the Line on Beat

"Sheena, it figures you'd be in that room—even with all of this. What's with that room?"

The voice came first—sharp, knowing. A challenge wrapped in casual curiosity.

Then came the walk.

A runway stride, deliberate, like the world was hers and hers alone.

The door swung open without hesitation. No knock. No warning.

Bethany—Beth Martha Colucci, by birth certificate.
But no—codeswitching. Not here. Not now.
Beat.

That was the name that mattered. The name that held weight, carved into studio sessions and street corners alike.

She stepped inside like it was a gauntlet, shoulders squared, chin high. She had long since corrected anyone who dared call her by the name she had left behind.

To the world—outside of hospital records and their mother's insistence—she was simply Beth.

She was undeniably beautiful, a fact that had trailed her since childhood.

At Jean Childs Young Middle, then Mays High, teachers used to call her Sheena's little twin.

But where Sheena's beauty carried a quiet gravity, Beth's was kinetic. Loud. Demanding to be seen.

Her skin, warm caramel just shy of ivory, caught the light effortlessly, a contrast that had always separated them.

Her braids tumbled down her back—intricate, deliberate, professionally crafted.
Golden and honey-blonde strands wove together, darker roots adding depth. Each movement caught the light like liquid gold.
Soft curls kissed the ends, the detail that only came with top-tier styling.

Everything about her was intentional.

Not just beauty. Status. Presence. A woman who didn't just have money—she knew exactly how to wear it.

Beth leaned against the door frame, one hand on her hip, her stance dripping with effortless bravado.

The oversized Louis Vuitton hoodie—a Dapper Dan original—draped over her frame like armor, the Slim Money Records logo flashing from the tee underneath.

It hung just low enough to tease what lay beneath.

And that?

A sequined Louis Vuitton mini skirt that didn't just whisper—

It screamed.

Around her neck, a thick gold chain caught Sheena's eye. Too flashy. Too gaudy.

Quintessential Slim.

Sheena, ignoring the subtle shift in the room's air pressure, pushed out a soft laugh under her breath.

"Damn, You might as well have 'A Slim Records Production' stamped on your forehead."

Then, seeing it in her mind's eye—*A Slim production.* Tattooed on her neck.

Beth's eyes flicked around the room, lingering on the freshly made bed, high-thread-count sheets crisp against the light.

Her gaze dipped to the neatly tucked suitcase.

"Look at you. Back in her room. Guess you're finally ready to reclaim the throne, huh?"

" Thrown? I didn't come back for this."

She met Beth's gaze evenly.

"And you know it."

Beth scoffed, stepping fully into the room without waiting for an invitation.

"No, of course not. You came to write your little poems, play perfect sister for a few days, and—" Beth's smirk sharpened.

"As I heard in the streets— you already play'n with 'Day' before you disappear again. Like always."

The last jab landed. A quick pulse shot through Sheena's body.

Beth's words had a pugilistic rhythm—like rebellion in a precinct interrogation room or a tough client running their mouth just enough to make you lean forward.

Sheena didn't flinch.

She studied Beth—really studied her.

Noted the bravado stretched tight over something raw. The way her jaw clenched, it was like she was holding back something too sharp to say out loud.

The restless fingers fidgeting with the hem of her hoodie—a tell-tale sign.

" I left to go to school -to heal. You're still that little girl who used to trail behind me, begging for attention."

Beth's lip curled. "A—what—a-tion-attention?"

Sheena exhaled, slow and steady. "I was there, Beth. I'm here now. But you can't see me."

Her gaze flicked to the thin gold chain, the oversized logo armor.

"Not buried beneath all that gold."

Beth scoffed, rolling her shoulders like she was shaking something off. "What the hell are you talking about? You abandoned me. Came when it was convenient. Mostly not. Left quickly. Stay judging. And now you're a damn family therapist?" She let out a humorless chuckle. "Damn, you are special even if you're a smart-ass. Really—the ass part- no, definitely the ass part. Even if Mama probably thought you were an ass too- because Daddy sure did."

The shift inside Sheena was immediate.

Bitch really just pulled Mama into this? How childish.

That quiet click—when apprehension lets go and instinct takes over.

She leaned in, her voice calm but locked in.
"So now," she exhaled, voice steady, weighty.

"I'm about to cross the line from contemporaries to 'beat that ass' parent mode."

Measured. Deliberate.
Not loud—never that.

"I gotta check you now. 'Cause I get it—your 'baddest bitch' attitude was—no, probably is—necessary in the worlds you climb through.
But let's be clear.
I'm the baddest bitch's oldest sister.

And if you don't control your attitude—yes, your attitude—and stay fair?
Cuz—and I said cuz on purpose—make no mistake about it, I will not drop down and climb through the gutter with you.
No, I'll just turn you around, bend you over my knee, and climb through your high-yellow, high-and-mighty ass."

Beth flinched.

Not much. Just enough.

The left-right motion of Sheena's head caught her off guard, a rhythm Beth couldn't track.
Beth took two steps back.

The space got smaller.

Her laughter came sharp and bitter—more shield than sound.
More defense than deflection.

Her tone shifted, softened—like she had just stepped out of the rain and hadn't fully dried.

"Heal?" The word landed hard, spat like something foreign.
"That's what you call it? Leaving me alone with him? With this house?"

Sheena stayed still.
But Beth didn't.

Her hand sliced through the air—wide, wild, consuming.
As if gesturing at every corner of the room.
Every buried memory.
Every damn ghost.

What Sheena didn't see—what she couldn't place—was the scent still lingering in Beth's nostrils.

Smoke.
Fire.
Flames.

The ones that had swallowed their father, Steven, weeks after Sheena left for college.

The report had said he didn't die in the fire itself.
Said it was a heart attack—as if that changed anything.

Didn't matter.

The scent had haunted Beth for years.

She had scrubbed.
Repainted.
Rebuilt.

And yet—it never truly left.

But it took years before she could stand in this house and not smell the burning.

Sheena's voice softened, but her spine stayed steel.

"You know that's not true."

Beth's expression twisted, part fury, part disbelief.

"Auntie Joyce was here every day. She offered to take you in full-time, but you wanted to stay at Mays. I didn't leave you, Beth. I left to make sure I could come back whole."

Beth's nostrils flared. She wasn't buying it.

"Whole?" she echoed, tone razor-sharp. "What does that even mean? While I was stuck here, you became Howard's golden girl, stacking degrees and living your best life. Thriving."

Sheena let out a slow, controlled breath.

"I know it wasn't easy for you, Beth. But don't rewrite the story to make me the villain."

Silence stretched between them.

"I was eighteen," Sheena said, steady, honest. "I was barely holding myself together."

Beth's voice came sharp, slicing through Sheena's words like a blade against stone.

"Oh, so now you're the therapist too?" Beth scoffed, shaking her head. "Look at you, all calm and wise, speaking your truth like a TED Talk. But tell me, big sister—if you're so healed, why does this house still shake your voice?"

Sheena leaned forward, "Because pain doesn't just disappear; you don't outrun it. You don't silence it by throwing money at renovations or calling yourself a new name. You face it."

Beth's jaw tensed. "Yeah? And where was that wisdom when I was the one left here? While you were off finding your 'truth,' I was drowning in his."

The air between them thickened. The weight of too many years, too many silences, pressed in.

"I didn't leave you," Sheena said, her voice softer now. "I tried to save you."

Beth let out a bitter laugh, shaking her head. "Save me? Sheena, you never even looked back."

Sheena stepped forward, her voice low and measured. "Because I couldn't. If I had, I might've never left at all."

Beth swallowed hard, something shifting in her. Her fingers toyed with the hem of her hoodie—the same nervous tic she had as a child.

And then, for the first time, her voice broke.

"I waited, you know," Beth whispered, gaze fixed on the floor. "I waited for you to come back and get me."

Beth, crying, was the 13-year-old trapped beneath Louis Vuitton armor.

Sheena's breath hitched—Beth's sweet scent, familiar and fleeting, made her proud. 'Beth...'"

Beth shook her head quickly as if shaking off the weight of the confession. Her walls went up again, her voice regaining its edge. "Forget it. Doesn't matter now."

She turned toward the door, shoulders stiff, but Sheena wasn't letting her leave with that.

"Beth."

Beth paused.

"I see you now."

For a moment—just a flicker—Beth hesitated like she wanted to believe her.

But then she scoffed. "Good for you."

And with that, she was gone.

Sheena stood there, staring at the empty doorway, the ghost of Beth's words lingering in the air.

I waited for you to come back and get me.

She closed her eyes, exhaling deeply. This wasn't over. Not even close.

Because now?

Sheena wasn't leaving without her.

Beth's phone erupted with sound—loud, intrusive. Slim was FaceTiming.

The hook to his hit song blasted through the room like a war cry:

Northern niggas slide through just to get slayed,

New Orleans Wardies soft like powdered beignets,

Alabama boys fold quick—Red Tide Bengay,

ATL streets? Built from red clay. Shit, nigga, we ain't got no time to play!

The bass rattled the walls, each line a challenge, a taunt that had already set fires across the South. New Orleans wasn't laughing. Alabama damn sure wasn't. Slim was playing a game that had real consequences, and everyone knew it.

Beth smirked, picking up the call. "Hey, Thick."

Slim's face filled the screen, all grin and bravado. "Girl, bring that fine ass outside. I been waitin' too long!"

His eyes flicked past her—to Sheena. And just like that, the grin widened, shifting gears.

"Oh, what's up, Sheena?" He leaned closer to the camera, eyes hungry. "Damn, girl. You still got that thang."

Sheena's expression didn't flinch. "Hey, Slim. How you doin'?"

Slim laughed, flashing gold. "Better now, seein' you." He leaned back, tossing a thick stack of cash between his hands like a deck of cards. "You still try'na be legit? Girl, come on. Forget that criminology degree. Get wit' this crime thang. Make that money. You always been the baddest. And you know I been a fan since day one—back when you was wit' Big Bro Day."

That name.

It hit differently coming from Slim.

Sheena exhaled steadily. "That's nice, Slim."

Slim let out a loud cackle. "Man, I just saw Damien the other day, snoopin' around as usual. Playin' po-po." He dragged the word out mockingly. Then, with casual menace:

"If he weren't my fam', I'd have that police nigga marked as a snitch."

The room tightened. The words hung in the air, half-joke, half-warning.

Sheena saw it for what it was.

Slim wasn't just talking. He was testing the waters.

Beth, playing neutral, rolled her eyes with a smirk. "Slim, stop playin'. And I have my car. I could've met you."

Slim's grin faded for a second—just a flicker. Then he smoothed it over, brushing past her defiance. "Alright, alright. Beth, come on outside. Quit playin' with me. You know I'm out here."

Another toss of the cash.

"And don't keep me waitin'. Time is money, baby. Oh yeah—did you tell her about the ba—?"

"I told you a thousand times, Slim. I'm grown. I am not one of your artists. We are partners in this business."

Beth's voice was steady, cutting through the tension.

"And like I said, stop playing. You're gonna stop clocking me, take me off your drone vision, quit watching my cameras, and stop tracking me on the iPhone—hands off. I'm not your property. We roll together. Period."

Slim made the immediate adjustment—bodyguard to admiring boyfriend. It was always a quick shift with him.

He threw his hands up, flashing that gold-toothed grin. "Yes, mamma, once and for all, damn—" Then, lower, sharper, almost like he was talking to himself, "You gonna regret that. Thick I ain't jokin' and clockin'? Remember that now."

His voice deepened, slipping into something almost playful, but the overprotectiveness he had learned from Damien—his "big bro" long before he was Beth's man—still lingered beneath the surface.

Slim had been 13 when Damien was 18, hanging onto his every word, watching how he moved. The way he handled things. The way he protected Sheena.

And now?

That same instinct—that same need to control, guard, and claim— didn't just disappear because Beth declared herself independent.

"Don't call me next time you are in one of those luxury hotels, and the room service doesn't get it right. Or when you are on stage and the mic doesn't work. Your words—'We are partners in this business. I'm an equal. I can care for myself.' Remember, I'm not your help".

He leaned back, arms folded, lips twisting into a half-smirk, half-laugh—like the front seat of the Slim Comedy Show.
"I'm officially—checked.
Ass.
Thick.
Hands off.
Still, yo, man."
And just like that, be announced he was waiting outside. "Yeah, so but really- let's get going-".
He was off-duty. But now, he had to protect growing less capable artists, and he needed her expertise and artistry.
He turned on his one hit song—the track that had sold just enough copies to get him a grip, launching him from rapper to power broker.

Young artists whispered the same prayer: *Thank you for never stepping into the booth again—never lowering the craft.*

Feared or respected? Both.

Slim wasn't just a rapper. He was a leader—a street tactician, moving in rooms where deals were made before the ink dried.

The bass thumped through the phone, rattling the walls and vibrating like a taunt, a flex, a declaration.

Slim didn't need the mic anymore.

He had Beth now.

And Beth?

Most didn't know—she had bars. She had business. And Slim?

He had the name. She had the game.

But Sheena saw what she saw.

She exhaled, watching her sister soak it all in.

Draped in designer. Caught in Slim's world. Playing her role.

Sheena almost pitied her.

Like Malcolm and Martin. Like Nikki Giovanni and Nicki Minaj.
The debate raged on—who got to define a Black woman's power?

The streets or Spelman?
Survival or self-reinvention?
Respectability or rawness?

Beth embodied the question. Slim thought he owned the answer.

Sheena? She wasn't sure anymore.

Slim' s only hit load now:
Don't forget, in the A, we don't play,
We, the kings of the South, hold it down every day.
Pull up slick, hear the choppers where we stay—
Step wrong, and you'll see how the ATL gets ablaze.
Sheena exhaled, shaking her head. "I don't know what's worse—him calling you out there like a child or you letting him cart you around when you probably have more than two hundred thousand dollars sitting outside right now."
Beth stiffened.
Sheena didn't know.
Didn't know why Slim's voice made her stomach twist.
Didn't know why she hadn't touched her glass of wine tonight.
Didn't know why she rested her hand, instinctively, over her belly.
Sheena didn't know.
Beth bit back the sharp retort, opting instead for a smirk. "Stay in your lane, Sheena. Slim respects me more than you ever will. He's in his lane- puppy dogs get checked."
Sheena's eyes narrowed. "Respect? Is that what you call it?" She let out a humorless laugh. "Beth, if you think he cares about you beyond what you do for him, you're fooling yourself."
Beth felt a familiar itch—a simmering irritation just beneath the surface.
And just like that, Beth felt the itch.
The need to run. To leave before she let herself crack. Before she let Sheena in.

Hand on the door, she turned. "You don't know anything about Slim. Or me."

Her voice wavered. She caught it before it cracked.

Stay as long as you want. But don't expect me to roll out the red carpet just because you decided to come back.

And with that, she was gone.

Sheena sat there, listening to Slim's anthem still echoing—just a little off-beat.

Moment IV: The Ellison Ross Case-One of Many?

The file sat where Damien had left it, his touch lingering in the folds, the weight of his trust pressing against her fingertips.

Sheena hesitated, breath hitching as memory flickered—his eyes on her at dinner, and his fingers barely brushed hers when he passed it under the table. A quiet urgency. A message unsaid.

The file sat where Damien had left it, the weight of his trust pressing against her fingertips.

Sheena hesitated. His touch still lingered in the folds, a ghost of warmth against the cold, stiff edges. She could still see his eyes on her at dinner, the brief brush of his fingers beneath the table— unspoken urgency wrapped in something deeper.

But now, in the silence of her room, there were no distractions.

No Damien. No steady presence to keep her from what lay ahead.

Just her, the file, and whatever darkness waited inside.

His scent clung to the government-issued folder—clean, familiar, disarming. A contradiction. Like him. Like this. Like the space between who they were and what this case demanded of them.

Sheena exhaled, steadying herself. The diary still sat open beside her, its pages steeped in memory, but this—this was something else.

She flipped open the file.

The contrast struck immediately—sterile reports with

precise, detached language. And then, between them, his notes. Handwritten, unguarded. Sharp thoughts were scrawled in margins, meant only for her.

This wasn't just a case.

It was a message. A puzzle. A line she was about to cross, where love and danger blurred.

And Damien had trusted her to see what he couldn't.

April 1, 2025.

Officer Rodrick Gordon arrived at the abandoned playground of St. Anthony's Catholic School, the weight of dawn pressing against the skyline. The scene was grim. Ellison Ross, a light-skinned Black man, lay broken and mutilated—an image that stained memory.

Damien had slipped Sheena the report during dinner, a quiet exchange beneath the table, his fingers barely grazing hers. She peeled back its pages alone in her room, bracing for what lay beneath.

At first glance, it read like a standard police report—cold, clinical, routine. But as Sheena scanned the lines, the gaps became glaring.

Samantha and Heath Bower. Local homeowners. Members of Buy Back the Block. Their statement was brief: they had found the body while walking their dog. That should have been the end of it.

But one detail snagged.

Any further contact with the Bowers had to be directed through Maddox, Talmadge, and Perdue Attorneys at Law—Atlanta's most conservative, gentrification-hungry law firm.

Aren't they the firm that turned East Lake into a gated playground for the rich?

Luxury lofts. A golf course. Urban renewal. And for good

measure, they threw in an "equitable" charter school—just enough to make it sound righteous.

Sheena's thoughts sliced through the sterile language in the file.

I've heard about them all the way up in Chicago.
Same firm that made eminent domain sound like a favor.

Developers didn't just hire them—they hid behind them.
Used their legal jargon like riot shields, pushing out the very people they claimed to uplift.

If Atlanta's old money elite needed to erase a neighborhood or bury a lawsuit, they made one call: Maddox, Talmadge, and Perdue Attories at Law.

Sheena stilled. The name alone sent a pulse of recognition through her.

Maddox, Talmadge, and Perdue don't just handle real estate.
They handle erasure. They handle displacement.
A danger with a smile—a lynch mob in khakis.
They call it urban renewal. They call it progress.

But Atlanta knows better.
They orchestrated displacement.
Their playbook was simple: raise property values, push out Black residents, and call it progress.
And now, somehow, they were tangled up in a murder.
Sheena's fingers gripped the edges of the file. Damien, you have stepped into something profound, baby.
Her eyes flicked back to the report, searching for more.
Officer Gordon's name appeared, but his badge number was

missing. That was deliberate. A cop without an official trail. A case with no actual owner.

And then, the phrase that locked her breath in her throat: "Presumed homeless-related death."

Sheena frowned. She looked again at the victim's name. Ellison Ross.

A Xavier University T-shirt. Pressed slacks. A man who had been someone was reduced to an assumption.

This wasn't a homeless man.

They were either wrong.

Or they wanted to be.

Her phone buzzed.

She glanced at the screen.

Beth.

She is still on her Beat stuff.

But this time, it needed a different kind of attention.

The text read:

Queen Shee, Thick insists I inform you— followed by a Beth emoji with a baby bump.

Sheena stared at the message, her grip on the phone tightening. For a moment, the weight of the case dissolved into something softer, something warmer—a quiet, unexpected joy that tingled through her body.

Beth. A baby.

Urgency and joy swirled together, disorienting but undeniable. For all their fights, for all the lines Beth had crossed, Sheena couldn't help but smile.

She wanted this for her sister. For Slim. And maybe, somewhere deep down, for herself.

A familiar ache surfaced, one she rarely let linger. Her future had always been uncertain—professionally, emotionally, and now, physically. She'd long made peace with the likelihood that she couldn't have a child. It was an absence she had learned to carry.

But this?

Oh, my God, Beth- a baby?

She wasn't just going to be an aunt. She was going to be *that* aunt. The one who loved fiercely, who protected, who could be what Coletta would've wanted for this child.

A baby and a rapper-in the ATL? How is that going to work for the baby?

For the first time in a long time, hope flickered in a space she had kept locked away.

Then reality settled back in.

This wasn't just about a baby. It was a lifeline. The text had broken through the isolation of the moment, reminding her that even with all the fractures, they were still connected.

And Slim?

The thought of him wanting this baby—for his reasons, no doubt—humanized him in a way she hadn't considered before. It complicated things. Made them richer, more nuanced. This wasn't just about Beth or Slim. It was about what this baby could mean for all of them.

For a moment, Sheena let herself breathe in that possibility.

Then she refocused, exhaling as she pocketed her phone.

The work pulled her back in.

Ellison Ross. Even now, his name feels heavy. He was just a boy back then—my St. Anthony's schoolmate.

But in Sheena's mind, he was a Black body before he was a name. A site. A scene. The kind of body that, historically, could be left behind without consequence—where a crime could be committed with impunity, and justice could remain an afterthought.

She had spent too much time in crime labs, in courtrooms, in case files, studying how the world classified violence. Black victims became statistics. Black killers became archetypes. And yet, between those cold facts were stories—the truths that rarely made it into police reports.

And Damien? His mind moved differently. Sheena knew his

thoughts were caught in something more profound—not just the crime but the memory.

Ellison Ross. Even now, his name feels heavy.

He was just a boy back then—my St. Anthony's schoolmate.

A beautiful, effeminate boy with polished shoes, his voice soaring above the Metro Atlanta Boys Choir as they sang Lift Every Voice and Sing.

Ellison had a quiet grace that mocked the chaos of our all-Black Catholic school lives.

He was a target of a junior version of toxic masculinity—bullied by us boys who weren't taught to hate like white folks but were taught to hate Black men for being 'sissies.'

But Ellison never bowed to shame.

I envied his courage, even as I failed to defend it.

I shudder now at my weakness, wishing I'd been more assertive.

I'm sorry, Ellison.

Rory taught me how to say that—and mean it.

Sheena pressed her fingers into the report like she could pull him from it, demanding the city say his name—and mean it.

The ATL had spoken.

Now, it was her turn.

Say his name.

Ellison Ross.

Even in death, his dignity defied erasure.

Sheena's gaze drifted outside. *Why here? Why him?*

The questions weighed on her, heavy as granite at Westview Cemetery—Atlanta's most famous resting place.

Damien's voice echoed in her mind. *I think you're right, babe. This case is bigger than Ellison.*

This wasn't just a murder. It was about Atlanta's soul.

Sheena leaned back, letting the pieces click into place.

Damien gave her this file because he trusted her to see what he couldn't.

This wasn't just about finding a killer.

It was about restoring humanity—to Ellison. To Damien. To Atlanta.

Somebody wanted the truth buried.

Sheena was about to dig it up.

The taste of tequila lingered, fading.

The heat of Damien's kiss still pressed against her memory.

Beth. The baby.

Sheena nestled into her teenage bed; the mattress still twisted in that one spot—a reminder that some things never smooth out.

Beth hadn't held back with the linens.

European white goose-down comforter—luxurious but grounding.

She pulled it tight, sinking into something warm, something safe.

Just for a moment.

Then, a smirk.

"That girl—Slim's baby mama."
Shaking her head, she let the thought drift into sleep.

Moment V: After the Ghost Crossed the Line

Sheena woke to the weight of the night before.

The ghosts of past trauma.
Beth's rebellion—sharp-edged but softened by vulnerability.
The crimes stripping Atlanta of its soul.
And beneath it all—the lingering memory of Damien's scent.
Soft. Protective. Steady.

She sat up, stretching, feeling a shift before she could name it.
Something had settled. Something had changed.

Funny how the past never really leaves.
It doesn't fade—it waits. Lurking like a shadow, stepping into the
light when least expected.

Last night was more than memory. It was revelation.

The house... this room...
It wasn't just about what had happened there.
It was about what she fought to keep from taking from her.

And Beth... sweet, stubborn Beth.
Soon to be Slim or Thick's child's mother a
Maybe a girl?
Another mama- Black, brilliant, and bold.

The case.
The bodies.
Those sites aren't just crime scenes.
They were speaking.
Calling out truths ignored too long.

This isn't just about who or how.
It's about why.
And then—Damien.
He kissed me the same- his tender kiss.
More a part of her than she had realized.
She exhaled, pressing a hand into the mattress, grounding her-
self in this truth.
She loved him.
I have always loved Day. I always will.
But love as children, love as teenagers—that was easy. That was
stolen kisses at my window, soft whispers in the dark, the promise
of always.

Who are we now?
Who are we as adults? After distance, after choices, after everything we've lost and everything we've become? Where is he with his wife?

Are we still us?-Us? After all this time?

Last night didn't change the world.

But it unearthed her. Propelled her to know that she deserved more.

She had seen where she had been.

She had faced what she feared.

She had decided what she was ready to fight for.

And just like that, the spirits did it all in one night.

She swung her legs over the bed, pink-polished toes pressing into the plush throw rug Beth had picked to cover the scuffed hardwood.

A faint smile.

Beth had tried in her own way.

Her phone buzzed.

Google Calendar Notification:

Keynote Speaker, 4 PM – Concerned Black Clergy: Crime & Community Healing

The nudge she needed.

Sheena stretched, rolling her shoulders. Coffee first. Maybe a workout.

But more than anything, she needed to see Damien.

The thought alone warmed her, undeniable.

"What can I do with my downtime?" she murmured, a small smile forming.

Then—through the quiet hum of morning—she heard it.

The chime of a local Episcopal church bell-

Bing... bing... bing... bing.

Soft at first. Then again— bing... bing... bing... bing.

Faint, yet deliberate. A sound that didn't quite belong, yet refused to be ignored.

A sound that didn't belong in the chaos of Atlanta—yet felt placed there just for her.

It wasn't just a bell.

It was a call to action.

An altar call- and it wasn't even Sunday morning.

She closed her eyes just the same; in her mind, the voice of pastor back in Chicago- the Rev. Dr. Otis Moss III raised a thought of conviction—rich, heavy with purpose-stepped in hope,

It would be nice for you to see Damien- after last night.

The moment settled deep.

She stood slowly, feeling the rug beneath her feet once more.

The weight of the day loomed ahead.

But so did something else.

Something lighter.

Something softer.

For sure -it wasn't nighttime anymore.

It was daytime somewhere in the ATL.

CHAPTER 3

THE LIGHT OF DAY

Moment I: It's Day Time

Damien never rushed his mornings.

Steam curled around him as he stepped out of the shower, heat still kissing his skin, the weight of last night settling into his muscles like a memory.

The scent of warm bath oil filled the air as he smoothed it over his chest, shoulders, and arms—each stroke slow, deliberate, indulgent.

The plush rug beneath his feet whispered of her touch. That thought alone made him smirk.

His lips, still damp from steam, curled into a knowing grin. He licked them, savoring the moment as if the rug beneath him was a runway meant for kings.

And just as Silk, hailing from Atlanta, climbed through the hook into Damien's soul, he let himself go with it.

He sang without thinking.

He felt without guarding.

His scent lingered, nutmeg-spiced and rich, rising from the heat of the shower's pulse.

His skin was Trevante Rhodes brown- the dark golden top of a perfect pound cake, softened by steam but rich with depth. He knew when to be silent, to take in a deep breath scented with cucumber and quiet understanding, letting her words be delicious wisdom.

Despite a world that often forsook Black beauty, a man well cared for.

But he wasn't beautiful because the world found him profitable—he was beautiful because he loved himself—shoulders back, never in shame.

His ex-wife had taken for granted his cocoa-dusted frame, the muscle that curved just beyond the reach of his towel—evidence of a man rebuilding, healing, becoming.

This Day moving like the perfect riff of your favorite love song. This is Damien, the a walking receipt of what he hoped to be to her.

He was Black masculinity wrapped in a dark whisper of self-assured allure.

A M-A-N.

Not just in body, but in presence.

Deeply resonant.

Almond, roasted masculinity.

Still, coming.

Then—

Beep.

The front door unlocked.

He didn't flinch. His people had the code. It was probably the cleaning crew about to start their examination early. He reached for the towel, wrapped it low around his waist, and moved to meet them before they got too far inside.

But when he turned the corner—

Caramel. A fitted jogging suit. The smell of coconut-saffron-infused silk.

He exhaled a soft, surprised laugh. Damn. He had just been thinking about her while singing Silk on a loop now vibrating through his chest.

Then—

"Sheena".

The immediate rise of Day—undeniable, unguarded, bold in her presence.

Her eyes dipped—slow, deliberate, drinking him in like she had all the time in the world.

A smirk curled at the edge of her lips, a flicker of amusement meeting something deeper.

Beneath the towel, a bump loomed.

An impossible thing. A promise wrapped in muscle and heat.

A desert worth crossing.

She had felt it years ago, knowing its presence without ever daring to touch, claim, have and hold.

Back then, she had lingered at the edge—tasting the possibility without taking the journey.

But now?

Now, it was time to cross.

Sheena's lips parted slightly, not in surprise, but in realization. "Hmmm."

Not a giggle. Not a gasp. But something heavier. A knowing.

A quiet delight in what was hers to see, to want, to take.

She smiled, half-shy, half-knowing. "Hey, Day. I hope you don't mind me coming by."

Damien just stared, caught between last night and right now.

"Oh, girl, I don't care that you came by," flipping like he was spitting game, shaking his head. "You know this is your spot."

Sheena leaned against the counter, eyes steady on him. "I wanted to come in and hang with you last night." She exhaled, tilting her head just slightly. "But I had to get through the night myself—big girl panties stuff." Then, softer now, like a realization settling deep—

"But now... I could be reeeeady."

He smirked, stepping a little closer. "And here you go—'reeeeday'—not a singing critic like last night, huh? First thing in the morning, popping up, judging my vocals."

Sheena playfully snapped her fingers—soft but commanding, like a rhythm only she could lead.

And just as Damien moved to step toward her—

"Kiss me, Day."

The words came soft, yet certain, a command wrapped in honey.

Sheena closed the space between them, pressing closer than they had ever been.

The air between them thickened, charged with something deeper than just desire.

It was understanding.

It was memory -pulled from the way you knew it would always be.

It was home.

Sheena had already laid herself bare to him years ago—not in body, but in truth. She had allowed him to have her many times through words unspoken and tender kisses never had.

It was Daytime.

Damien wasn't a man to hesitate, but with her, he did—if only for a breath. He needed to take her in. To see her.

He reached for her, and she came willingly, tilting her chin just slightly, parting her lips before their mouths met.

At first, it was wet, precise—a kiss that held intention and carried patience and control.

Then—

It was wet, irrational—a kiss that had no more boundaries, that needed no more permission. A kiss that took, that gave, that demanded surrender.

Somewhere between breath and movement, Sheena unzipped her jogging top, letting it fall from her shoulders. Her jogging pants slipped away in a smooth descent.

And that was when Damien saw it.

At the G-string's edge, a discreet tattoo.

One word. One name.

Day.

Damien's throat tightened. His breath slowed.

He didn't say a word, but his fingers traced over it, his thumb brushing just enough to feel the ink beneath his skin.

Sheena smirked, eyes half-lidded as she whispered, "What? You surprised?"

Damien didn't answer. He let his lips trail lower, making his response known without words.

The weight of the moment sat between them, heavy and inevitable. Warm- the winter blanket on a free body on the most chilly days.

His fingers traced the side of her face, reverent, possesive, knowing. His voice, low and deliberate, cut through the stillness.

Silk schmoozed, *"Let's make love."* The w ords w ere D amien's now. And they weren't a request—they were inevitable.

A tug.

Every time I think about

All the little freaky things you do

Sheena's back arched.

Feels so good to be inside

I'm glad you let me in between your thighs."

Now, the song was just narration.

Her voice was breathy, open, the final surrender.

She turned back at him- her head, lips parted, breath catching as Damien's hand—firm, firmer but patient- guided her back closer. His thumb skimmed her jaw, his palm cradling her cheek as he took her in.

He exhaled against her skin, his voice slipping into the space between them, hushed but irresistible.

Toss your body back and forth.

Turn around

So I can watch you ride, yeah.
A slow purr—soft, sweet, surrendering.
Sheena thought-
I didn't know it would be this good—oh, shit. Day, that's—oh, that's your spot.
"Let me have you, Sheena. I need you. I want only you".
Damien pulled her firmer.
She felt his breath before she felt his lips.
"I wanna hear you tell me it's all mine, mine, mine." Silk or Damien's voice was a quiet demand, his weight settling into her, his claim undeniable.
She felt his hands before she felt his weight.
And in that moment, the rhythm wasn't just the song—it was them.
Sheena let go.
Now, their bodies moved—pounding, throbbing, satisfying. Needing. Trusting.
Damien took her there.
"Pull it, Day. Pull it, Day. Pull my hair, Day. Pull my hair." And he did.
Sexual harmony—cultivated over a lifetime of missing.
"Pull it Daaaay."
A breathless moan, stretched, breaking at the edges—
"Ooooh, Daaaaaay… Puuulllll— that's it—thaaaat's iiiiiiiittttt."

Moment II: Em interrupts Sheena's Daytime

A lifetime of new love had started—rooted in deep sensuality, yet stretching beyond the physical.
The weight of them.
The heat of them.
The urgency of now.
It was the same urgency they'd felt back when they first kissed—

On Cascade.

In the hallways of the ATL's unprecedented public-"private" Benjamin Elijah Mays High School.

Or tucked away in the food court at Greenbriar Mall.

But this?

This was different.

This was grown. Whole. Certain.

This was love rediscovered, fully realized, fully claimed.

I think we're in (in) too (too) deep (baby) Don't wanna pull out—

Dvsn's melodic erotism throbbed through the air, the bassline humming low, a pulse between them. The song didn't just play—it settled deep, threading through their limbs, collapsing their bodies into a moan—not just pleasure, but recognition.

I just wanna go down, in history, how you like

As the one who makes you comfortable

Cause your lips, they got me feeling very vulnerable...

The rhythm cascaded over their skin, a slow, intoxicating pull deeper—sweeter and sweeter like a body-heavy ellipse neither wanted to break.

BZZZ. BZZZ.

The phone jittered against the counter—urgent, insistent, breaking the heat between them like an uninvited guest.

Sheena cocooned deeper into the sheets, into Damien, unwilling to let the moment slip away just yet.

His chest rose, still pressed against hers. His hand was in her hair. His breath, was still there. The bassline of Dvsn still humming in the sheets.

Reality. A blade cutting clean through silk. Confident. His love. Her mother's grit. Sheena's intellect.

Just sixteen- but thirty when you were not right.

At The Lovett School, they called her "Em—Checkmate."

Not for how she guarded the paint—

but for how she cornered people in conversation.

For a second, Damien didn't move. Didn't blink. Didn't want to leave this moment.

But she was waiting.

And some loves can't be unless others are kept well.

It was FaceTime.

He exhaled, centering himself—ready to hold the other half of his heart.

A slow smile spread across his face as he answered, camera off. "Hey, baby."

The response was immediate—sharp, bright, full of attitude. "Hey, Daddy! Why's your camera off?"

Em's voice filled the space—teasing, relentless, and wiser than her years. No matter how old she got, she always managed to check him like a woman twice her age.

Damien exhaled through his nose, amused. He already knew how this was going to go.
"Em, baby, listen—"

"Uh-uh, don't 'baby' me. Turn the camera on!"

Sheena smirked beneath the covers. The girl had presence. That mix of fire and affection was all Beat at fifteen.

"Right now, I just got out the shower," Damien lied, knowing she wasn't buying it.

"Daddy, it's eleven o'clock. You just now showering? Aren't you supposed to be at work?"

"I am," he said, rubbing his forehead. "Just getting myself together."

Em let out an exaggerated sigh.
"Turn the camera on, Dad. Stop playing."

"I'm not doing that right now," he said, lowering his voice to stay in control. "What do you need, sweet pea?"

There was a pause. Then, a little more edge in her tone:
"Daddy... you got somebody over there?"

Sheena had already gone still, listening.

Em gasped dramatically. "Oh my God! You do! I knew it. One of those Instagram—"

"Ay!"

She burst out laughing. "I'm just sayin'—I saw your followers, Daddy."

Damien groaned, closing his eyes as Sheena muffled her laughter.

"Baby, there is no Instagram anything, okay? What do you want?"

Em huffed, still grinning. "Mmm-hmm. Well, if somebody's over there—and I know she can hear me—you better treat my daddy right. Because I don't play."

Sheena let out a laugh, covering her mouth. The way Em talked reminded her so much of Beat at that age—unapologetically bold, protective, and with a heart too big to ignore.

"What do you want, baby?" Damien asked, chuckling despite himself.

Em sobered slightly, though her voice stayed warm. "I need something."

Damien stretched, tilting his head back. "Em, I just sent your mama three thousand dollars. What could you possibly need?"

"You know how she is," Em said with a sigh. "She's living large, Daddy. She works hard, but she spends harder."

Damien chuckled. "Girl—"

"Besides," she continued quickly, "you know she doesn't want me playing basketball."

That got his attention. "What's going on?"

"I killed it last game. Coach said I've got real potential. I want to play with the AAU team this summer."

He already knew what was coming. "How much?"

"Five hundred."

"For what?"

"I need shoes. The good ones," she said confidently. "And maybe a travel sweatsuit."

Damien smirked. "You know Raven Johnson won a state title and a Natty at South Carolina. You trying to be like her, you better put in Raven-like work."

Em groaned. "Daddy, really?"

"I'm just saying…"

"I *am* putting in work! That's why I need the gear. C'mon, please."

He sighed. "All right. Let me sit down with your mama and talk it through."

"Don't tell her I asked. You know how she is."

"I won't say anything," he said. "But being a mother's not just about buying things and looking good."

"I know, Daddy. And even if she never loved you, I love you. I'm grateful."

His throat tightened. But before he could respond—

"Also… can I get that candy, though?"

"Emily DeBerg."

She giggled. "You know, Em-D. Like that old group EPMD. But seriously—come see me later, okay?"

"I've got a meeting, but after that, I'll bring it to you."

"Love you, Daddy!"

"Love you too, baby."

And just before the call ended—

"Hey, whoever you are—I know you can hear me. Don't play with my daddy. I don't play either."

Click.

The FaceTime ended. The only interruption Damien ever allowed—because some loves can't be unless others are kept well.

Sheena had a pillow pressed over her mouth, trying not to laugh.

"You laughing?" Damien asked, turning to her.

She wiped her eyes, laughter spilling over. "Absolutely. Because if you don't get those shoes, *Auntie IG Chick* is gonna get dragged."

Lovemaking had just ended, but now they were fully wrapped in something else—something more playful, more sacred.

Beneath the sheets, Sheena stretched, trailing her manicured nails along Damien's calves. She hooked her foot around his, rubbing gently.

"It's the shoes, Day," she said, mimicking Em's voice. "Get the shoes, Daddy."

Damien chuckled, the laughter in his chest settling into something deeper.

"Get me those shoes," she whispered again, this time more intimately.

Her fingers glided slowly up his thighs, touching him with a reverence that felt holy.

The morning—or maybe mid-morning—melted around them.

Time blurred.

Sheena felt held, grounded. Safe.

And in the quiet aftermath of intimacy, she found herself doing things she once only dreamed of—silly, childlike things she used to suppress.

But here, in Day's bed, she reclaimed something.

The innocence life had tried to steal.

Years of being a Black woman in America had taken so much.

But in the right man's arms, she healed.

She reached for the bottle of body oil on the nightstand, dipped a finger into the smooth liquid, and began tracing letters onto Damien's chest.
S-H-E-E-N-A.
His skin was warm beneath her fingertip, the oil catching in the morning light. She took her time, like inscribing something sacred.

Then, without thinking—no, without needing to think—she started humming.

The melody slipped out before she even realized it. The words followed, like a whisper from another time—

A song they had written together in 11th-grade math class.

A lifetime ago.

"Yo, it's Sheena on the scene, reppin' B.E. Mays,

ATL fire, we were born to blaze."

Damien's brow furrowed slightly, a lazy grin tugging at his lips as he looked up at her, his arms still draped around her waist.

"What are you doing? What are you singing?" His tone was half-teasing, half-knowing.

Sheena smirked, tracing another slow swirl on his chest before slipping into the hook, her voice softer now, more melodic:

"Beloved in the ATL, where the streets don't sleep,

From the boulevard grind to the passion, we keep.

It's a vibe, it's a movement, it's the city we claim,

ATL, be-loved, in the heart, in the name."

She didn't realize she had closed her eyes until the last note faded, leaving only silence and Damien's chest's slow, steady rise beneath her hand.

When she opened them, Damien was staring at her—deeply, knowingly, like he was seeing more than just her face, more than just this moment.

His fingers brushed against her wrist, stopping her, holding her there.

"Damn," he murmured. His voice wasn't playful anymore. "We really wrote that, huh?"

Sheena swallowed, nodding.

"Yeah. We did."

A beat of quiet passed, but it wasn't empty.

It was full.

Full of all the years.

All the ways they had loved each other in the dark, even when they hadn't said it out loud.

BeLoved in the ATL.

The words stretched between them, lingering in the air, in the sheets, in their skin.

Sheena shrugged, her giggle bubbling up naturally. "Impromptu artwork," she mused, dipping her finger back into the oil, drawing the final swirl of her name across his chest.

Damien exhaled a quiet laugh. "Oh, so now you're kicking me out of the production credits? You just gon' jake my bars?"

She grinned, humming lightly again, the memory slipping between them like a shared secret, like a song only they knew.

The song wasn't just a song.

It was them.

It had always been them.

And for the first time, they were BeLoved in the ATL.

Damien's hand found hers mid-stroke, stopping her just as she finished tracing the last letter.

His touch was firm but tender. His eyes searched hers, holding her there, steadying her.

"You still surprise me," he murmured.

Sheena smiled, leaning down, pressing a soft kiss against his chest—right where her name shimmered in the oil.

Then, just as effortlessly as Em had claimed "Don't play with Em's Daddy no Day", that same deep protection rose in Sheena, unspoken but undeniable.

She had never seen Damien as fragile, but suddenly, she felt it—how much this Black man had deserved to be loved and had missed it.

And now?

She was determined that he would never go without again.

Her voice, steady but low, carried the weight of her realization.

"Damien... what happened with Em's mother?"

Moment III: Daytime, Tamika's Way

Sheena's breath was still warm against Damien's skin, her fingers idly tracing the remnants of the oil she had written across his chest. The song they had once written together—BeLoved in the ATL—lingered in the sheets, the melody still humming low between them.

And again she asked it.

"Damien… what happened with Em's mother?"

Sheena wasn't the type to pry. If anything, she had been too careful—always leaving space, always letting him reveal on his own time. But this morning, something had shifted. Maybe it was the weight of him finally in her arms. Maybe it was Em's voice, so protective of her father, forcing Sheena to understand who had come before her. Damien deserved another look.

Either way, he knew this wasn't a question he could dodge.

Damien exhaled, his fingers brushing over Sheena's wrist before settling against her waist. "You really wanna know?"

Sheena didn't answer right away. Instead, her fingers moved first. A slow, lazy glide across Damien's chest, tracing patterns only she could read. Not rushed, not probing—just there. Feeling.

Her palm flattened, warm against the muscle beneath, pressing into his heartbeat, steadying him before she even spoke.

Like she wasn't just asking about Tamika.

Like she was asking about the man he had been when he loved her.

When Daytime was so far out of reach, they both would've gone mad trying to hold onto it.

Damien exhaled, the breath slow, dragging across Sheena's forehead. His fingertips found the dip of her spine, resting there, firm but gentle, his touch answering before his words did.

She didn't push. Just held him. Let him be held.

And in that, Damien realized—this wasn't about Tamika.

This was about him.

About whom he was before Sheena came back into his life.

Before this morning, before the way she had folded into him, not just her body but her presence—like she had always been meant to be there.

She was asking him to tell her a truth he had long since stopped trying to explain.

And for some reason, this time, he wanted to.

Finally, she nodded.

So he told her.

The Beginning of the End

"I met Tamika while she was home partying during Spring Break," he said, his fingers idly tracing Sheena's waist as if the touch kept him tethered to the present. "She was at Tuskegee, in her last year, struggling to fight her parents about not wanting to be a teacher. I was still a cop back then."

Sheena's brow lifted slightly. "So this was… Justin's? Limelight?"

Damien huffed out a small laugh. "One of those. She used to club-hop, always looking for the right scene, the right people."

"Sounds exhausting."

The Weight of a Question – The Beginning of Tamika's Story

Damien smirked, his voice carrying that easy cadence of a man who had long since made peace with his past—or at least learned to tell it without flinching.

"For her, it was necessary. Tamika always knew how to move in the right spaces, how to be where the power was—even if she wasn't the power herself. Even in high school, I knew of her."

Sheena's fingers stilled slightly on his chest, but she didn't interrupt.

"Tamika went to The Frederick Douglass High School. And unlike Keisha—our ex-mayor—she wasn't about that straight educational grind. Nah. She was more in-crowd than intellectual. More labels than leadership."

Sheena exhaled slowly, already seeing it. The type. The girl.

She didn't say anything, but Damien caught the way her lips

pursed slightly, the way her silence filled in the blanks. Mays girls and Douglass girls? They weren't ever really gonna be friends.

"The night I met her, she was with the enemy—some cats I was cool with who had gone to Doug," Damien continued, his fingers tracing slow, absent-minded circles against Sheena's waist. "They was telling me, 'Man, she fine, Day. But she 'bout them dollars.'"

Sheena still didn't say anything, but Damien could feel it now— her energy shifting, her breath slowing, that way she absorbed his words and folded them neatly into whatever quiet judgment she was making.

She didn't have to say it.

He already knew.

The minute he said Douglass, Sheena—Mays High, stepper, Atlanta through and through—had already dismissed Tamika. Filed her away as another pretty girl who moved where the power was, rather than being power herself.

And maybe, for the first time, Damien saw it too.

"We hooked up the first night we met," he admitted.

Sheena didn't flinch, didn't tense, just waited for the rest.

"She went back to school for her senior year, and I didn't think about her much after that." He shook his head. "Then she called me outta nowhere, talking about she was pregnant."

"And she thought it was yours?"

"She thought it was her boyfriend's at first," Damien corrected. "Did a whole damn Maury moment. Turned out, I was the father."

Sheena let out a slow exhale.

Damien continued. "She came back to Atlanta. At first, she had her family's backing, but she didn't want to marry me. Thought I was… beneath her."

Sheena's lips parted slightly.

Damien chuckled, but there wasn't much humor in it. "I was a cop. She was about to work for Delta Airlines as a flight attendant, and had plans to work her way into money. Me?" He shrugged. "I wasn't part of the package she wanted."

"But you married her anyway."

Damien nodded.

"Yeah. She didn't want to—but I insisted. I wasn't about to let my kid grow up without a father. Not like I did."

He exhaled, ran a hand over his jaw, then shook his head.

"About six months ago, Em hit me like—'Daddy, Mommy's friend said I was cute like her. Said we had a connection. Told me he had a buddy who could hook me up with some coaching. Said my convo was steady.'"

Damien's voice dropped—low, rough.

"I ain't no killer... but—"

The air between them thickened.

Sheena absorbed that quietly, her breath still pressed into his chest.

Her mind flickered back—a memory, a moment, a window, a boy.

Cascade. Late. Her childhood bedroom.

Damien standing there, outside, watching, waiting—like he'd been born to come for her.

And she knew. Had always known.

What if it hadn't happened? What if she hadn't left? What if he had known right after it happened? What if...

She knew.

Damien would have crossed the line.

And she wouldn't have wanted that.

That wouldn't have been right—not for them.

Not good for Damien.

Not good for what they could become.

I'm glad he stayed free.

She had no doubt.

And now, lying against him, feeling the steady rise and fall of his chest beneath her palm, she knew something else too.

It wasn't about Em's mother anymore.

It was about Em.

It was about her.

And it was about what it meant to be loved by a man like Damien DeBerg.

Sheena didn't speak—she didn't have to. Instead, she dragged her nails lightly across his chest, tracing the same skin she had already marked with her name.

Damien exhaled again like he knew exactly what she wasn't saying.

His fingers flexed against her hip, his grip sure, confident.

And for the first time, Sheena realized—

He may not do it himself.

But let somebody cross the line?

Let somebody fuck around and find out?

And the world would find out just how far Day would go.

"She was eight months pregnant when we got married. Her mom suggested we keep it quiet, wait 'til after Em was born, and have a bigger reception later. Less scandal that way."

Sheena scoffed under her breath. "Less scandal?"

"Yeah. But it didn't matter." He exhaled, rubbing a hand over his face as if dusting off something he hadn't touched in years. "The marriage lasted exactly one month. I mean, on paper? In actuality, fourteen years of hollow exile and broken trust, because Em is sixteen now. But Tamika had her attorney call mine, agreeing to pay all the court fees if we could make the official divorce date Em's birthday—November 4."

Sheena's brows pulled together, confusion flickering through her eyes.

"Wait... why?"

Damien let out a dry chuckle, shaking his head. "Tamika always teases that the day is Liberation Day—for her." His voice dipped slightly. "And Em, according to her."

Sheena stilled.

It wasn't a shock. Not exactly. But something about that cut differently now. Not just because she knew Em, she had seen how that girl loved her daddy, but because she could feel, even in the way he said it, how deep that wound ran.

She opened her mouth, then closed it.

Damien noticed. He sighed, running a hand over his beard before returning to her.

"Nah, go ahead. Say it."

Sheena hesitated, then, finally— "That's some cold sh—" She stopped herself, adjusting, tempering her words. "That's wild."

Damien smirked again, but there was something else behind it this time. Something tired.

"Yeah. That's Tamika."

Sheena watched him, taking in the way his chest rose and fell, like he was carrying the weight of something long buried but never really gone.

Em's birthday was her mother's Liberation Day.

Damien had signed the papers.

And yet, he was the one who had stayed and liberated.

Moment IV: While Away From Day

Damien's fingers traced the curve of Sheena's back, his touch lingering like the question still hanging in the air. The weight of their conversation sat between them—heavy, unbroken. His voice, roughened with something unreadable, cut through the silence.

"And now, your turn—I bird-wounded me with your two-year-ago news."

His tone was measured, but Sheena caught it.

That fixation. That unspoken thing.

Like a man who already knew the answer but needed to hear it anyway.

Like a boy who once had a crush on his teacher, still waiting for a lesson he wasn't sure he wanted.

Sheena exhaled, tilting her head slightly, the weight of memory settling deep before she spoke.

"Scott Alfred Hogarth, IV."

Damien's fingers paused mid-trace.

"Criminal pro bono attorney. Harvard Law. University of Chicago undergrad. White, sincere, honest, safe—and guilty."

A smirk played at the corner of Damien's lips. "Guilty?"

Sheena chuckled lightly. "In his own way."

Scott's name carried weight in the right circles. His lineage traced back to William Hogarth, a long-forgotten English painter whose name still held whispers of prestige. His last name had placed him neatly into a conservative law firm that draped itself in justice while cashing checks from mass incarceration.

And Scott?

He had hated that.

It had appalled him, outraged him, the hypocrisy of it all. Inspired by Obama, he had thrown himself into public defense, fighting for the poor, Black, and Brown. He could have done anything, leveraged his privilege for generational wealth—but he chose the trenches.

Or, at least, he thought he did.

Sheena had admired that.

And in his way, he had loved her.

Loved her enough to try.

To listen. To adjust. To press his privilege into service.

To dress sharper, soften his presence, shift his approach.

By white boy standards, he was "cute."

But he would never be a Black man.

And that? That was the line that would always remain.

Because Sheena wasn't just brilliant.

She was an intelligent Black woman.
Not just PhD-intelligent, but something more ancient.
A wisdom you don't read in books—you live it.
You earn it by surviving.
By knowing when to be still.
When to move.
When to fight.

Scott could never truly understand.
No matter how much he listened, how much he tried to empathize.

Because what Sheena carried didn't come from privilege or proximity.
It came from Black trauma and Black resilience.

You don't *study* that.
You survive it.

You rise after the world has taken from you—
just because your Blackness made it possible,
and your womanhood made it permissible.

And Sheena knew the truth.

The essence of the Black soul will always remain untold by the white gaze—no matter how well-intentioned.

To that end, she carried this belief like a gospel:
Every Black woman is a Ph.D. at the fissure of their intersectionality—
with a concentration on original humanity-woke when your divinity has them wishing they were asleep.

Scott had pursued her with patience, with quiet listening. But he had never seen her.

Because to see her was to know Frankie Beverly wasn't just a name, but a feeling.

It was to dance to him.

To understand that real red Kool-Aid didn't come from a store-bought packet, but from somebody's mama in the kitchen, with a sugar ratio only she could get right.

It was being at Howard University's quad, arguing over who in Slow Hall was finer—only to know none of them could ever touch Day back in Atlanta.

And Sheena?

She had too much in her to pretend otherwise.

She had been marked forever.

Tattooed at the G-string line with Day's name long before ink touched her skin.

Scott had never been the one who could ask her to cross the line.

Even if she had crossed over for a few.

She had known it was over the moment she got her hair done.

They had been caught in the middle of something heated, tangled in sheets when Scott reached for her braids.

And she stopped.

Mid-stream. Cold. Immediate. Unthinking.

Not just hesitation—resistance.

As if every Black woman before her, every ancestor who had ever laced shells through their locs and stood unbowed, had stopped her hands before he could take what was never meant to be understood.

She hadn't needed to explain why.

Just like those before her had never been able to explain it to Missy.

And further still—he was too mechanical.

Too precise. Too careful.

She could feel it in the way he touched her—calculated, measured, knowing just enough to be wrong.

Because he would have never pulled it right.

She had ended it because while away, she had become whole.

She had become mature, certain.

But still knowing, deep down—

Daybreak ain't Daytime.

Sheena let out a slow breath, staring at nothing in particular.

Damien was silent.

Then, his fingers, still warm against her skin, flexed. His voice was low, teasing, but edged with something real.

"So, what you saying?" he murmured. "He ain't pull it right?"

Sheena turned her head toward him, smirking. "You tell me."

And just like that—

Damien moved.

He didn't ask.

Didn't hesitate.

His fingers found the base of her now flowing hair, wrapping just enough to remind her who she had always belonged to.

"Pull my hair, again, Day."

Moment V: The Day Must Go On

The silk sheets still carried their scent. A slow, lingering warmth that should have been enough to hold them in bed just a little longer. But the day had no patience for lovers.

Damien exhaled, rolling onto his back, and staring at the ceiling like it held the answer to something he didn't know how to ask.

Sheena watched him, the weight of their conversation still settling between them like an unspoken truth. He had let her in, let her touch something raw beneath the surface. But now, the world outside was calling him back.

His phone buzzed again—this time, a text.

HQ. Now.

He pinched the bridge of his nose, his other hand still idly tracing circles on Sheena's thigh. "And just like that…" he muttered.

Sheena stretched, rolling onto her stomach and propping herself up on her elbows. "They need you?" Her voice was quiet, but there was something else underneath it. A knowing.

"They always do," Damien said, swinging his legs off the bed. He sat there for a moment, rubbing a hand over his head before standing up, and reaching for the pair of sweats he had discarded sometime last night.

Sheena's eyes followed him, the way his body moved with a quiet confidence, the way even in silence, he filled the room.

This wasn't just her lover. This was a man who belonged to something beyond them.

And yet, when his gaze landed back on her, there was a flicker of hesitation. Like maybe, just maybe, a part of him wanted to stay.

She smirked, stretching lazily, the sheets slipping lower over her back. "You gon' be alright out there, Day?"

He smirked back, stepping toward the bed, pressing a slow, deliberate kiss against her shoulder. "Yeah. You gon' be alright in here?"

Sheena rolled her eyes, but her smirk lingered. "I'll manage."

He reached for his phone, his keys, his badge—pieces of himself that belonged to the outside world. But before he could fully slip into that version of himself, she caught his wrist.

"Damien."

He turned.

Her fingers trailed down his forearm, slow, thoughtful. "Be careful. Whatever this is… it's bigger than just a case."

He nodded once, understanding settling between them.

Then, with one last glance, Damien was gone.

Sheena: The Weight of the Morning

Sheena stayed in bed a little longer after the door clicked shut.

The sheets, still warm from him, felt like they held the echoes of everything they'd just shared.

She traced her fingers over the space where he had laid, breathing in the scent of him—clean, dark spice, a scent that belonged to no one else but him.

And yet, the moment he left, reality crept back in. The world had found its way between them again.

She turned onto her back, staring at the ceiling.

Tamika.

The name lingered like an aftertaste. Not a threat, not jealousy, just… context. A piece of Damien's past that she now held in her hands.

But she had her own past too.

And she was tired of running from it.

She reached for her phone, flipping through her missed calls, her texts.

One name stood out.

Scott.

Sheena exhaled, her thumb hovering over the screen.

She had unfinished business of her own.

The past wasn't just Damien's to wrestle with.

It was time to face hers.

Moment VI: What's in the City's Light

The press conference came on, cutting through the lingering haze of morning. For Damien, it was like the TV had hijacked the room, replacing the music with something far heavier. The weight of politics had a way of shifting the air, of making the walls close in.

Sheena nudged him, her urgency sharper than the shift in sound.

"Day. Put your TV on," she said, sitting up, sheets still pooled around her waist.

The screen loomed larger than the windows, dominating the space, making it feel less like a hotel suite and more like the front row of a war being declared.

The Georgia Governor stood at the podium, a Republican through and through—business-oriented, flexible when it served him, rigid when the money dictated. He stood flanked by GBI investigators on one side and attorneys from the most powerful conservative law firm in the state on the other. Among them were Black pastors who had long since decided it was easier to get paid than to fight.

Little did Damien or Sheena know that Emanuel Cain was one of them.

The governor leaned in, voice dripping with authority, with finality.

"I want to emphatically say that all of this talk that would slow business in Georgia because of Atlanta—it's got to stop. There is no Wayne Williams 2.0. The WOKE Mob's fake news has got to stop those who would sow divisiveness- that damn Critical Race theory is ruining decent Georgians!"

Sheena's inhale was sharp. Damien's jaw flexed.

And as a marketing afterthought, a shriveled-up white fella identifying himself as a Georgia Gang host

"The GBI has told the Atlanta Police Department to look no further. These cases are not connected. There is no conspiracy. There is no serial killing. And let me be clear—this city's violence is the result of political incompetence at the local level. Other cities around Atlanta are thriving. Maybe it's time we consider annexing Atlanta into one of those more responsible municipalities because bigger isn't always better. And Atlanta has proven that."

The room stilled, the words slithering across the screen like a slow, poisonous tide.

"And Mayor Bond, this isn't about party. But let's not forget— we, as Republicans, hold the political upper hand. And for those who continue to spread hysteria, claiming conspiracy, or making baseless accusations that could harm Georgia's business interests? Be advised. The attorneys standing with me today are prepared to bring lawsuits against anyone who engages in reckless speculation or slander."

The message was clear.

Shut up. Stand down. Don't rock the boat.

Sheena exhaled, shaking her head. "So that's the game."

Damien was already reaching for the remote, flipping to Channel 2: Live, Local, Late-Breaking. They gave a more digestible, sanitized version of the governor's words—saying he and the mayor were "working together" to ensure the city's safety.

But Damien knew better.

The shit was officially hitting the fan.

And almost on cue—his phone buzzed. HQ. NOW.

The meeting, originally scheduled for 1 p.m., had been moved up to 12:30. He had less than 45 minutes to get across the city.

His mind moved like a chef dicing ingredients on a cutting board—sharp, precise, ruthless.

The governor just gave the green light to kill the case, "Check."

The GBI was done investigating.

The message to anyone fighting for Atlanta was clear: fall in line or become a target.

Damien stood, reaching for his pants. Sheena shifted, watching him dress, her lips pressing into a firm line.

"You good?" she asked.

He nodded, though neither of them believed it.

"I gotta go see M after this," he added, grabbing his keys. "Make sure she's straight."

Sheena slid out of bed, moving toward him, unbothered by the lack of clothing between them. She placed a hand against his chest, feeling the steady drum of his heartbeat.

"We already knew this wouldn't be easy," she said, searching his eyes. "You ready for what comes next?"

Damien exhaled, his lips curving slightly before pressing into hers—a kiss that wasn't just passion but a promise.

"Always."

They both knew the intimacy they had just shared wasn't about them anymore.

It wasn't just about the case. It was about what they stood for—values forged in the ATL's quiet corners and private corridors. Lessons whispered on Cascade porches, traded in the hallways of Mays High, carried through MARTA train stations, taunted on the blacktops of Adams Park, and sanctified in the pulse of midnight rides down Peachtree.

It was the city's rhythm—spoken in drawls, sharpened by struggle, and carried in the beat of the people who refused to fold.

They weren't just from Atlanta. They were stitched into its fabric.

CHAPTER 4

THE SYSTEM THROWS SHADE

Moment I: The System Throws Shade

Damien had two loves.

One had been violated—vengeance had been the only option. The other was being violated—justice had to be the only option. The difference was time. And time was cruel and crucial.

And here, in his car, the crash of the hi-hats, the drop of the bass, and Usher's haunting delivery caused Damien to have a mental collision.

Oh, oh oh…

Mm, you're gonna want me back…

It's the last words she said to me…

It's driving me crazy. Driving me crazy.

It looped and looped.

If I could rewind the time and get inside your mind…

It's driving me crazy. Driving me crazy. It's driving me crazy.

Sheena's wound had been inflicted in the dark, behind closed doors, where walls and silence swallowed screams.

But the ATL?

Atlanta bled in broad daylight.

Right here on these streets—under the glow of streetlights and campaign banners. Beneath courthouse steps where justice twisted itself into a cash transaction.

With Sheena, he had been too late.

With Atlanta, he was still in the fight.

But for how much longer?

How many more bodies would be sacrificed before the city's backbone snapped?

It's driving me crazy. Crazy. Crazy. Crazy baby.

Usher's revelation faded as Damien pulled up, his thoughts still tangled in the past—things that needed to be revealed, secrets yet to be told.

But outside, Atlanta had no time for nostalgia.

The city was loud, alive, and on fire. MAGA hats bobbed in the crowd. Street preachers screamed salvation, advocating for humility.

The noise wasn't just sound—it was a war zone, and Damien was walking straight into it.

The chants crashed against each other like fists in a street fight.

"Make Atlanta Great Again! MAGA, damn it, MAGA!"

"Jesus—get saved, damn it!"

"Be like Clarence Thomas, one of the 'good ones!'"

Their words weren't just noise—they were weapons flung like bricks through the air. Damien walked through the storm of voices, jaw tight, hands loose at his sides—an officer trained not to react, but a man who felt every insult claw at his skin. A bead of sweat slid down the back of his neck. Not from the heat. From restraint.

A woman in a red baseball cap caught his eye.

Damn.

That bleach-blond, caveman-looking Congresswoman.

The walking Confederate flag with a spray tan.

Her entire career? A scam—since the day she jumped off one of her daddy's roofs and barely fumbled her way into UGA.

Lose an election? "Rigged!"

Win one? "God blessed America! Oh, I love Jesus!"

A cheating-ass affair with a coworker, all while being propped up by Georgia's so-called "righteous Evangelicals."

Running her mouth about "saving America" while gutting the very people who built it.

She made Jim Crow look subtle. Mass incarceration looked like God's justice. God's love. He thought, "Yeah. Real Proverbs 31 energy".

Damien shook his head, looking away.

Too late.

She'd already ruined his appetite.

Damien set his fork down, slow, deliberate.

"What, you with them? You one of those damn woke cops?"

Her words were acid in the air, sharp and careless, empty of any real political weight—just something she'd picked up off FOX or a Proud Little Boys' group chat and, like a good sycophant, parroted without thought.

But it wasn't the words that made his stomach twist.

It was the smirk.

Unearned entitlement.

That smug little curve of her lip, the quiet dare in her eyes. Like she expected him to flinch, to prove her right.

And maybe, if he was a different man, he would have.

But Damien just continued forward, exhaling slowly. What she wanted was a reaction. A fight. An excuse.

And he wasn't about to give her a damn thing.

He'd seen that smirk before—

In courtrooms.

In precinct halls.

On the faces of men who smiled just like that before denying justice.

It was the smile of certainty. The smile that grew wider at the phrase, "Orange is the new black."

The belief that she belonged here—Damien heard it through her, through their bravado. *Ours. Mine. Mine—all mine.* The hollow victory cry of mental midget childish children who had sold their souls to the devil—the orange devil in a red MAGA hat.

Being American meant preying on the weak and rewriting America's fractured history.

That he was the outsider.

He exhaled, shaking his head as he turned away.

Laughing to himself, *Ah, Congresswoman—please, spell 'woke- but then again- you look like you just woke up from a rough night sleep.*

Moment II: Shade Inside Too

The shift from outside to inside was suffocating. The moment the glass doors slid shut behind him, the noise of the protests flattened into a dull murmur, as if the city itself had been muted.

Inside HQ, Atlanta was stripped of its pulse. No trap beats, no scent of street food drifting from vendors, no fire in the voices outside. Just recycled air and the dull hum of a coffee machine that hadn't been cleaned in weeks.

Here, Atlanta wasn't streets, culture, or people. It was a ledger. A deal. A brand. And brands didn't bleed. They weren't dragged from their homes in the night. They didn't scream in the backs of squad cars. Brands didn't die.

They were polished, marketed, protected—even if it meant burying the very people who gave them their value in the first place.

The machine had always functioned that way. The Black upper class stayed in power by knowing exactly when to bow— "Mo' tea, Suh?" —just enough—to the white business elite. In return, they kept their seats at the table.

The cost was clear.

Black working people, the ones who built this city, the ones who stayed and fought for it. The ones who kept the streets swept, the kids fed, the elders cared for. Committed public school teachers rejected "school choice" because they knew it was a hustle—knew the cheating scandal was a hoax engineered by the white business elite. Knew that "anti-critical race theory" was just code for anti-nigga.

And what did they get for it?

Left to fend for themselves.
Gentrified out.
Policed into submission.
Erased altogether.

Damien refused to breathe deeply with Sheena or hug his daughter in a city where the air was stale with gunpowder and cowardice.

The streets would remember him as a man who loved—even if it killed him.

And in this case?

Black preachers, politicians, and bureaucrats were supposed to take notice.

Damn—ain't y'all supposed to care?

Faith. Collaboration. Pragmatism.

Preachers preach faith—but it ain't faith if you ain't involved.

Politicians push collaboration—but it ain't collaboration if the only thing getting set aside is you and the convention.

Bureaucrats swear by pragmatism—but it ain't pragmatism if all you do is retire and become a consultant for the same folks privatizing what we built.

And yet—

Y'all niggas lie to yourselves, lying to us.

They were supposed to stand up for the people—not stick the people up.

But instead—

They sold blessings for bank drafts.
They called poverty a personal failure.
They blamed students for systems designed to fail them.

"Tithing is your connection to your blessing."
"Vote for me—you're poor because you're lazy."
"As a principal, I lead by data. They don't learn because you don't teach."

And Damien's so-called "theory of a fictitious crime"?
Wrong kinds of victims.
Wrong city.
Wrong time.
Atlanta was still fighting to prove itself "business-friendly"—
"Too busy to hate."
Bullshit.
Because power never hated money -just people it couldn't use.
Never hated development deals—just the local public schools

full of poor Black and brown children that didn't justify a private, gated golf course in their community. "We drew names". The lottery system decided which of these kids were "worthy" of a charter school seat because "the Black mothers were tired of Black teachers failing their Black children".

Never hated tax breaks for those who had enough.

It was only ever too busy to care.

A ghost was moving through all of it—organized, masterful puppeteers with brown-faced puppets whose stages were pulpits and political platforms.

Not just surviving the game but thriving in it—playing it from the inside out.

Moving pieces. Pulling strings. Making ethereal promises.

Making sure you didn't see them looking and never allowing you to see.

Making sure they kept Atlanta clean. Isolated. Random.

But Damien knew—the ATL was in him. Nothing about this was random.

He entered the building, each step measured, counting the distance between him and his next move. The precinct buzzed with its usual rhythm—telephones ringing, officers in quiet conversations, the occasional burst of laughter breaking the tension in the air.

The HQ access code had barely left Damien's fingertips when his mentee, Detctive Ayers Kent, was already on him.

"Detective DeBerg, let me holla at you for a sec—I need your..."

Damien barely looked up. He already knew the tone, the hunger in Kent's voice. Young. Eager. Looking for a shortcut up the ranks? A mentee Damien had loaned out to the Gang Unit, trying to prove himself.

"Kent, I'm sorry, dude. Hit me later—unless it's an emergency."

Kent didn't take the hint. His stride didn't break, his voice dipping just enough to make it clear he thought he had something worth stopping for.

"You know it's always urgent in these streets—" Kent's voice dropped lower, a conspiratorial edge creeping in. Then came the wink—too casual, too familiar. "I got hitched on a report I turned in wrong. But when I went to pull the perp—a gang member…"

The whisper. The bobbing head. The index finger bouncing up and down, like a yes-man on his way downstairs.

That was the tell.

Whatever Kent needed, it wasn't about paperwork.

Damien exhaled sharply, adjusting his jacket. These young cats. Always eager to play the game but never patient enough to learn it. The ambition was there, sure. But the thinking? The patience? The long game? That was in short supply.

"Kent, I heard you, man. Both times—shit, all three times." Damien sighed. "I'm headed upstairs. It'll keep. Trust me—your young thugs aren't about to take over the A in the next 48 hours."

Kent smirked but didn't let up.

"Nah, Dee. He's not just some name in a case file." Kent tilted his chin toward the elevator. "He's downstairs."

Damien's brow furrowed. "Gang Unit?"

Kent nodded. "Yeah. And he's got a story you might want to hear."

Now Damien was listening.

A gang member in custody didn't mean much.

But a gang member in custody, volunteering to talk? That meant everything.

Still, everything downstairs couldn't compare to what was waiting for him upstairs.

The elevator doors slid closed. Next stop—the meeting he had to give his minutes to.

Moment III: The Conference Room or a Plantation?

Damien stuck his head out of the elevator like a cautious turtle, the blast of air-conditioning hitting him sharply and suddenly. The shift was immediate—cooler, sterile, a stark contrast to the heat of beat cops fresh off of the streets below.

A lift to on high, but the question lingered—was this Heaven or Hell?

A taxpayer's spectacle, polished floors gleaming beneath the weight of corruption and whispered deals. The place where power moved in silence, where justice was often a matter of negotiation rather than truth.

Eyes were on him.

Not paranoia. Presence. The persistence was necessary to drive non-democratic agendas.

He rolled his shoulders forward, exhaling the last traces of the conversation with Kent. Downstairs had its kind of urgency, but up here? This was where decisions were made, where people played the game behind closed doors.

And Damien? He wasn't just here to listen. He was here to be heard.

Then his phone buzzed.

Not his work phone. Not a number he could ignore. Tamika.

He always answered her calls. Even when he shouldn't.

The screen lit up again.

It was a text.

Call me before you talk to her.

I'm so sick of this shit

Damien's mind drifted to the Northside Hospital Maternity

ward for a moment.

Sixteen years earlier.

Tamika—the woman he never wanted to marry and never wanted to marry him.

The woman who never wanted to stretch her body to be a mother.

She had already made up her mind.

She wanted to end the pregnancy.
But her mother had given her no choice.
"Finish what you started—Clark College and this pregnancy."
So, Tamika did both. One with honors—summa cum laude. The other just honorable enough.
Not out of love. But out of spite.
Pompous. Unshaken. Relentless. The same way she did everything.
She had thrust the newborn into his arms to pick up a comb and lip gloss.
"Here's your daughter—you desperately wanted me to have her. She looks like me."
Em's tiny body was warm against his chest, soft, fragile—yet full of life.
His heart clenched. The third woman he had ever truly loved.
His hands were steady. His grip sure.
He tucked her close, held her tight—and never let go.
Then.
Until now.
And forever.
He hit her back—frustrated.

W-U. Em's good. Got her.

His head lifted in a half-smile—just enough to acknowledge the faceless somebody nearby.

Damn. This chick.

If not for Em loving her mother, he'd have dragged Tamika to court for permanent custody yesterday.

Damn, Tamika. You're a full-blown horror show.
He slid the phone back into his pocket and stepped through the frosted glass doors.

Now the Hunger Games—the psychological bullshit—was beginning.

Assholes on deck.

Then, rising out of the purposeful misted fog, a voice cut through the sterile air.

"They're in the conference room waiting for you, Detective. Can I get you anything?"

Damien nodded, appreciating the professionalism. It had the smoothness of a concierge—the ease of an elite country club. Polished. Pleasant. Everything perfectly in place.

But *they* and *conference room* landed in his chest like a trapdoor.

"The captain of homicide called me in?"

He rolled his shoulders, keeping his face unreadable as he stepped past the desk. "What's up with *they*?"

He had walked into enough situations to know—when too many suits were in one room, it wasn't about giving orders. It was about control.

The scent of coffee lingered in the air. Not cheap—Nicaraguan, fruity, with citrus notes.

But beneath it?

Something off.
This wasn't going to be a conversation. It was something else. He stepped inside."
Immaculately decorated. Glass-polished. Moneyed. But none of that mattered.
All he saw were bars, gleaming badges, and conservative suits—too conservative for the work they claimed to do in Atlanta.
Their suits were armor, insulating them from the blood, sweat, and tears it took to lead an urban city—from the decisions that kept the real ATL breathing.
Strong leadership had always defined Atlanta. From Maynard to Andy, Bill to Shirley. The dynamic Kays, Kasim, Keisha, Andre—each carving their legacy in the city's blueprint. City councilwomen and men, like Michael Bond, serving on small salaries but giving back in true ATL servant leadership—not for status, but for the people.
And the preachers? You couldn't tell Atlanta's story without them. The ATL has an unshakable spiritual truth as deep and true as the Georgia red clay—one that defies facts, transcends fiction, and refuses to dim.
Em heard him crying out— *"Preach, Black woman, preach!"*— rejuvenating, watching a truth.
"Preach, Black man, preach!"—celebrating Dr. Martin Luther King Jr.'s birthday.
It is upheld by those who carry the light, like Bernice King. Jamal Bryant. Raphael Warnock. Kevin Murriel. Keyanna Jones. Aaron Parker. Keith Hammond—
and all those like them who came before.

Standing in pulpits. At podiums. On street corners. By the bedsides. With those who mourned the loss of lives too young.

Not just preaching— not promoting- but protecting. Defying the kind of madness outside and now inside.

Speaking truth to power.

No—the suits lived in strategy meetings.

Damien lived in the streets.

In here, the parade processional- top-heavy six-figure salaries.

Seated at the head of the long conference table.

Not the ATL- generic Atlanta. The Georgia that claimed Atlanta would be nowhere without it.

They understood policy. He understood the weight of an RIP T-shirt at a cookout.

A voice sliced through his thoughts—smooth, hollow.

"Detective DeBerg. Thank you for joining us. This is an important meeting—we won't keep you long. Just some high-level guidance to help you close cases safely. Because, as you know, your oath is to the city. Welcome."

Damien barely heard the words.

Not because he wasn't listening—because he was reading.

The body language. The voice patterns. The too-perfect delivery. This wasn't a briefing. This was a script—and he hadn't been given his lines.

This wasn't collaboration. This wasn't support.

It was theater.

Not Sherlock. Not Hitchcock. This was Rocky Horror creeping through Atlanta's veins like fentanyl.

And the man leading the meeting—the one shaping every syllable like it had been workshopped for optics—felt more like Mr. Roarke.

Then he saw it.

The phoniness in the voice.

A voice that wore a badge but had never truly been police.

Senior Office Consultant Morgan Caster.

They had started together. The difference? Morgan finished college. Got a master's in criminal justice. Word was, he was even working on a doctorate. Much learning. No knowledge.

Much learning. Too little knowledge. No backbone.

All degrees, no discernment.

All access, no courage.

A résumé built on nodding at the right time.

A handshake too weak to hold the weight of truth.

Morgan had never done the work. Never walked the beats. Never stood between a kid and a bullet meant for someone else. He had rank. Not respect.

He was strictly policy. Internal affairs. A man of reports, procedures, oversight.

But not brotherhood.

And Damien understood that in a bad way.

Morgan was the kind of guy good cops loathed and bad ones took for granted. Not because he was corrupt. No—Morgan would never do anything immediately criminal.

He was just the kind of cop who didn't get it.

If "snitch" was a word on the street, Morgan was its progenitor.

It seeped out of him, laced every move he made, and echoed in everything he did.

Not dirty. Just dangerous in a way you couldn't put handcuffs on.

And then Damien noticed something else.

His immediate boss, Lieutenant Carr, wasn't in the meeting—nor was the interim captain who had summoned him to this so-called "collaborative high-level strategy session."

The people who should have been running this? Absent.

Instead, Morgan, a leech, sat among those who defined justice as "just us."

Morgan straightened his tie, adjusted his tone, and spoke as if reading a script handed down from above.

"Detective, there is no conspiracy, no serial killing, and nothing worth upsetting Atlanta's good reputation. There is no reason to disrupt these fine people from the GBI and their partners at the firm. These are good folks. Atlanta is a good town. So drop it and stay out of the city's business. You got that, Detective?"

Yeah, that's what Morgan said.

But what Damien—and everyone who loved the ATL—heard?

Ole Morgan doing his best to speak fo' his massah.
"I'm not gonna hold them long to chastise us—'Boy,' there is no conspiracy—no serial killing or anything worth upsetting Atlanta's good reputation. We most certainly don't wanna keep these fine mens away from their valuable work of scaring other 'woke folks' in other parts of Georgie. Oh bye da way-call da Georgia Gang and tell'm wez gonna be good just like their pretty lil black gale Republican host say we should be -good and stupid."

The skinning and grinning slobbered off Morgan's lips—tick, tap, tick, tap, tap.
Every syllable caramelizing, slow and syrupy, as if dipped in Massa's bourbon.

Then came the real call from the Big House porch—fiddle and all.

"Detective, we appreciate Officer Morgan explaining this to you in simple terms we hope you can understand."
Damien felt the weight of the GBI agent's smugness settle on the room like condensation on a muggy summer day.
He exhaled slowly. *How do people become so damn shallow? So manipulative?*

They really can't say our names because they don't give a damn about knowing our names.

Morgan smiled. Ate it up. He enjoyed performing his role as proxy, soaking in the pats on the head—for his people.

"We know you've put in a little time on this case," the agent continued, "and have found exactly what we already knew—nothing systematic is happening in Atlanta. Unless you want the MAGA Initiative instituted immediately, you will stay in your lane. Solve individual crimes individually. Let us determine the patterns. We do the thinking work. You do the grunt work. Understand? You do understand-don't you?"

"Excuse me, sir. MAGA?"

Like a waiter refilling a water glass, Morgan jumped in.

"Ah, the 'Make Atlanta Great Again' initiative Detective Damien."

Now, rubbing his hands together like some 1958 Georgia Tech water boy, he nodded.

"Sure, sure. The governor and our friends at the law firm of Maddox, Talmadge, and Perdue have a plan—to keep Atlanta out of the hands of those who 'love' the city but create all the crime. The gangs. The violence. The ones who do nothing but eat chicken wings at J.R. Crickets and have babies that grow up to be gang members.

The people who keep you too busy for thinking man's work, Detective."

Damien exhaled slowly.

"Damn. This dude here".

"Excuse me, detective"?

The lecture had turned into a full-on House Negro Minstrel show, and Damien wasn't having it.

But the moment that sealed it?

The agents and the attorneys stood up. Walked out like stormtroopers—casual, precise, untouchable.

One of them slid an envelope into Morgan's hand— *Here, errand boy. Go on down to the cabin and give to that boy who thinks he's man. Go on-get-get.*

Morgan took it eagerly.

Silence.

The lion and the scared lamb were left alone in the room.

The lamb spoke first.

"Detective, I am surprised at you. You have been playing this game for too long. Those men love Georgia. Love Atlanta. Love it enough to keep it from being destroyed by sloppy detective work and bad rumors. This is not a game. Not to me. Not to them. Not to this department."

Morgan pushed a file forward.

Thick. Manila.

Red letters stamped across the top: EMBARGOED BY GBI – IN CARE OF APD

"Detective, years ago you did sloppy police work. Some things never change. And just like the streets talk, so do the people who want time off their sentences."

Damien's eyes locked on Morgan.

"And that dealer—the one who did your dirty work on Mr. Shem Dathan? Let's just say that this file goes active if you don't stay in your lane. And the person you try to arrest? He won't be your prisoner. He'll be your cellmate. Because you know, Detective—you don't have to pull the trigger to be guilty. You just have to supply the gun and the getaway."

Lions know poisoned meat.

Then, Morgan delivered the final blow.

"Detective, I hear you're divorced. You have a 16-year-old daughter 10th grader at The Lovett School. She plays basketball. Leave here. Live a quiet life. Raise Emily or excuse me, Em. And maybe that PhD criminologist Sheena Colucci- you brought in from Chicago for this 'serial murder' case will finally give you a chance after all these years. Don't mess this up like you did your marriage."

Damien's body went hot.

Not because of the threat.

Because Emily's name and Sheena's presence had just come out of Morgan's mouth.

"Are you done?"

"No. Do you have any questions? Do you understand what's at stake?"

Damien's voice was ice.

"Are. Weee. Done?"

"Yes, Detective. We arrrre done… if you are done with your egotistical witch hunt."

Damien rose.

Two things in mind.

Exiting the conference room to the elevator.

First, he was not done.

And for the love of God, would they put their hands on Em or Sheena?

I'll burn the whole damn system down saving the ATL and my family.

I put that on everything.

On Mama's grave.

Try me— and see if I don't will pull up.

The elevator consumed him-covered his anger when it closed "those cold-"Trump lov'n mother fucker".

Moment IV: Headed Down to More Shade

Then it ejected him just as quickly, still mad- but focused and slightly less claustrophobic.

Then.

Tamika. On cue.

Damn. This chick.

"Damien, you don't have to come."

Her voice was smooth, polished—but the cadence? That was the tell. It bounced in that damning way, like she was already two steps ahead of him.

"Em isn't playing basketball anymore. She doesn't need those Skechers—I want her in girlie stuff now."

Here we go.

Tamika wasn't asking. She was informing him. Because that's how she moved—present the decision like it had already been made.

"Tamika—"

"No, Damien, listen." Her tone never changed—calm, controlled, edged with that effortless c ondescension. " She's n ot interested anymore. And before you assume this is about me? No, I didn't force it. She said it herself. She's done. And frankly? I'm relieved. Basketball wasn't gonna get her anywhere. She needs to focus on her future. You should be glad she's thinking ahead."

His jaw was clenched.

Tamika never understood sports. Not that she couldn't—she didn't care to.

She liked a certain kind of daughter.

The polished kind. The curated kind. The too concerned about her looks kind- "A pretty girl in Atlanta can go far".

The kind who never sweated out her hair over a basketball game.

"You undermine me every time."

Her voice—silk over steel.

"And yet you wonder why she plays you the way she does."

Then, just like that—the pivot.

"Oh, by the way, did Em mention she has a boyfriend?"

A deliberate pause. Then, smoothly—

"One that reminds me so much of you. Isn't that something?"

Damien exhaled sharply.

She never missed an opportunity.

"You should worry less about crime in Atlanta," she added lightly, "and more about what's happening in this house. With your daughter."

The line hung there. Then—

"Did she at least tell you she passed her driver's test?"

His pulse ticked.

"She did?"

"Mmhmm."

He looked around the APD lobby like he hadn't walked through it a million times before. But now?

Now he noticed everything.

And across the room—Kent.

Headed straight for him.

Waving something like a damn lottery ticket.

Or maybe an A+ on his homework.

"I let her use my car."

Damien muted the phone, motioning to Kent. "One sec—it's my daughter."

Back to Tamika—

"And she already lost the garage door opener."

The hell?

Kent was getting closer now, voice urgent. "DeBerg—you gotta come downstairs. This is hotter than Big Daddy's chicken grease."

Damien's patience thinned to damn near nothing.

"Tamika, put Em on the phone."

A shuffle. Then, Em's voice—bored, irritated.

"Daddy, I got her in check."

"Don't talk to your mom like that."

Tamika cut back in. "See? That's exactly what I'm talking about. She's like this because of you."

Em sighed. Teenage girl exhaustion.

"Daddy, you can see me later, okay?"

Then—click.

The call dropped.

Damien inhaled. Sat with it.

He wasn't in the room with them.

Not stopping M from knocking her mother out—

Metaphorically.

But it still felt like a loss.

He unmuted.

"Kent—what, man?"

His phone rang. Again.

Tamika.

Exhale. He gave Kent the stop sign-again.

This time, he let it ring. Once. Twice.

Then—answered.

"Oh yeah, Damien, I need—"

A pause. A deliberate one.

Like she was thinking about her needs first.

Then, her voice shifted. Not annoyed. Not demanding.

Assumptive.

"Listen."

His shoulders tightened.

"For somebody who fancies himself some big-time detective, let me put you up on game. Don't be having people come by my house, checking on me, asking me all these damn questions—because let me be real clear, Damien, I don't have anything to tell them."

Pause.

Damien settled in again as best he could-*Damn everything is hard with you.*

Damien stood up straighter- a board trying not to break.

"What- Tamika- I'm at work-I really don't have time to keep going back…"

"What- yes you do—GBI. That damn GBI came by here today. Asking about you. About me. Em. And Sheena Colucci."

His stomach dropped.

Tamika kept going, not realizing the weight of what she had just said.

"And you know what I told them?"

Another pause.

The kind only a woman raised on Atlanta Housewives drama could pull off.

"Nothing."

Silence.

Then, her voice—smooth, poised.

"But Damien, if you keep pulling this petty mess, if you think you're gonna send folks to check on me—then best believe?

I might just start talking."

His pulse hammered.

Not at her pampered threat.

No.

At what she didn't even realize.

The GBI wasn't there because of him.

The GBI was there for him.

For what he held more valuable than anything.

For all he loved in this world—besides Sheena.

He wasn't even willing to let them fuck with Tamika—because she was Em's mother.

Period.

A slow, hot rage burned beneath his skin, curling tight in his ribs.

He swallowed it down.

Tamika didn't know.

But now?

Now he did.

And if the GBI was sniffing around…

He was closer than he thought—but to what?

To who?

The questions tangled like tripwires in his head, but then—

"Oh, and another thing."

Damien clenched his jaw.

Here we go.

"You finally hooked up with Sheena?"

Mmm. The smirk in her voice took the room hostage.

The dagger twisted—just enough.

"Took you long enough."

Damien's fingers flexed over his phone.

Then, silk over steel—"Don't have her around my daughter. We do Roja Roja. Not bitch scents."

Then—click.

Dead air.

He still smelled burnt toast.

The bitterness of it sat in his chest.

And Kent—he had not become enough of a detective under Damien's tutelage to recognize what was happening.

What Damien was about to do.

The sacrifice.

Kent had pulled him down to the basement, sure.

But the work in the Gang Unit wasn't just bang, bang.

It was Bang. Bang.

Bodies stacked quick. No hesitation.

"Homicide is us, nigga—real quick. Drill, drill, bitch!"

Damien exhaled, staring at the screen.

The weight of the conversation settled.

Tamika thought he had sent the GBI.

But the truth was worse.

They weren't coming for her.

They were coming for him.

Kent's arm moved—silent, like a school crossing guard ushering him into the abyss.

Behind Kent, the elevator doors yawned open.

A small step in police lore.

A giant step for his career.

For his love.

For his life.
The elevator—
A tomb.
A descent.
Headed straight for Dante's Inferno.
The basement.

Moment V: YD Tells About Evil Shade

The room was dim, humming with the low flicker of fluorescent lights.

Damien sat across from YD, watching the younger man's restless movements. Fingers flexing. Leg bouncing under the table. His eyes darted to the room's corners, like he expected someone to be standing there.

Kent leaned against the wall, arms crossed, unreadable.

Damien settled into his chair, calm, measured.

"Alright, young brother, why am I here? I do bodies—not Drill, not street shit."

Kent nodded, sharp and firm—conducting YD like an orchestra, moving to a rhythm only the streets could compose.

YD sniffed hard, exhaling through his teeth. "Youth detention ain't pretty," he muttered. "Me, I know. Gon' probably end up in 'Big-Bo' one day. They say it can be hell. But I ain't scared, though."

Damien leaned back, his whole body open—giving YD time.

YD's voice cracked, just slightly, as he embraced the space, the moment—the unusual warmth in a world that usually gave him none.

He didn't see it, but Damien's embrace wasn't just for him—it was for Kent, too.

To wake him up.
To make him see.

Kent didn't know it yet, but he was standing at the same cross-roads Damien had faced once—before he had Shem killed.

Before he learned the weight of what it meant to take a life.

Before, he started seeing people, not just problems.

Damien had sat Kent down months ago and told him plainly:

"The people you'll be dealing with are mostly Black boys—people, human beings, alive but not well. Trapped in an upstairs system designed to make them into the niggas they scream they are.

"Do more social work than police work. These are our boys—hell, now too many of our daughters.

If you don't see them, trust—the streets or a judge's suite won't see them".

And when you return to Homicide, you'll see what I couldn't at your age."

Kent tapped his watch, impatient. "Come on, little puppy—eat for me."

He hadn't yet digested the meal Damien had put on his plate.

YD shifted in his seat, his cuffs rattling. He wouldn't meet Damien's eyes.

Damien let the silence stretch before tapping the table—just once. A sharp sound. Enough to break the tension.

"Tell me something, YD. How long you been caught up in this?"

YD scoffed. A dry, bitter sound. "Man, since forever." He shook his head. "You think I had choices? I've been in the system since I was six years old. Youth detention. Juvenile. Back and forth. You come out? You go right back in."

Damien leaned back. Six years old.

"And your people?"

YD shrugged, but there was something stiff about it. "My people?" He let out a laugh, but there was no humor in it. "My people were the system." His fingers flexed, cuffs clinking. "Black women and street hustlers. I called every woman over thirty Mama or Auntie. I ain't know nothing else."

Damien nodded slowly, absorbing that. He had seen it before. Kids are swallowed up by the city and spit out by a system that only knows how to punish, never protect.

"So why Homie Thugs?"

YD flinched just a little. It was quick, but Damien caught it.

YD licked his lips. "Man, it was for protection." His eyes darted to the corner, like something unseen was standing there. "Prison system crazy, man. All levels. You roll with who you roll with. Homie Thugs look out for each other, always have."

Damien said nothing. Just watched him.

YD shifted again, then exhaled, shaking his head. "You know how it is." He gave Damien a tired look. "You get in, and the streets name you. I was just a little kid in and out of youth detention. So they first called me Youth Detention—real creative, huh?"

He smirked, but his eyes stayed dark.

Damien let him talk.

"So then it got shortened to Yo-D. Then Yo-Doggy. Then Yo-D-E." YD scratched his arm. "But I've been in and out so much? They lost track of my birth name. Hell, I barely remember it. So after a while?" He sniffed, voice going flat.

"I was just YD."

Damien exhaled through his nose.

Funny thing about the streets—

The higher you got, the shorter your name became.

And YD had climbed.

Damien let the weight of that settle before speaking again.

"So why do you care now?"

He didn't wait for an answer. Instead, he reached for Kent's keys and unlocked the cuffs, letting them fall heavy against the table.

YD flinched at the sound.

His fingers twitched, hesitating—like he wasn't sure if he was allowed to move.

Then, slowly, he rubbed each wrist, massaging the raw skin with a kind of care so rare, it almost felt foreign.

A long silence.

Then—

YD's voice was barely above a whisper.

"I told you."

He swallowed hard, his throat working like the words were stuck there. "I don't want him to do no one else like he did, Buddy."

The fluorescent light buzzed overhead.

Damien's chest tightened.

Because this wasn't just a confession.

This was the closest thing to faith YD had ever spoken.

His voice cracked at the end, betraying the words. He swallowed hard, sitting up straighter like he could recover.

"Man... in jail, you expect it. They call it breaking. Buck-breaking. You see it coming—you know who's hunting you.

But this dude? YD shook his head. He out here. Free. Smiling at folks. Shaking hands. And when he hunts? His voice cracked. Man, they don't even know they're prey till it's too late.

He ain't making boys into men. He is making men into boys. And there ain't no love in it.

Do they say the streets ain't got no love? He scoffed, but there was no humor in it. This dude? He's the only one who means that shit."

"I mean—jail, hell?" He gave a dry laugh. "'Cause this dude I'm 'bout to tell you 'bout? Man, he's the Devil. Real talk."

Damien exchanged a glance with Kent.

"Who?"

YD shook his head, rubbing his forearms. "I don't know his name. Never did. But I can describe him."

Kent shifted slightly. "You never got a name?"

YD licked his lips, his hands flexing. "Nah, man. It was always at night. Always buzzin'. But I know he a preacher."

Damien's eyes sharpened.

"How do you know that?"

YD laughed, but there was no humor in it. 'Cause he was always gettin' preacher calls. Especially from this one deacon."

He shifted again, fingers tapping against the table. His leg bounced harder.

"One time?" YD's voice dropped. "The deacon was loud. He was in there screamin', talkin' bout—'Twelve thousand dollars just missing! The Master's Twelve is gone from the offering!'"

Damien straightened slightly. Kent stilled.

YD sucked his teeth. "And you know what Preacher says? He say—'Damn, you son for coming at me. Did you call my armor-bearer before you called? You probably have it, but I forgive you."

His fingers clenched and unclenched on the tabletop. His breath was shaky.

"And then he always said somethin' else. Every time. Talk'n tongues like my Grandma when she be gon'n into the spirit."

Damien leaned in slightly. "What did he say?"

YD's lips barely moved. "Quos deus vult perdere, prius dementat."

Damien blinked.

For a second, his brain lagged. Then—click. That's not 'Tougues'.

Latin.

The phrase stirred something buried deep—Catholic school. St. Anthony's Catholic School had taught him much Latin, especially specific Latin phrases of moral conduct. He'd heard it before, but it felt wrong here, out of place.

Why the hell is some street preacher using Latin?

Kent noticed the shift in Damien's face. "What?"

Damien exhaled sharply, running a hand over his chin. "That's Latin. Means... 'Those whom a god wishes to destroy, he first drives mad.'"

YD pressed his lips together, not making heads or tails of Damien's investigator talk. "That's when he always did somethin' freaky. Nasty."

Damien's stomach tightened.

YD shook his head, voice tightening, like he could still hear it echo.

"Man... that boy, Jonathan—he ain't back down. Even when he should've.

He laughed—high, nervous, bold. Went straight in.

"Oh, I'm puttin' you on blast. Snapchat. IG.

Hell, I might make you famous on YouTube—tell 'em you swallow.

Your sexy-ass? Your handsome-ass preacher self?

You about to be everybody's favorite viral clip.

I'm your social media agent now.

And my job? Is revelation.

Everybody's about to see what's been hiding in plain sight.

And don't get it twisted—ain't nothin' wrong with the closet.

Ain't nothin' wrong with bein' gay.

What's wrong?
Is actin' like you not,
while shamin' folks who walk in the beauty of their truth.

You out here playin' purity politics,
but you still dippin' in the same fields—
that's the problem.

Closets don't keep secrets forever—especially not yours.

So the only real question is—

how many hot boy parties you gon' sneak into

before you finally come out in the light?"

YD stopped pushing back. His hands were shaking now, whether from fear, memory, or the weight of truth.

"Then he said it—
clear as day.

Said he was gonna tell everybody.

Tell 'em…
The preacher liked to get… freaky. "
His voice cracked on the last word, and he blinked fast—like he was trying to keep something buried.
Damien exhaled sharply, shaking his head.
His fist curled tight, and he gave it a slow, frustrated shake—aimed not at YD, Jonathan, but the twisted truth laid bare on the table.

"Let me be clear," Damien said, voice low but firm.
"Ain't nothin' wrong with being gay.
What's wrong is hurting another human being.
What's evil is using God as a shield to hide behind—while you leave pain in your wake."

Kent nodded slowly, then turned toward Damien.
"Yeah, that part," he said, voice steady. "People gotta let people be people. Period."

Then, softer, with conviction:
"We're here for you—for everybody tryin' to bring the truth forward.
Go on, man. You got this."

Then his jaw tightened. His hands balled into fists, cuffs rattling against the table.

"He said it—then he hit Buddy in the face with a hammer."

Silence stretched across the room, thick and unmoving.

YD shifted in his seat, his knee bouncing under the table. His fingers twitched like they were trying to shake something off—something that wouldn't let go.

"I jumped out that car—I ran like I ran track or somethin'," YD said, breath catching in the memory. "Buddy was okay, but he ain't HT. I kept runnin'."

His words sped up—

like his body was still in motion,

like fear had never stopped chasing him.

His eyes darted toward the corner of the room before settling back on the table. He looked haunted.

"I ain't never seen the preacher again." The words came slower now, like he wasn't sure if he wanted to say them.

His wrists rubbed against the metal cuffs, and he sucked in a breath, forcing himself to keep going.

"But the other day? I heard on the wing 'bout a guy who got killed."

He swallowed again, his Adam's apple bobbing.

"I knew it was Buddy." His lips pressed together before he shook his head. "Damn that preacher—wit' them tongues and that temper—he couldn't even take a joke."

He exhaled, the sound shaky, almost broken. His shoulders sagged, like the weight of it was finally pressing down on him.

"Just did, Buddy, for no reason." His voice was barely above a whisper now.

His fingers twitched.

"That shit ain't right," he muttered.

Then he slumped back in the chair, staring at the ceiling like he was searching for something that wasn't there.

"Just be what you is," he said, softer now. "Not what you ain't."

Silence.

"And then it just went downhill from there."

A chill rolled through the room.

Damien's jaw tightened. "And you're saying this now because?"

YD's hands trembled. He looked up, eyes wet but hard.

"I ain't no snitch," he whispered.

Then his voice steadied. "But I don't want him to do no one else like he did Buddy."

A longer silence.

Damien studied him, then flicked a glance at Ayers.

They flipped on the recorder.

Later, as Damien stepped out of the building, his mind spun.

That phrase—*Quos deus vult perdere, prius dementat*—still rattled in his head.

YD's words weren't just about a murder.

This wasn't just about murder. It was about power.

The person who killed these men wasn't just striking out in anger—he was trapped by what they knew. His victims had unknowingly exposed a caged predator.

But in a city with a thriving and influential gay community, why would someone kill over a crude joke?

Unless… it wasn't just a joke.

Unless what was at stake was more than reputation, more than pride.

A preacher?

A man of God?

And when the truth threatened to spill past the pulpit, what else could he do?

But kill?

Whoever this preacher was, he wasn't just killing people. He was controlling them.

And now?

Sheena was about to meet him—prosōpon me prosōpon or face to face.

I have to tell her- I have to because on my life I going to go with this- they got what they wanted a fight with their bully asses. I need to connect with my boy, gotta hit Rory.

Moment VI: Rory Calls Out Shade in High Places

The peppered protesters throughout the city carried a particular urban stench—strategically placed, deliberately agitating.

Surface street congestion layered over hot, sticky asphalt, amplifying a shared irritation with no party lines.

Vitriol pulled from their lungs like a lousy drag on Pall Mall Gold Unfiltered cigarette—yellowed teeth flashing between chants:

"Make Atlanta Great Again!"

"Get saved!"

"Stop the woke mob!"

"Protect unborn children—love your neighbor as yourself!"

"Love your neighbor, but put them damn immigrants on ice!"

At every red light from Atlanta Police Headquarters, through caution lights, then caught again by the bumper in front of him, Damien endured them—the Governor's non-city-resident sycophants, shipped in like hired hands to choke the city from within.

The national government's neoliberal machine had empowered the Georgia gang—these self-righteous keepers of "Southern heritage"—to punish Atlanta the way they had punished Obama, not for anything he had done, but for simply making the gumbo goodness of the American dream available to 'urban lepers.'

Now, they stood here, wrapped in red-hooded righteousness, Bubba and Bubba-ettes storming state capitols, easing up constitutions, twisting scripture into slogans that could fit on a bumper sticker.

"God is love—but He's got borders!"

"Guns before grits, prayers before programs!"

"Jesus Saves—but not on government welfare!"

The new theocracy of convenience.

Conservatism without consciousness.

A movement so disconnected from plausible cerebellum function that even their historians wouldn't recognize them.

And yet, here they were. At every stoplight. Every turn. Every inch of Atlanta.

And Damien?

He was trapped in it.

Then—in the heart of Atlanta's most prestigious residential neighborhood—

The doorman-elevator combo ushered Damien up too many floors to count, straight into Rory's skylined "church."

A foyer of glass, wealth, and elevation.

"Welcome to therapy, church, or whatever you need, good friend."

Rory wasn't even in sight, but his presence was curated. The walls—lined with specifically chosen Black art—spoke in his absence:

"Wealth."

"Take Black Excellence Seriously."

"We didn't 'move on up'—check history, we BEEN up."

Before Damien even saw him, he smelled him.

A mint-kissed breeze, full of eucalyptus and the promise of clarity and composure.

Then—Rory.

Just off the grand view of Atlanta, standing like he belonged to it.

"Damn, Alvin Ailey—how much did you pay for that?" Damien asked, glancing at the art.

Rory waved a hand. "You just gon' show up in the afternoon, Detective—last minute, no wine, no warning—crass as hell. Boi, stop."

Yeah. Damien had made the right decision coming here.

Because the sight of this Black man—living above the fray, but ready to outthink it, sue it, and if needed, die for it—meant one thing.

The Talented Tenth.

Damien's love for Rory ran deep—moved him to Rory as naturally as Sheena had moved to him.

Two Black men, unashamed to hug, unafraid to share what most Black men never get—never take—because they've been forced to act like they don't need it.

Conditioned to believe warmth was weakness.

Because white patriarchal tradition had raped them of it—stripped them of the basic, human comfort that should have been theirs.

But not here. Not between them.

Damien stepped back and had a flashback conversation with Tamika when she had asked, "Can a man love another man and not be gay, Damien?" They were out together- not in romance but in humanity- "I'm not gay- but I'm confident that I know me and you don't".

Rory pulled back first, smoothing down the front of his crisp dress shirt.

"I love you, Damien—but this shirt has to stay crisp for my Zoom call with a new client. They're trying to put a lot of green money into my Black pocket, so now I gotta listen to more Trap music and pretend it's my life's soundtrack."

Damien let him go.

But his voice was tight.

"I love you too, bro. But I need your insight. This is hittin' hard—it could take me down. And if this shit gets out—" He exhaled, jaw tense. "Forget loving Sheena. Forget seeing Em until she's 21—if Tamika has her way."

Rory's easy smirk faded.

His eyes flickered with something sharp.

"I see you're shaken. Did something happen with Em? Or at—?"

He didn't finish the thought.

Instead, he sank into the plush, light-gray Dresden sofa, letting it pull him into the kind of controlled comfort only understood by those who knew—

All problems can be solved with patience, persistence, and time.

God only knew he had won his traditional Savannah family over the same way.

Black, beautiful, gay, and proud.

Out in the light.

Loved—despite their initial hesitation.

"Ok, so Sheena came over this morning- oooh my God".

Rory always seemed to want for Damien what he wanted for himself, even if much of what he wanted in intimacy seemed to elude him too often.

"Damien, I told you, I told you months ago you need her- to reach out to her. I'm soooo happy for you, maaaaaan".

The reverence in his voice didn't ask for details; it only applauded Damien's resilience.

"But, that's the problem after all these years- after all this way- I didn't see this coming".

Damien saw himself with no legal move. "I have- lied to may self- I don't tolerate that from even Em- I actually enjoyed it- I needed it- Damn- this shit gonna come out".

The system raged on, letting Black bodies pile up—justice chipped away, discarded, forgotten. And worse than that, Sheena, the woman he desperately loved, and his daughter, the child he was fighting to raise, would be left in peril.

That's why he had never told Sheena. Because deep down, he had always believed what he did was right. If it was right then, it was right now—given the right set of circumstances.

And yet, if he went along to get along, no one with something tangible to lose would blame him. The ones who told—who did what YD had done—weren't men with anything at stake. Only men with nothing left to protect made that kind of commitment.

But if Damien was going to truly love Sheena—not possess her, not claim her the way Shem tried to, not the way porn hustlers threw tips at girls like tokens—if he was going to be a real friend to Rory, if he was going to raise his daughter with the values of both the Talented Tenth and a servant's heart—he had to go through with this.

No move.

No way out.

No more waiting.

Checkmate.

Rory leaned forward, voice steady, sure. "Damien, this is not that difficult—Sheena has loved you since that rap y'all wrote in the 11th grade—BeLoved in the ATL. But love ain't grown or real until you've been through some things. And going through something means you gotta come out with trust and a shared vision."

Damien exhaled, his jaw tight. He had heard Oprah say something like that once. On the few afternoons he had been home to watch.

Rory didn't let up.

"And you can't have a shared vision without trust. Trust is fresh air—something both of you gotta breathe on your own, without pressure, without fear. No manipulation. Just truth. Otherwise, y'all aren't partners. You're just two people trying not to drown."

Rory let it sit for a second, then added—

"And she can't swim for both of you while you're drowning."

Damien's jaw tightened.

"At some point, it has to be growth. Otherwise, it's just good sex."

A courtroom of judgment swept through their brotherhood.

Not from guilt. Not from shame.

But from Truth itself—searing them together in the shared struggle to live it.

Rory held his gaze.

"You can't be Sheena's 'Day' and live a midnight lie."

The words settled, final.

Then—as if the session was over, as if they both knew the truth now—

Damien exhaled. No more running.

Rory sat back. "Damien, this is not hard. You gotta tell her the truth. Fight their asses. And let the chips fall where they may."

Damien ran a hand down his face. "Rory, man… if I do this? She might walk away for good. And they threatened Em—"

Rory didn't hesitate. "But if she stays under false pretenses, you'll never be the man who can love her the way she needs. And Em? You'll be taking care of her with clipped wings, trapped in a cage. And that ain't gonna work. Tell her, Damien. Tell her."

Silence stretched between them.

Damien dropped his head, letting it bob slightly, like a buoy tossed on a stormy sea. He was ashamed that he had even made this a question.

Then—he caught something in Rory's face. That quiet confidence in him.

The kind of confidence that allowed a cisgender Black man, raised in a world that tried to limit him, to be this close to another Black man and not flinch.

Damien stood, resolute.

The elevator doors were already open—waiting to take him down to his fate.

Then, Rory stood too. One last story. One last lesson.

"Damien, you got this—it's gonna be fine. Sheena loves you. You both love Atlanta. And Atlanta loves us."

A pause. Then—

"Did I ever tell you my favorite Bible verse?"

Damien turned slightly, waiting.

"I learned it at Ebenezer," Rory continued, his voice steady. "One of Dr. Joseph Roberts's last sermons, a few years before Dr. Raphael Warnock took over. Luke 9:51—Now it came to pass, when the time had come for Him to be received up, that He stead-fastly set His face to go to Jerusalem.

"For eternal love, you have to be willing to face eternal truth. No matter how this all turns out—pursue truth, and love will follow."

Damien held his gaze. The words were meant for him, but something about the way Rory said them felt personal.

Then—Rory exhaled, a quiet resolve in his tone.

"I have to face this every day, Damien."

"What?"

"Being a gay Black man in conservative law spaces. In a tra-ditional Black family." His expression was unreadable. "A family determined to love me… as long as I accept me."

Damien let that sit.

"And you did."

Rory smiled—not bitter, not broken. Just certain.

"I did." He nodded. "I had to."

And there it was.

The line between him and Bishop Emanuel Cain III, whom he had known since they were freshmen at Morehouse, was a mutual companion.

Both were raised in faith-heavy, traditional families.

Both choosing whether to own their truth or suffocate in their shame.

One chose light.

The other?

Darkness. Deception. Death.

"Just so you know, Damien—this case you're on? I might be getting involved. Publicly."

Rory's voice was steady, but Damien could hear the weight behind it.

"The Atlanta Black Gay Men's Alliance—of which I'm a board member and legal consultant—is preparing to take direct action if this thing keeps escalating."

And there it was. Another layer. Another pressure point.

Now, Damien wasn't just tangled in it—he was sinking.

The case wasn't just a case anymore. It wasn't just a matter of justice, or love, or loyalty.

It was personal.

It was political.

And it was about to explode.

The elevator doors slid shut, sealing him in.

The descent began.

But Damien had the feeling he wasn't heading for the lobby.

He was free-falling straight into the fire.

Moment VII: Throwing Shade on Cain's Game

At the very moment, Damien was being pelted with salivating Evangelicalism, birthed into slurs—

"Make Atlanta Great Again! Damn you!"

"Jesus is right and white! Damn your woke mob—give us our country—we mean, our city—back! Damn you in our Lord's name!"—

while he was pushing through the heat, the noise, the fevered desperation of men who never really owned Atlanta in the first place—

Sheena stepped into the light.

The conference ballroom was cool, high-ceilinged, and packed with bodies more used to discussing pain than performing it. And yet, they had come—to listen, to learn, and maybe, unknowingly, to witness the beginning of a shift.

She paused at the edge of the stage, letting the room settle around her like a hush that knew its place.

She was the keynote for the afternoon session.

They didn't know it yet, but Atlanta was about to hear its other voice.

Inadvertently but purposely, she closed her eyes—a moment of grounding and intention. When she reopened them, she gave a slight nod to the audience and herself.

She took them in—all of them.

Some of the preachers carried the scent of sophisticated cologne, their suits tailored sharply and better suited for a European Italian designer runway show than the streets where their congregations lived and died. Others wore clergy collars, stiff and starched, the kind more fitting for a confessional than a conference on justice.

But then, there were the quiet ones.

The ones who didn't sit in the front row for optics. The ones whose faces weren't carved in pride but etched with love, with purpose. Their suits weren't perfect, their hands weren't soft, and their eyes held stories of days at hospital bedsides and long talks with lost persons.

They weren't here to be seen. They were here to listen. To learn.

The outside of the program documented the contrast in plain sight:

The Atlanta Concerned Black Clergy's 10th Annual New Jim Crow & Caste Dismantling Symposium

Then—discreetly, yet thoughtfully, in deep gold lettering at the bottom:

Omni Hotels & Resorts is committed to diversity as we value the opportunities it brings to our business.

Yep. They had to let them know.

Going forward, real Black money would only be spent with organizations and businesses committed to what was right. This would be led by real, committed black preachers.

Even during troubled times.

Even despite the Predator-in-Chief's second term.

A hush.

The intersection of Black womanhood, deep intelligence, and a relentless commitment to humanity settled over the room. The weight of history, of struggle, of survival. Always reeling from the wounds wrought by supremacy—the patriarchal nightmare that molested without care, lied and stole with impunity, and elected without regard for character, let alone democracy.

Sheena stepped to the podium.

"Good evening, and thank you, Reverend Doctor, for that gracious introduction. My political science undergrad, Master of Divinity, and dissertation committee would all assure you that while my résumé is long, my rewrite and editing time is even longer."

Loose. Confident.

Understanding the moment—not just now, but the moment.

"I would be remiss to stand before such a robust group of theological servants and not begin with my theological shero—Dr. Jacquelyn Grant."

She paused, allowing recognition to settle.

"Many of you know her well. In her seminal work, White Women's Christ and Black Women's Jesus, she writes: 'In analyzing the nature of God in Jesus Christ vis-à-vis the variety of human conditions, these theologians have argued that there is a relationship between Western-articulated theologies and Christologies, and Western supremacist ideology—which tends to perpetuate the oppression of the oppressed.'"

Silence, thick with recognition.

Sheena let the words breathe.

Twenty-seven minutes later, even those with little to no theological training understood her message.

Then, she brought it home.

"Finally, circling back to where we began—"

Her voice sharpened.

"In this moment, we cannot allow our desire for safe streets, good schools, and full bellies to be held hostage by wolves in sheep's clothing—those who call for greatness in God's name while doing the work of the adversary when no one is looking."

A pause. The weight of truth settled on the room.

"But we are not alone."

She lifted her chin.

"I have—we have—leadership to follow."

Dr. Jacquelyn Grant. Michelle Alexander. Isabel Wilkerson. Alicia Garza. Patrisse Cullors. Opal Tometi. Valerie Cooper. Eboni Marshall Turman. Kimberlé Crenshaw. Nikole Hannah-Jones. Tamika Mallory. Shavon Arline-Bradley.

All Black.

All brilliant.

Blue-collar, white-collar, no-collar—

and some who should've had a bishop's collar.

And then, the name that gave voice to Sheena's own personal story—

"Tarana Burke—gotta say it twice now—Tarana Burke."

She let the applause rise. She knew she was preaching now.

"And last, but certainly not least—our Queen. My homegirl. The woman I look up to—Reverend Dr. Bernice A. King."

A moment passed, thick with reverence. Then Sheena leaned in for the final word:

"And finally, we must never forget the unsung sheroes—

Atlanta Public Schools educator, spiritual advisor Dr. Chuanitra Merrell, entrepreneur, and our contemporary version of Madam C.J. Walker, Ms. Vivian Arnold.

Women who hold us down, steady us, love us—without applause.

Because true spiritual mothers don't need recognition—

but today?

They gon' get it."

Thunder.

From those used to receiving thunder.

She had them.

She had outed wolves in sheep's clothing and turned over tables without flipping a single chair. The air over the ATL felt different now—pregnant with day where there had recently been so, so much night.

The people in the room felt it.

Most appreciated her—respected her—and loved her.

Damien was there.

Not in body.

Earlier, she had invited him into her body. But more than that, she had welcomed him into her spirit. His presence was steady, familiar. A contrast to the others—the ones who only saw her as something to use. Not servants but manipulators.

She realized that after all of these years, she was willing to walk in the confidence that he loved her.

Not just for her brilliance. Not just for the fire in her words. But for who she was when the mic was off.

And yet—

Love couldn't shield her from the war she had just walked into.

But she didn't know that.

Not yet.

Then—

The green tea she requested had already been placed just off-center of the seat she was asked to take.

Lemon filled the air. A small detail, but an intentional one. Care. Thoughtfulness. The kind that came naturally from the young Spellman-ite who had volunteered alongside her sorority sisters.

And then there was him.

The young brother pulling mic cables, sneaking glances at her like she hung the damn moon.

Smitten.

Proud.

Proud to be in the room. Proud to be with her. Proud to be part of The Omega Psi Phi Fraternity, Incorporated—the Dog Team of Service, even if his purple golf shirt was a shade too conservative for The Perfect 10—Quedafi-Dewey's Ques, "The Mother Pearl Made!"—she remembered from Howard University's Alpha Chapter. True Bruhz, committed to uplifting our people like all dedicated Omega men worldwide.

The first five questions were routine. Expected.

Then—

The shift.

That's when it always happens.

When people get too comfortable.

When truth starts creeping in.

That's when the real battle begins.

The air shifted.

Most in the audience didn't notice. They were still caught up in the rhythm of Sheena's words—absorbing, nodding, reflecting.

But Cain noticed.

His posture remained composed, his expression unreadable. But his stillness wasn't patience for those who knew how to see—those attuned to the imperceptible tensions of power. It was containment.

Sheena had spoken the truth. Not about him, not directly. But truth doesn't need to name names to be deadly. And that was the danger.

Cain's deacon, seated just a few feet away, swallowed hard. A flicker of discomfort crossed his face. He had heard sermons, lectures, and power plays—but he had never seen Cain react like this.

Sheena had done something few had ever managed.

She had named his crime without even knowing it.

Because love doesn't hurt.

And love doesn't live a lie.

Cain glanced at her.

Cain saw in her the thing that would one day undo him.

The effortless power. The kind of confidence that wasn't loud or performative—because real power never has to be.

And that was the problem.

What if they—my congregation, my followers—really started to believe that power wasn't something that had to come from me or my church?

Cain was a preacher who had long conditioned his flock with one repeated line, one memorized commandment: "We can't meet Bishop after church—you don't want to disrupt his anointing. Get in touch with him on Monday during business hours. Oh, we forgot—the church is closed Monday through Saturday."

The thought flickered through his mind before he could stop it. Because Sheena spoke with the depth of a woman who saw through the marketing charade.

And that was the real threat.

Because women like her—Black women who loved, thought critically, thrived, and served without regret or submission—brought light into dark places.

And his darkness could not afford exposure.

Then and audience member latter reveled as Cain spoke, "Well, Dr. Colucci, first let me say—thank you for honoring all those women. Yes, some of them have done good work, even if some are... shall we say, a bit woke, maybe leading our people down paths that are less important in the eyes of God.

But I must ask—why does it seem like you take issue with the clergy? With us? Especially when it comes to prosperity. What are you really saying here? What's your challenge with men— and women—of God being prosperous?"

Sheena smiled tightly.

"Thank you for that question, Reverend—"

" Ah, Bishop. Bishop Emanuel Adolphus Cain, the Third— please, Bishop, if you must. I am prominent in this body—the Body."

Sheena took a measured breath and scanned the room. The audience was engaged. Expectant. A heavy weight fight-the bell-"Bing".

Cain's presence. His energy.

It *raged* from the corner of the room—thick, volatile, unholy.

Then—
He lurched forward.

His hand slammed the mic—
His mouth covered it—
and from somewhere between his gut and his God, came:

"Oucccakattacatt!"

A sound.
Not a word.
A summons.
The audience-all heads jerked back-breath held.
Then. Raw. Violent. Coated in manufactured glossolalia—
the kind that ain't never cast out nothing real,
but always commands control.

And just like that—

The coiled silence before the storm.
Then she responded.

"Thank you for that question, Bishop Cain."

"I say to that what Dr. Robert M. Franklin, former president of Morehouse College, says in his pivotal book Crisis in the Village: Restoring Hope in African American Communities. He writes—and I quote:

"'The prosperity gospel may be even more insidious and dangerous because it subverts particular elements of the Jesus story and of classical biblical Christianity in order to instill a new attitude toward capitalism and riches.'"

Let me be clear—the prosperity theology is a sleep theology.

And I'm wide awake.

We're wide awake.

We're woke, and we won't apologize for it.

Because what we believe in is a life modeled after Christ—a life of love, sacrifice, humility, and service.

Any theology that replaces servanthood with status,

any preaching that elevates greed over grace,

and any church that confuses material wealth with spiritual power—

is not just missing the mark.

It's stealing from our people.

And I don't believe Jesus flipped tables in the temple just so we could turn around and set up Cash Apps at the altar."

She paused.

Let the echo of that truth find its rhythm in the room.

"I'm not here to attack the clergy. I'm here so that your work don't become criminal. I'm here to remind us we are called to shepherd souls, not build empires.

And if that makes me controversial—then maybe the gospel still works."

Then came the deeper turn:

"When we talk about belief—particularly Christian belief— we're talking about something foundational.

An internal structure.

A sacred architecture of the soul.

We are talking about personal growth with African principles as old as Egypt.

The salvation of Jesus is—all at once—the restoration of the soul and the restoration of community.

And community is only restored when 'the least of these' are protected."

A quiet murmur of agreement rippled.

"As we move through life, we encounter new layers—beliefs about our value, our place, our identity.

And those beliefs are constantly under pressure—by trauma, by success, by failure, by systems of oppression.

So belief isn't just something you change—it's something you shape.

Something you cultivate.

Something to be held in reverence, inside a sacred community of like-minded believers—the ecclesia.

The church."

Cain's face reddened.

A voice—his own, but twisted with indignation—burst out without consent:

"They are sheep, woman—sheep!"

The room jolted—momentarily unsure if they'd heard him right.

But Sheena? She didn't flinch.

She met his eyes—only briefly.

Then spoke softly. Gently. But with precision:

"Some people believe their job is to change others.

To control belief.

But belief doesn't work that way.

Our job isn't to control.

It's to model.

To serve.

To stand in truth, and create space—for people to walk in their own God-given grace.

We have enough light among us.

Enough since 1619.

Enough of His light—no, Her light—

to trust the truth.

Not these evangelical, pseudo-religious trope traps."

Then it happened.

A small tell.
Almost imperceptible.
But she caught it.

She saw it then.

The barely-there tension in his jaw. The way his deacon's gaze flickered downward, uneasy.

A man like Cain—a man whose entire existence was predicated on controlling the beliefs of others—could not afford this conversation.

Because belief was power.

And power with a shot of manipulation was Cain's currency.

The audience applauded; some nodded, others took notes.

But the moment had already passed beyond their grasp.

Cain knew it. Sheena knew it. His deacon knew it.

The air between them was thicker than theology.

This wasn't a speech anymore. This was a war.

And Sheena, unknowingly, had just landed the first blow.

Moment VIII: Your Shade Illuminated Our Truth

Hands were shaken. Camaraderie flowed freely. Plans were being made. Books were bought from vendors, particularly at the booths sponsored by Medu Bookstore of Greenbriar Mall—where Nia Damali advised each leader on their next necessary literary consumption, doing her part for "each one teach one."

As a group, they pooled their love and effort, creating a sanctuary of safety for warriors who would soon leave a place where they mattered—to face purposeful darkness, wrapped in the verbal tropes of love:

"Make Atlanta Great Again. Jesus loves you. Stop the Woke Mob."

Just beyond the Medu Bookstore table, a sub-assembly orchestrated itself around Dr. Sheena Colucci—the Socratic method was at play.

"We in the criminal psychology space attempt to suspend our bias—this allows us to see people for who they are and why they are."

"Dr. Colucci, is that how you were able to help the Chicago Police Department solve the group home abuse case?"

"Reverend, you got it. Most of what protects predators is done in plain view, but our biases put up barriers that keep us from seeing as clearly as we should."

"Ah, Doc Coloeshee, what you just said right there—that's it! Everybody ain't what they say they is."

Deacon McCainy didn't understand Sheena's theories well enough to explain them, but he knew truth when he heard it.

"Dr. Colucci, when you're done, can I have a private word with you?"

The other participants disbanded, meandering on in unison as if to honor the tutoring session that had just taken place.

"Hi, aaah… 'Deacon McClendon'?"

He was such a large man, his suit so dark, that standing so close, his name tag was obscured.

"Ah, yes, Mama Dr. Coloeshee. I don't have a lot of time—I mean, you don't have a lot of time for us. But let me get to the point, or we gonna lose our church. We been going backwards—the wrong way—for years. But if we don't stop now, it will be too late. I can't give you all the details right here—that ain't right to put our church business out in the street… his business out in the street. But—"

"Oh, one minute, Deacon, slow down. I got you. But we just met—I respect your office, but I have no idea what you're talking about."

Sheena saw his shoulders drop, his six-foot-six frame shrinking to five-six—the kind of humility that had no strength to survive chastisement from a superior.

Sheena reached up, placing a hand on his lowered shoulder, and in that moment, she became a healing advocate.

"It's our church. No, really, it's our pastor. He's broke bad. And he's smart, powerful, and we can't do nothing with him any more. He got everything on lock, and he's robbing the sheep. He's taking more money than we can give—The Master's, twelve thousand recently."

"Listen, Deacon, I hear your concern, and I would love to help, but—"

"No, Dr. Coloeshee—"

"Dr. Colucci."

"I'm sorry, no disrespect, Mama—Dr. Colucci, we have to have your help. You're not from Atlanta, and you won't be in with him, so you can see. We need you—our church needs you—or we gonna lose. And people may be hurt. Bad."

The room morphed into a private confessional booth with just the two of them inside.

The priest. The confessor.

She offered him her number and agreed that he should call to make an appointment, as she would be in town for a few more days, maybe a week. She'd sit down with him at the church to get a more in-depth perspective, though she made no guarantees that she could solve their problem.

Then, just as the Deacon took her card, his hand started trembling.

The immediate atmosphere eclipsed into an icy hush, thick with controlled resentment.

"Deacon McClendon, what are you still doing here? I thought I told you that as soon as the program was over, you were to go to the church dining hall and help the custodial staff clean. You know—your personal goal for this year is obedience."

"I'm on my way, Pastor, I was—"

"What have we here? Dr. Colucci, the girl who just had them drop the mic on me."

A slow, deliberate pause.

"I'm Bishop Emmanuel Cain, III—this bothersome person's pastor."

He spoke with razor blades, dressed sharp, and observed deeper than love would allow—because all he wanted to see were flaws and weaknesses.

"I know who you are. Meeting you finally—I saw you today on TV. So when you stood to question, it clicked for—"

Sheena had overstepped his agenda and didn't deserve to finish.

"Dr. Colucci, let me be clear. Atlanta is fine if we stop outside agitators from butting into church business. And I don't know what my Deacon told you—he is a rank liar, as are most of my sheep. You're in criminology; you know what I'm up against.

Don't mind him. And most certainly, don't get involved in all this Atlanta stuff—Atlanta was once great, but if she is to become great again, she needs tithing people being blessed, helping their pastor move God's agenda forward.

Don't buy into this nonsense.

"It's been nice to meet you.

Let me pray for you— Quos deus vult perdere, prius dementat."

Sheena's eyes widened.

Why is he praying in tongues... and not in Jesus' name?

At that moment, she noticed another man—Cain's armor-bearer.

The way he responded was as if Cain were calling a slave. Or a flunky.

The air in the confessional remained interrupted enough that Sheena, almost without thinking, put the paper with Deacon McClendon's number in her purse, not in her executive portfolio.

Whatever had just happened, she did not want to complicate the matter further by losing contact with him.

A buzzing vibration snapped her back to the moment.

Day.

He had texted her.

"We need to talk. I'll be at the hotel to pick you up. Dinner?"

Sheena exhaled, fingers brushing across the phone screen.

"Sure—I need to see you, too. "

Moment IX: Day picks up Shee in the Early Night

Damien arrived on time as Sheena patted the last attendee on the back trading numbers to keep in touch.

The evening was slowly turning into night where shade was less noticeable giving way to past shadows.

Atlanta at night was alive—humming with motion, spilling light onto the pavement, casting long shadows against buildings old enough to hold secrets in their walls.

Sheena exhaled, sinking into the leather seat, kicking off her heels as she stretched her legs. She was still electric from the event, still charged from the energy in the room.

"This afternoon was something else," she said, half-laughing as she ran her fingers through her curls. "The engagement, the energy—people were really locked in."

Damien glanced at her, his grip on the wheel tightening. "That's good. I figured it would be."

She nodded, staring out the windshield, her thoughts trailing off. "It's wild, though. One of the pastors—it brought me right back to my father. Not in a good way."

Damien's fingers flexed, but his voice stayed steady. "Yeah?"

Sheena sighed, watching the streetlights flicker across the hood. "Yeah. Just the way he spoke, you know? That kind of love that isn't really love—just control wrapped in devotion. He didn't say it outright, but you could feel it."

Her voice softened. "The way he dismissed every challenge. The way he expected people to follow, no matter what. That kind of love suffocates—it tells you it's for your good while it steals the breath from your lungs."

She didn't say his name.

She didn't have to.

Stephen Colucci.

The ghost was always there—sitting between them, whispering in the spaces she never quite filled in.

Damien exhaled slowly, gripping the wheel. The neon glow of Paschal's came into view as he turned onto Northside Drive.

Sheena smirked, shifting the mood. "Oh—did you give Em that candy for 'dem shoes, Daddy? 'Dem shoooooes."

Damien chuckled, shaking his head. "No. Tamika called right when I stepped out of a critical meeting. You know how these things go—complicated when they don't have to be. But Em's gonna get it, and whatever else she needs."

Sheena reached over and put her hand on his thigh, rubbing it slightly.

His tone shifted. "But there's something more important we need to talk about- us."

Sheena rolled her eyes playfully. "Ah, 'us'?" She leaned back, tilting her head. "I just asked you to pull my hair, not buy me a ring, Detective. Read the room a little better—damn, Day. Pull it. Puuuull it."

Damien swallowed. Her laughter missed its mark.

On autopilot, he turned past the valet, pulling into a shadowed space behind the restaurant.

Sheena frowned. "Why are we back here—what's wrong Day, did something happen at work"?

She sat back in the car closer to the window- Damien needed room.

Damien cut the engine.

"I need to tell you something before we go inside."

His voice was low. Weighted.

The air in the car changed.

Sheena turned to him, expectant. Curious. Unaware of the wrecking ball about to hit.

Damien's hands stayed on the wheel, his knuckles pale in the dim light.

Then he exhaled.

"Sheena... it's about Shem."

The air shattered.

She turned to him, waiting. Expecting something—but not expecting what was coming.

Damien's hands were still on the wheel, his knuckles pale in the dim light.

Then he exhaled, finally letting go of the truth he had buried for years.

"Sheena... it's about Shem."

The air between them shattered.

EMBARGOED flashed in giant red letters.

The words stared back at him like a verdict already passed.

Damien's voice was low, raw. "What's in the file is true. And I did it."

Sheena's breath hitched.

Damien kept his eyes on the dashboard, his fingers gripping the wheel like it was the only thing keeping him steady. "And it's gonna come out."

She shook her head, slow at first, as if she could stop time, as if she could un-hear what he had just said. "What are you talking about?"

He turned to her then, eyes dark, heavy with something she hadn't seen in him before—not like this.

Regret. Resolve. Something is breaking open.

"I was young, Sheena. And he hurt you. He hurt us. He stole from us. And I couldn't let that stand."

Sheena's heartbeat slammed against her ribs.

Damien swallowed hard. "I thought he might even try Beth. I thought I was doing what had to be done."

The walls of the car pressed in. The night outside felt impossibly close.

"Sheena, I need you to hear this from me first." His voice cracked, but he pushed through. "I am not that man anymore. But I did what I did, and I have to own that."

Sheena closed her eyes.

In her mind, she was no longer in the car.

She was on a plane—just after boarding.
The cabin lights dimmed.
The seatbelt sign blinked overhead, sterile and cold.
Then—an oxygen mask dropped into her lap.

That's what she needed now.
Air.
Space.
Time.
A way to breathe again.

But there was none of that here.
Only him.
Only this moment.
Only the truth she never asked for.

She turned her head too fast, her temple knocking against the passenger-side window.

The thud sounded louder than it should've.

Startled her.

Shamed her.

Damien exhaled sharply, steadying himself. "If I don't stop now and back down," he said, his voice a low, grave rhythm, "everything I've been working toward will fall apart. And this city?"

He glanced at her but didn't expect her to meet his gaze.

"The real killer will rip Atlanta apart."

His voice dropped, even lower. Confessional. Specific.

"But you had to know first. Before it all breaks. I need you to know why I did it. And that I have always loved you."

She couldn't move.

Her breath became airless.

I can't breathe.

Eric Garner.

Her mind clung to the name like a life raft in a storm.

It wasn't just about Damien.

It was about every man who had ever decided what justice looked like without asking who might pay for it.

It was about survival disguised as sacrifice.

It was about how men like Damien had been taught that love had to *cost* something—or someone.

She turned away from him again, slower this time.

But the window didn't offer escape—only her reflection.

Her face, pale.
Her lips parted, trembling.
As if trying to speak a language she no longer believed in.

"Oh my God, Damien."
Her voice cracked like a dam giving way.
"No—you didn't, baby. Say you didn't."

But she already knew.

And then—she saw i
Not in his tone.
But in the stillness.
The way his hands gripped the wheel like a verdict.
The quiet war behind his eyes.
The subtle twitch in his jaw when she said *say you didn't.*

She saw it.

The thing that buried good black men.

The thing that broke them open and dared them to call it
love.
The thing that lived in the bones of men like Damien—the
thing that got them killed in bar fights, that justified one-night
stands, that made them ride for their homies and sell dope to come
up for their women-but really for their own egos.
That thing—toxic masculinity disguised as love.
Sheena knew Damien was human. She knew he was capable.
But capable of this?
What Damien had brought her into town for—without even
knowing it—was her expertise. Most people looked at crime and
asked who or what. Sheena asked why. And when she asked why,
she stopped listening to what you said. She watched instead.

Your hands shake ever so slightly as your words layered beautifully, textured like a lyric. Your eyes narrow, playing hide-and-seek. That smirk saying, "Catch this.

I did.

Catch this.

I didn't do it.

Or I don't know. But, I do".

Or maybe you said, "I don't know, but your head twitched and bobbed like you were vibing to a Future lick —knowing damn well you were standing dead center in the crime.

Was Sheena overthinking it? Maybe. But then there was this.

Damien had said: "I killed Sheena because…"

Because.

That was the part that stopped her cold.

"I killed Sheena because he hurt you."

"He was a bad man".

Bad.

But what did Damien do? He didn't come for me. And Shem wasn't bad. He was like many Black perpetrators—spiritually lost.

White supremacists labeled us bad, locked our communities up wholesale, and sold us on hold-for-sale. But Sheena knew better. There was a difference between being bad and being evil.

And Damien—he had done street shit to get his way in a world already behind the gate of a game rigged against him. Sheena couldn't help but apply her craft to him. Because that's what he was now.

Not Damien, the man she had loved.

Not Damien, the man she had made love to.

Damien, the suspect.

The narrow, slender thread of forensic psychology beneath his brokenness told Sheena two things.

One: this perp was indecisive.

Two: this perp killed,

Sheena was excellent at her craft-and Damien was convicted

-no trial necessary. That's what made her dangerous in her field. She didn't need to see to know. She didn't need a man's lyrical, slick, heroic talk to step out of her stance.

"Brother, you not gonna catch me slipping."

She was a forensic psychologist specializing in street knowledge and had heard it all before. The hesitation, the half-truth, the smooth words wrapped around jagged edges.

I heard it all before. All of your lies-sweet talk- baby this- baby that.

The R&B song spoke for itself. That's where it came from. That's where it always came from. Because at the end of the day, a man's words were just music, and Sheena knew how to read past the melody.

Was she overthinking it?

Nah.

I heard it all before.

She didn't care much for what people said. She read the body, the subconscious mind, the things people couldn't fake. And what she saw in Damien was indecision.

And indecision wasn't sexy. I wasn't grounding-stable-mature-she knew you couldn't build intimacy on it.

She pressed her palms to her chest, forcing air into her lungs. She needed to get out of this car.

She needed to move. She pressed her palm to her chest, forcing air into her lungs. She needed to get out of this car. She needed to move.

And yet—she was frozen. This block from her Day would block their light, love, and future.

Moment X: No Shade-Just Not Us

Sheena's breath was shallow, her heartbeat thundering in her ears.

"Open the door, Day." Her voice wavered, but her resolve didn't. "I love you—but not like this. Not... this."

She reached for the handle, but his hand brushed her arm before she could steady herself.

Maybe it was instinct. Maybe it was a reflex. Maybe it was just him trying to steady her step down.

But an unwanted pull is an unwanted pull.

Sheena yanked her arm back.

Her eyes met his, and in that second, she wasn't looking at Damien DeBerg, the man she loved. She was looking at every man who had ever thought love was a grip instead of a hand to hold.

She turned away before the tears could come. Before she could second-guess herself.

Her purse brushed against her hip as she stepped out of the car, and for a flicker of a moment, he saw the slip of paper sticking out of the side pocket.

Deacon's number.

But Damien said nothing. Nothing at all.

Sheena straightened her shoulders, exhaling slow. The weight of the past, the weight of the moment, pressing against her ribs.

A valet in a crisp white shirt stepped forward, but Sheena lifted a hand before he could speak. "No, I'm fine, sir. I will be dining alone tonight."

Damien sat there, watching her walk away, the heat from the confession still burning in his chest.

The lie he had lived with had been unknown—until now.

And now that it was known, would it block Day's light?

Would it stop him from solving the ATL's serial murders?

Would it stop him from loving the only woman in the A he had ever loved?

Some lies—some lies block the light.

And now, he didn't know if he would ever find his way out of the dark.

His phone buzzed against his thigh.

Text: Sheena: RUOK? I luv u.

His whole body dropped- his shook. His thumb hovered over the screen.

But some lies—some lies block the light.

And now, he didn't know if he would ever find his way out of the dark.

His phone buzzed again.

Text: Sheena: RUOK?

A longer beat. His thumb hovered over the screen.

Then, finally—

Text: FWIW... Luv u always.

He exhaled. The weight of the night settled deeper into his chest.

He stared at the message, watching the words linger on the screen—like an echo of something slipping away.

And for the first time since he told her the truth—

he wasn't sure if love was enough.

And for the first time since he first laid eyes on Sheena Elise Colucci all those years ago at —since their rap battle at that Mays high school talent show, since that day in the back of Math class when they wrote the rap song that defined them—Beloved in the ATL—since every touch, every laugh, every heated argument that only ever led them back to each other's spirits—

—he felt something break.

Maybe it was trust.

Maybe it was the belief that love could outrun consequences.

Maybe it was just the cold realization that some things, once done, could never be undone.

But as he sat there—engine humming low and sad—

something played on the radio. He couldn't hear it.

Some mistakes don't get second chances.

All truth comes due.

She wasn't coming back.
Not this time.

Because now she knew—he hadn't done it for her.
He'd done it for himself.

The weight of that truth settled deep.
His head throbbed. His hands clenched the wheel.
Then—he struck it. Hard. Twice.
As if punishing himself.

Because that's what he'd done.

He had thrown shade on himself.

CHAPTER 5

TWO LOVES-SISTERS AND BROTHERS

Moment I: A Sister Carrying Me

Looking out at the morning skyline of Atlanta, Sheena didn't see Cascade. She didn't see the city that had raised her, the one she once believed in.

She only saw the gravitational, undeniable pull away from her two loves.

One had collapsed in her arms under the weight of unspoken words. The other was collapsing around her. Atlanta, once the Black Mecca, now seemed to be making a mess of Black lives.

She traced slow circles on the cold glass, her reflection staring back at her—silent, unyielding. Last night lingered in her mind. She had wanted him to pick her up for dinner with two goals in mind. Now, only one question remained.

Her fingers fidgeted, restless. She needed to move. Light-headedness crept in as she exhaled, her breath fogging the glass as if searching for answers in the fading warmth.

Her phone lit up on the nightstand. Tina. Returning the call Sheena had made before falling asleep.

She exhaled and picked up. She created a mental tally of what had gone wrong.

"Okay, girl, how did your session go?" Tina's voice was already teasing.

Sheena fought off her strained voice, stretching her legs. Here we go.

"Oh, I can tell you—it went well."

"Girl, I ain't talking about that. I knew you were gonna do well at your conference. And I know you went over there yesterday. I wanna hear about Daytime."

"Girl, before I even get to that, I got a few other things to catch you up on."

"Ohhh, saving the best for last? I'm in."

Sheena poured her overflow into Tina's cup. And Tina, like always, held it, rolled it around, and offered back pearls.

"Good for work- now get to the Day part already".

"Oh, wow. That doesn't mean that."

"Girl, it's not over."

"Trust your gut, but realize—he was young."

Tina sighed. "Are you being Sheena or Shee? Girl,

sometimes you gotta give up control- men- no, a man- no, your man-your Day-not Damien…"

"I'm always here for you. I'm ride or die, you know that. But no matter what you do—do what your heart tells you, not your head."

Tina's voice softened. "He's always gonna be my Day. 'Cause even if y'all never get together for real, he's always gonna be in you. He was in you the day we met."

Sheena closed her eyes.

"And girl—pearls are made in a living organism, not just by pressure. You were built to endure. You were built for this. For love. For life. And yeah, love can be messy, but it's worth fighting for."

"Thanks, Tee, I gotta go. A lot to think about, and like I said,

I need to check in with Beth. And then… this church. These two organisms? Immediate pressure."

"Love you, sexy cowgirl—ride it, girl. 'Pull it, Day, pull it—please keep pullin' it.'"

Sheena giggled, soothed by the warmth of being nurtured by her dear friend.

"HBCU, college-educated bitch, bye-bye already."

Tina laughed. "I know what y'all got goin' on down there. Y'all got that BunnaB, 'cause it's hot up here. Dah-dah-dah—Ice Cream Girl. See? I knew you had that sophisticated hoe in you."

The call clicked off, ending what might as well have been the final part of her sorority hazing session.

Sheena smirked, shaking her head as her phone shifted in her hand, as if it too were nodding in admiration for Tina's wisdom.

She glanced down at her manicured nails, freshly painted pink, done to match the tailored outfit she had planned to wear today with Day. Her thumb scrolled.

Beth.

She pressed her lips together and glanced back at the skyline.

Tina always knew her best.

And now—Beth's voice was on the other end.

Moment II: Me Carrying My Sister?

If Beth's voice had been so present—"Sure, pick me up. It'll be good for us to hang"—it was strangely absent now, lost in the jasmine-scented hush of the plush studio foyer.

The office oozed peace and calm, a panoramic display of art, wealth, and stable business, brought to life by the IG model chosen to decorate the walls—gaze fixed, an emblem of power.

Sheena gasped. "Wow. Who knew?"

Even though she whispered it, the receptionist noticed—but was too professional to acknowledge.

"Yes, ma'am. Can I help you? Welcome to Slim Too Thick ATL Entertainment."

Sheena turned to the voice.

The receptionist's tone was polished, her words clipped and deliberate.

But that wasn't what Sheena heard.

"Welcome to Aston, Bitton & Chamberlain—attorneys at law. Specializing in high-end entertainment law for artists with hits only. Please believe it."

A law firm.

That's what this felt like.

The scented air, the furniture, the platinum plaques on the walls—they didn't just suggest success. They whispered it. Money. Power. Strategy.

The atmosphere wasn't just professional; it was intentional.

International.

We in the Atlanta entertainment scene are international.

Respect.

She blinked, steadying herself.

She slowed now, glancing around. The office, nestled in a Midtown Atlanta station, felt inconspicuous—unremarkable, even. But if she had known it was just steps from Patchwerk Recording Studios, she might have expected a buzzing energy, maybe even a hint of bass slipping through the walls.

Instead, the air was thick with something richer, smoother—like slow jazz pressing against the space, a Coltrane breath suspended in time.

Whatever was happening behind those soundproof walls was meant to stay there.

"Yes, I'm Dr. Colucci."

She started strong, but her words stumbled under the weight of the platinum record gleaming behind the receptionist.

Her eyes caught her reflection in it.

She swallowed.

"I'm here for my sister."

No, she corrected herself, standing a little taller.

"No. I'm here for my sister, Beth."

Soothingly, almost cooing, as if not to disturb the Atlanta Symphony Orchestra, the receptionist murmured,

"Beat, your guest is here."

Then Beat's voice moved like poetry, politely inviting them onto the red carpet running the full length of the narrow hall.

The walls on each side stood like museum curators—not just holding the building up, but commanding presence.

"Please look to your right and to your left—observe how we've turned gold and platinum into green and street cats into big dogs."

Then. In the depth of the studio.

"Whew! Keep dat!"

A well-dressed hip-hop figure clearly at work on something meaningful spoke in rapid-fire style like a cornerman during a heavyweight fight.

"Beat, you battling Boss Lady—sharp as an ax—you kill'n the game!"

Sheena whinced- "There is a serious artist in the booth-damn-he takes them seriously".

Buttons twisted- ticks performed.

"Did he just ride Beth like 'Boss Lady"?

Wait—

Then Sheena heard the next line rumble from the belly of Beth in character as Beat aka Boss Lady to the delight of her producer-employee— "Cold chap'n you like the Braves tomahawk!"

Sheena leaned against the console, arms folded, the low hum of bass vibrating through her bones. Through the glass, Beth—no, *Beat*—moved with command, adjusting her headphones with an ease that suggested she'd done this a thousand times.

She wasn't just in the booth—she owned it.

And then—there it was.

She heard what the producer- engineer heard. What the world already knew.

Beth's voice filled the studio—confident, undeniable, carved in stone.

"Pull up in Hartsfield, you'll see the jet fuel is on.
I been killing hoes one by one since the day I was born.
Slim—call him Thick, 'cause his middle finger strong,
Betta not try ply'n us—when you do, things go wrong...

Cold chop'n like the Braves tomahawk!
My pretty—Cold chop'n like the Braves tomahawk!
ATL city—Cold chop'n like the Braves tomahawk!
My kitty—Cold chopped you like the Braves tomahawk!"

The words wrapped around Sheena like a slow revelation, each syllable cutting through her previous assumptions.
his wasn't just bravado.
It wasn't just flexing.

It was possession. Ownership. Control.

Beth wasn't playing. She wasn't falling.

Beth's voice cut through the studio speakers, distorted through a walkie-talkie:

"Hey, big sis—Sheena, I see you. What you think?"

The revelation came from an unexpected source.

"Damn. Big Sis, you somebody."

Sheena turned toward the voice.

He flicked the button with care, his focus unwavering.

"Beat don't even ask Slim—the co-owner of this shit—for a critique."

He threw up a casual salute toward the booth, signaling to Beth that she had his full attention.

"In fact—nobody.

She barely listens to up-and-coming GOAT's—except Loto, the Queen of the ATL, Monaleo, Cash Doll, Megan, Nikki. And you know Cardi B—her cipher twin, her competition."

He eyed Sheena with something close to amusement.

"But what—you? You must be the shit to be on her mind like that."

Sheena sensed it now.

The weight in the room. The hierarchy. She wasn't just standing next to some hype man. She was in the presence of someone *accomplished*—someone who didn't waste time.

She met his gaze.

"What's your name?"

A slow smirk—his eyes still locked on Boss Lady.

"Arturo Fuente. Aka the Burner Earn'ah."

A beat passed. Then—

"Yep. That's what you smell. You hit?"

Sheena's eyes were hazy now, wrapped in the expensive cigar-blunt smoke cloaking her like a veil.

"Huh?—I have, but nah, not now. Thanks."

Sheena remembered. Her and her sorors, in the comfort of no one else, passing a blunt, laughing, inhaling the good, good.

She clocked it now.
This wasn't some reckless, messy spot.

This was work.

The mixing boards. The respect. Professionalism weaved through the haze.

And somewhere in it all—

Love.

Love from Beat.
Love from her sister—the same sister she had just given up on.

"Damien—really?"

And love from her new weed man—whose name she didn't even know five minutes ago.

"Damn, girl, you did that."

He exhaled, letting the bass rumble beneath his words.

"I'm your agent now—shit, Beth. Beat, yo' girl good."

Arturo let the music breathe.

A trap adagio.

Sheena had spent years avoiding this world. She had assumed
it had swallowed Beth whole.

Beth was not lost.

She was leading.
It hit her with a quiet force, unsettling in its simplicity:
She had never truly listened.
Not just to Beth's music but to Beth herself.
Sheena had spent her life mastering the art of moving forward,
of carving stability from chaos. In the process, she judged what
didn't fit her vision of control, respectability, and safety.
But Beth wasn't looking for a handout.
She was bouncing bars, collaborating with hip-hop stars—
buying the help luxury cars.
She wasn't caught in someone else's game.
She had built something of her own.
And Sheena had refused to see it.
She felt the weight of that omission settle in her chest.
Had she ever given Beth the space to be her whole self?
Had she ever considered that Beat wasn't an act but a truth?
The realization warmed her as much as it unsettled her.
If Beth could be both Beat and Beth, then maybe Sheena could

exist beyond the rigid, disciplined version of herself she had clung to for so long.

Maybe healing didn't mean holding the world at arm's length.

Maybe, for the first time, it meant stepping closer.

And wasn't that the same wall she had put between herself and Damien?

Sheena glanced back at the booth, watching Beth slip effortlessly into her verse,

her voice cutting through the track like glass.

Sheena smiled—something small but real.

For the first time, she wasn't just hearing her sister.

She was listening.

Beth was in Sheena's face before she could even push through the haze.

Thumb up.

Verse? Hotter than fire.

"Arturo, save that. I'll be back tomorrow—or the next day—to cut it out."

"Tell Slim—this the verse they can add to that movie soundtrack. The one he was talking about."

"I don't think it's strong, though. You know I gotta stay drippin'."

"The A got a whole new group of besties—BunnaB is blowin' up."

"I like that *No Drought*—dah-dah-dah—*Ice Cream Girl!*"

Beth's characteristic dramatic pause channeled Morris Day when he was with The Time,
talking about "777-9311."

Then Beth, the entertainment industry collaborator, movie soundtrack maker—

"And if not? I'll give it to somebody else."

Now, Beth, the music executive, switching lanes as easily as she did in her own

"I ain't puttin' that on my album, though."
Beth took a purposeful stride back toward the mixing board, fingers grazing the dials as if the conversation had already ended.
Sheena hesitated. "Beth, did you—"
Beth lowered her voice, just enough. Auturo caught the cue, kept working, knowing better than to interrupt.
Then, prayerful, offhand, but code-switching to the sound of the factory whistle—
"Girl, let's go. Dah-dah-dah, we out."
And just as they moved, tossed over her shoulder, proud, light but loaded—
"By the way, Arturo, this is my big sister—BunnaB- say it again—dah, dah, dah."
Beth—the entertainer—switched lanes again.
Sheena wasn't sure if she was hearing Beat or if Beat was hearing Beth—
but it no longer mattered.
Because something softened.
Like a mother at her child's game—watching for the first time.

Only Damien could relate.

Like when he went to Em's games.

And right there, in that moment—they were closer than ever. Sheena saw it. She saw Beth. She saw them.

Beth had been victimized and had lived in pain—for her. And Sheena hadn't seen it.

He was hard on her, too. Different. Different reasons. But hard just the same.

He had divided them on purpose.

Sheena exhaled, the weight of realization pressing against her ribs.

Beat. Her talent—her ability to code-switch, to chase the bag without losing herself, and to be authentic—had always been her power.

And here Sheena was, always trying to carry Beth.

But what if she put it down?

What if Beth didn't need carrying?

For what it was worth—Beth, Beat, had straight Hartsfield-Jackson jet fuel coursing through her. It had kept her moving. Had help shape her. And maybe—just maybe—it would heal them too.

In her thoughts, Sheena became less animated than her sister, tilting her head to side in another, more somber rhythm.

But what—if anything—could ever heal Sheena and Damien?

Us? Us. Day and I?

She looked back at yesterday—how close they had been.

How far they had fallen.

Day and I are in the dark.

Because something had cut them and chopped them.

And it wasn't the Braves' tomahawk—

This isn't our BeLoved in the ATL-our rap hit- the orginal.

At times like this, Sheena did what she always did.

She focused on the work.

She **left** before the weight could settle.

"Sheena, pay attention. I'm ready for you to get me out of here."

Beat's voice pulled her back.

"I love work—but a girl gotta know when to let go."

Wow.

After all of this, it was time to go.

It was time to go to church.

Moment III: Sister and I at God's House?

Sheena and Beth stood at the back of the vast, empty auditorium.

The room should have felt hollow. Too much space. Too much air-conditioning—a biting, artificial chill emphasizing the work of prosperity, not the work of people.

But it didn't feel empty.

Because Cain was everywhere.

At every aisle break, his image loomed. His picture mounted at strategic points as if the ushers themselves might forget who ran this place.

The stage—standing in for the altar—felt more like a performance set. Dim lights. Big presence. The pastor's presence- this was his house.

Every angle, every wall, every corridor, he was there.

Cain on a plane.

Cain on a train.

Cain playing golf.

Cain on stage.

Beth saw good marketing- Sheena thought-

Cain, Cain, Cain I am.

Sheena chuckled, but it was the kind of laugh that didn't quite make it to her chest.

She thought of Dr. Otis Moss III back at Trinity in Chicago, how he had once taught on John 3:30—"He must increase, but I must decrease."

This pastor—he wasn't decreasing. And he didn't seem like he planned to anytime soon.

Jesus. Where is God in all of this? This entertainment? This spectacle?

Maybe God was tucked behind one of the pastor's posters.

She exhaled, then snickered to herself.

Ebenezer, here in Atlanta, was large—but warm..

If she still lived here, it's where she would go.

Trinity, her home church, was massive—but it had spirit. Service sought justice while feeding your soul.

This? This is a financial institution with a choir.

A pastor for profit—out for profit.

You know what they say about transactional relationships—no romance without finance.

That was the truth Pastor Cain lived by.

And yet—ironically, trying to focus on something that needed less judgment- she reached for Damien- Day's light.

Not physically. But deep down, she wanted him there.

Even though she knew.

Given the circumstances.

She deserved the cold into which she had walked.

"Hey, sis."

Sheena turned to Beth, who stood with one hand resting on her belly.

The other? Pointing.

Her finger stretched toward the stage, toward a large figure moving through the projected light.

Not Pastor Cain—the center of the show. The man. The myth. The legend.

This was a man of no reputation, Deacon Ogbomosho McLendon.

His Geechee father had given him the only African-oriented name he knew. And it fit—perfectly.

Not Cain. But still powerful in his own right.

Not Cain. But still standing in his house.

Not Cain. But still in control—for now.

McLendon wasn't a fool. He had invited them for a reason.

This wasn't just church.

This was a fight for what was left of it.

The giant was upon them.

But his steps were soft as cotton.

Before Sheena could brace for it, he wrapped them both in a warm, grounding embrace—the kind she wished Stephen had given if he hadn't been drunk and a loser.

Not stiff.

Not performative.

Just… right.

"Daughters—welcome to God's house. Or… what's left of it."

The words would have been funny—given the grandeur, the opulence, the sheer ostentation of the space. "Welcome to the house Cain built", But real spiritual people? People walking by faith?

They didn't give a rat's ass about the outer.

And neither did this Godly giant.

"Y'all come with me this way. Can I get you something to drink? Water or juice? You know we keep us some juice in this place."

Then, with a smirk—"And since the pastuh ain't here, I won't have to charge you, either."

Sheena caught it. The easy, playful jab.

Beth, on the other hand?

She was in ornament heaven.

Her eyes locked on the crucifixes lining the hall—stained glass shadows flickering against her skin as they made their way toward the conference room.

Sheena might've answered Deacon McLendon. Might've engaged.

But she had no cash.

"Thank God I ain't thirsty," she thought, smirking to herself.

And that? Just off of the conference room that had just consumed like a vault was Cain's most clueless hood ornament.

The plush conference room swallowed them whole, the heavy wooden doors sealing them inside like a vault.

This wasn't just any meeting.

This was Cain's inner sanctum.

Sheena and Beth stood with deliberate poise, their hands lightly resting on the backs of the high-backed chairs. The seats waved like the choir on Sunday baptism morning, polished and ready for devotion.

Smiles measured, but warm.

Posture upright, intentional.

Their presence saying, "We are good little girls. We mean no harm."

Deacon McClendon, steady and deliberate, pulled out a chair for Sheena.

Before she could take it, a voice sliced through the room—sharp, edged with authority and fatigue.

"I would be remiss not to introduce you to Mothah Ellena Benton."

Sheena and Beth turned.

An elder woman sat just on the otherside of the glass, watching them on her big-screen TV—her expression unreadable, yet knowing.

She measured every bit of church business that unfolded in the Trustees' Conference Room, seeing everything, revealing nothing.

Sheena took her in quickly—the navy suit modest but pressed, the way her hands rested over her stomach as if she had already decided this meeting was both necessary and a waste of time.

McClendon smirked, lowering his voice in something between playfulness and truth.

"Oh, what big eyes she got— but she can't hear you."

His inappropriate, sandpaper-dry giggle tickled both Sheena and Beth in the worst way—

The kind of sound that didn't belong anywhere

except maybe between the slow, wet smacks of pudding and green beans in an old folks' home.

She ain't deaf, but the Lawd took some of her hearing, seeing how she used to be a gossip.

"But hey, I'm just tryin' to make light."

Beth parachuted in from the streets, floating on McClendon's air for just a moment before leaning into Sheena's ear.

"Your Deacon friend got jokes."

Her whisper carried the kind of amusement that only came from clocking game mid-play.

He glanced at Mother Benton, the teasing slipping into something closer to reverence.

"She my sister. But she too old for pastah to replace her. And too old to care."

Beth stifled a grin, but Sheena felt something else settling in her chest—a quiet recognition of what was happening here.

They weren't just meeting Mother Benton.

They were about to leave a trail.

Sow a seed, even if they may not like the harvest.

Sheena took note of the way Mother Benton studied them, her gaze passing over them once, then again, as if committing their faces to memory.

This woman didn't miss much.

She was old-school church folk—the kind who watched everything but understood only what fit her world.

She'd sit through Jeopardy! every evening, calling out answers with conviction—and getting every single one wrong.

Yet, when it came to people, to business, to church politics?

She knew exactly what was going on.

And, unknowingly, she would make sure the Pastor did too.

Moment IV: Sister, I and the Master's Missing Twelve

Deacon McClendon sat heavy in the old church chair, his shoulders rounded like the weight of his father's name still pressed on his spine. His hands rested on the wooden table before him, the veins rising against his dark skin like roots struggling against stone. The ledger sat open, pages thin and delicate, but the truth it held was anything but.

His voice was thick with regret, each word pulling him deeper into the pit he had dug with good intentions.

"The thing about it is, I bear the cross now." His voice wavered but did not break. "I never was the man Deacon my father is—was."

Sheena sat across from him, rigid, absorbing the confession before her like a prosecutor listening to a guilty plea. Beside her, Beth exhaled slowly, her gaze drawn not to the man speaking but to the high ceilings, the stained glass filtering warm light over her like a baptism.

McClendon shook his head, his thoughts unraveling. "I liked it. He made me feel good. Pastor, that is. When he first came, a candidate for us, his daddy had a great reputation. But my daddy was still alive then. He'd come to church with his cane, sometimes a wheelchair. But he was respected because my daddy had put in the work. Cain's daddy had grown up—parallel, my daddy. My daddy, with no education or hard work, came up from the Georgia fields. Cain's daddy, Cain's daddy..." He paused, his eyes searching the past for something solid. "Mohawk. He all right. But my daddy say don't trust that kind."

Beth let the words settle, her fingers lacing together in her lap.

McClendon sighed. "And sure enough, we brought him in. Half the people didn't want him. Then I started getting him water, opening the door for him, going to get his stuff. He made me feel good. He pulled me in. He pulled me. Then I pulled everybody else in."

His hands clenched into fists, then slowly relaxed.

"I had enough clout from my daddy. The other deacons may have had one, two, three votes in their family, but the congregation was a good size. And I had my daddy."

Sheena saw it then—the sickness of pride, the addiction of proximity to power. He wasn't the first man who had sold his soul for the warmth of approval.

McClendon's voice dropped, the syllables slipping, the language breaking like a crumbling foundation. "My daddy on his deathbed told me don't do it. Say that ain't your pastor. Let God pick your pastor." His throat worked around the words. "But I picked him… 'cause he made me feel good."

Beth's posture changed. She was still sitting straight, but the awe was leaving her. The moment's heaviness was catching her at the edges, like shadows creeping up a wall.

McClendon blinked rapidly, staring at his own hands. "I used my daddy's righteousness. I was, at one time, a good man. I knew how. I learned it from him. I don't got it now. I done lost it. The longer the pastor has been here, the more I lost, 'cause the worse he got. He going up… I'm going down. But we got to stop it. Help us make it up—more righteousness for him…" His voice cracked. "I get someone hurt."

Sheena flinched at the phrase.

"Someone's gonna lose their religion, their hopes, 'cause of me and my pitiful, broke spine."

The words punched Sheena in the chest.

The word of God says, confess your sins one to another.

She remembered that scripture. But there was something else in this room—something heavier than scripture, something pressing its palm against the back of her neck. She could feel Beth sitting beside her and the reverence coming off her like heat. Sheena wasn't sure if Beth was caught in the sermon or caught in the unraveling.

McClendon exhaled hard, his hands shaking as he slid something across the table—a giant, dog-eared receipt book.

Sheena blinked. The thing was old; the pages yellowed and curled, the ink faded but legible. It wasn't what you would expect from a church of this size, not in a world of spreadsheets and accounting software.

McClendon's voice was hoarse. "I couldn't even take care of the Master's Twelve."

He lowered his head into his hands.

Beth furrowed her brow. "What do you mean by the Master's Twelve, sir?"

Sheena turned toward her, pressing a hand on her sister's forearm—a silent signal. You don't have to be in this. But the question was already in the air.

McClendon lifted his head, his eyes red and exhausted. He tapped the ledger, pointing to the last entry, his voice barely above a whisper.

"The Master's Twelve. He stole twelve thousand dollars. It was the second offering we had taken that day. And that twelve thousand... was to honor all of the disciples."

Silence thickened in the church.

Beth's fingers twitched. She was listening now in a way that had nothing to do with worship.

McClendon kept going, his words coming apart at the seams. "We was gonna use that money at a shelter. For battered women. 'Cause we had women in our community who been battered. Bruised. Abused."

Sheena held her breath.

"We even heard tell that there was some women in this community who had been violated in a way that no woman should."

The words sliced through her. The floor beneath her might as well have cracked open.

She saw Shem's face. Saw her tears.

A rush of fury bloomed in her chest, bright and hot, mixing with something deeper.

McClendon coughed, his hands tightening around the ledger. "And that twelve thousand… was gonna be for them."

Sheena gritted her teeth.

That was it. That was the knockout blow.

Because this wasn't just about a pastor skimming money. This wasn't about a greedy man bleeding the flock dry.

This was about what could have been. What should have been.

That money—that twelve thousand dollars—

Could have been the hand that pulled someone out.

Could have been the thing that kept a woman safe.

Could have been the thing that stopped Shem from ever needing to cry like that.

Sheena exhaled—long, slow.

She had come here to listen. But now she knew.

She couldn't leave.

She wouldn't.

Because the work was too valuable- demons don't stop. And if Damien could fight for her, in the best way he knew how…

She had to fight for this church.

Even if it meant that Damien would never touch her again with the warmth and the deepness that had once made her feel whole.

She wouldn't.

Because the work was too valuable- predators don't stop. And if Damien was hers she must fight now. If Atlanta was in her it had to be a fight.

She must fight for this church- now.

Even if it meant Damien would never touch her again like back at Mays when they were teens- innocent, authentic, real-the warmth and the deepness that had once made her feel safe.

Because some things—some crosses—were too heavy for one man to carry alone.

Sheena sat up in the church conference chair, tall, looking like she had just stood up in the pulpit.

"Well, we will see what we can do to get back the Master's Twelve."

Time to fight.

Moment V: Sister Give Back the Master's Twelve

Sheena was reeling.

What she had just learned wasn't just unsettling—it was confirmation.

Her mind—sharp, trained, relentless—had already begun piecing together the next steps.

Cain wasn't just corrupt.

He was a manipulator at best.

A thief at worst.

And if she was honest with herself?

Probably both.

Deacon McLendon needed help.

Mother Benton? She was a lost cause.

Bless their hearts.

Sheena inhaled slowly, forcing clarity through the weight pressing on her chest.

But even as the strategy took shape, another thought kept pressing in—

Not warm, but lonely.

Would it be fair to call Day after I sent him away?

She let the question sit.

Turned it over.

I felt the weight of it.

Because that's precisely what Damien had done at the beginning.

He had called her.

Brought her in.

Made her part of his world.

And now she was the one at the crossroads.

Should I call Damien and invite him into this? Like he did for me?

Or should I stand firm in the distance I created? Do I really want to stay away from him? Does he even want to consider us now?

As a professional, she could justify it.

As a woman, she couldn't ignore it.

And that? That was the actual fight.

Beth shifted beside her.

Her body was still, but her breathing had changed. The soft, rhythmic inhales she had maintained throughout the conversation were gone, replaced by something uneven, something breaking.

And then, quietly at first, she spoke.

"Sir... I've been a sinner."

Her voice was raw, her hands trembling as she clutched her stomach.

"This is the first time I've been in church in years. And I don't know if God loves me. But... I've made a lot of money, though."

Sheena turned to her sister, her mind scrambling to understand. But Beth wasn't looking at her. She was looking down—her hands now resting protectively over her stomach.

Sheena's breath caught in her throat.

Oh my God.

Beth had never said the words. Never admitted it. But now, here it was.

Beth was pregnant. Sheena saw their baby-their child- in the pure glow in the mother's eyes-in the precious touch of the belly still mostly flat.

And for the first time, she spoke a truth that had been buried deep inside her.

"That was the father I had," she whispered, her voice nearly breaking. "I used my father to get what I wanted."

The room felt smaller.

And then, the tears came.

They weren't the performative, defiant tears Beth had shed before. They weren't the angry, rebellious ones she threw at Sheena like daggers when they fought. These were different.

These were the tears of someone who had seen the reflection of her own soul for the first time and recoiled at the sight.

Deacon McClendon, in that moment, appeared different to her. His worn, lined face, the sorrow in his eyes—he wasn't just a deacon anymore.

To Beth, he was a priest. A confessor.

And the tears brought words.

"I knew that my father didn't love my sister," Beth admitted, her voice raw and guttural. "But I took everything he gave me. All the candy. All the gifts. All the shoes. The clothes. While Sheena sat in that room... abused."

Beth's body trembled.

"I'm so sorry, Sheena."

Sheena's eyes widened as Beth laid her head on her shoulder, her hands grasping her like a child clinging to something steady in a storm.

Beth, the one who had always fought her. Beth, who had built walls of sarcasm and pride to protect herself. Beth, who had laughed off anything that hurt too much to say out loud—was now breaking apart in her arms.

Sheena didn't know what to do.

Her sister had spent her whole life hiding from truth. And now, truth was bleeding out of her like a wound festering too long.

Beth lifted her head, her eyes swollen with tears.

"But I'm going to make it up."

Sheena tensed. Wooden like a fraternity paddle.

Beth's voice cracked, but she kept going. "And Sheena, I know I put music out there—"

"No," Sheena said sharply, shaking her head. "Beth, stop."

But Beth wasn't done. "I just want God to love me."

Sheena felt something shift in the room.

The walls of the church, the very air around them, seemed to tighten and close in as Beth said it.

And then, almost as an afterthought, Beth whispered, "I know I've called myself Beat."

And there it was again.

Made a lot of money.

But I'm going to do better.

Deacon McClendon, recognizing that this was no longer about Cain, no longer about corruption—about a soul in desperate need—reached across the aisle.

"Now, now, now, dear daughter."

His voice was warm. And in that moment, he became something more than just an old, weary churchman.

To Beth, he became a father.

And to Sheena...

She felt something familiar for the second time today, for the third time today. Something that reminded her of Damien.

Not in the way he touched or held her, but in the way he had always seen her.

And the weight of it all—the intensity of whatever was stirring in this church—was being challenged by something else.

Something deeper. She thought beyond the walls of this church:

He always told the truth and fought for what he believed in, even until his mother's death- he fought for her to get well and was never angry at his dad for not being there...

The intimacy and love between a man and a woman in intense, thrilling situations was always present.

But before anyone could process what was happening, Beth suddenly stood up.

She wiped her tears, lifted her chin, and exhaled sharply.

Then, she reached into her $15,000 designer bag and pulled out a stack of cash.

Sheena blinked.

What the hell?

Beth counted it off quickly, her fingers moving with precision. She was calm now. Resolved.

"Sir," she said, her voice steady, "this is… twelve thousand dollars."

Sheena stiffened.

She knew Beth had money—knew she had made good money. But she hadn't known this.

Beth extended the money to the Deacon.

"I don't know who took it," she admitted. "But this will help you, sir."

Deacon McClendon, eyes still wet with emotion, hesitated before reaching forward and taking it.

Then, without a second thought, he picked up the old ledger and wrote it down.

His voice was thick with awe. "God answered the prayer… from my daughter. Our lost daughter."

The words struck Sheena deep.

Deacon's voice cracked with something close to relief. "Done gave back the Master's twelve… when the old pastor wouldn't care for the twelve."

Sheena inhaled sharply. "Sir—sir—"

Her voice stuttered. She never stuttered.

But the moment was already moving.

McClendon bowed his head, and he was praying the next thing she knew.

And it wasn't the grand, performative prayer she had grown used to.

It was simple.

"Lord… first, the Master's twelve was taken away by a wolf. But just as the Lord was given to us by a virgin, you gave us back the money… from this fair maiden."

Beth's breath hitched.

Sheena saw the tears spill down her sister's face again.

But this time, they weren't tears of guilt.

They were cleansing.

Peaceful.

McClendon lifted his eyes to the heavens.

"Not because of the money, Lord. But because of the Blood. Wipe her sins clean."

Beth's shoulders shook.

Sheena held onto her.

And then, the words came—like scripture etched into the walls of time itself:

"Just like you did for Martha and Mary at Bethany... You stopped her from being too busy. Now, Lord, give her what she's gonna to live for you- nah, with you."

It felt as though the very heavens opened.

Sheena felt it.

And she heard it.

"Bethany."

The name settled between them like something ancient, something sacred.

"That's her real name—on her birth certificate. My father refused to call her that, because my mother insisted."

McClendon exhaled, his voice thick with revelation.

"Of course. Bethany. The place where the Master raised Lazarus from the dead. The same way He's raising this girl straight into His saving grace. And the same way He's gonna use you... to bring this church back from the dead."

Beth cried herself into rebirth.

And Sheena wiped her tears as payment for purity.

And then—

Piercing through the air.

Like Glinda the Good Witch floating in uninvited.

Like the sudden crash of an Apple computer over a school PA system.

Mother Benton's voice broke through the other side of the glass.

She didn't just speak—she engaged, a windup doll set in motion, every word soaked in devotion and duty.

"Yeah, Passah, they two of the nice young womens—one of 'em rich, a showgirl I think, 'cus she just gave another Master Twelve to us."

Sheena's stomach twisted.

"The Lawd giveth and the Lawd taketh away—"

A pause. Then—her voice dropping into obedient submission.

"I sho will, Passah. No, Passah. Yes, Passah. I hear you, Passah. I will, Passah. Bye now."

Click.

Beth, unfazed, filled out the receipt book for cash.

Bethney Colucci

(404) 344-2062

3421 Cascade Dr., 30311

No hesitation. No second thought.

Slim might be gangsta, but he was no criminal—anymore.

They paid their taxes.

And then some.

The air inside the church conference room was thick, unmoving.

Something had shifted. In everybody—even Mother Benton, whose hearing aid had caught just enough for her to store it away for later, ready to announce it like the evening news.

God knows, retired or not, a professional gossip never really quits.

And in that moment, Sheena knew what she had to do.

She may have thought she was done.

But she wasn't.

This was bigger than her.

It may be a thrill ride.

It may be dangerous.

And she knew Damien may be busy.

But she had to contact him?

Just for professional reasons?

He said he was always there for her… right?

Because whatever was happening in this church, whatever was coming next—

As she and Bethany walked out, she was in it.

"Bye now, nice to meet you, Deacon. I don't think they heard my goodbye—anyway, Passah say he saw them on the church cameras, said he recognized one of 'em. I gave him the show-girl's number—said he wanna call her to thank her for the second Mastah's Twelve. Ain't that nice? I'm glad I could help them nice young ladies—they so sweet."

Deacon McLendon had long since learned to tune out his too-old sister.

But this time, the bells of heaven were ringing in his head—at the help to come, and the help he had given?

Moment VI: Brother Carry Me Today

Damien's eyes snapped open and blinked hard, catching the first burst of sunlight beaming through his solar panel-sized foyer window.

Grant Park Zoo—is already alive.

School kids scrambling to be first inside the giant yellow mobile classrooms.

Teachers fumbling with clipboards, voices popping off instructions like alarm bells for the neighborhood.

A pulse of Atlanta—sweeter than ice cream, less strict than its traffic.

None of it registered.

His eyes were open. But closed.

Willie B—long gone, but still swinging in his mind.

That damn tire. That glass cage. Seeing life clearer than Damien could see his own right now.

Where the day before had started with her in his arms, today began with the weight of everything he'd lost.

It ended in the worst possible way.

Losing Sheena.

He faced the risk of losing his job if he did what he knew.

Fuck it.

Maybe it was overdramatic, but this shit felt like the worst of times and the best of times.

Because the only thing good about it?

He still had Em.

And he still had his boy Rory.

Then—

"Damn, now y'all gonna make me cut my wrist."

The radio had been a whisper in the background, but now? Now, it was screaming.

Mary and Musiq turned the memory of last night's shattered crystal into a musical haunting—hollering, condescending through his soul.

If you leave... then baby, I'll leave...

But if you believe you'll do best without me—

The words pressed against his chest.

But I have no doubt—

That we can work it out...

Fuck the radio.

Damien cut it off with a sharp flick of the wrist.

Whatever swag he had left, he had to go see Rory.

"Yeah, Day, come over—I hear it in your voice."

Damien didn't even try to play it off.

There were just some things that only bourbon infused with brown sugar could fix.

He thought, *Fuck time.*

Before he knew it, he was in Rory's, his spiritual brother's expensive high Buckhead condo.

"Why you gotta live in a damn condo with a damn valet who

always got his damn hand out—like a rich-ass homeless man? On some real scam shit—'You don't have to tip, sir'—with his damn hand out. Damn."

Damien's words scratched at Rory's ears like an infant crying, raw and relentless.

Rory didn't flinch. He felt it. Every "damn" was a teardrop, and Damien was bawling without shedding a single one.

Rory took it in, let it sit, let his boy get it out.

"Damn, boy… this shit got you hard."

He exhaled slowly.

"But I'm here for you. I'm hard and soft. I'm here."

His voice dropped, solid but open.

"You can cry here. You ain't gotta be hard with me."

A pause.

"I know this shit sucks."

Damien sat in the plush therapist chair—soft, expensive, and uncomfortable.

It felt like the inside of a casket.

If Rory had closed it?

He might never have climbed out.

But in the instant before that thought could settle too deep, Rory's assistant appeared.

She was a middle-aged Hispanic woman, charming in a way that wasn't forced, just natural.

A certified chef, she cooked for Rory, ran his space, and knew his rhythms.

She also knew Damien.

Knew him well enough not to ask if he needed water.

Knew him well enough not to let on that she sometimes listened.

Silently, she handed him a liter bottle of San Pellegrino with a crystal glass—a thin lemon slice floating inside, casual, deliberate.

Before Damien could reach for it, Rory reached over and popped the top.

The fizz broke the silence.

A slight, crisp sound.

The smallest gesture.

But it transformed his casket into a therapist's seat.

And Rory's smile—**easy, knowing, steady—**was the only invitation Damien needed.

A place where he could reach down.

And start the process of hurt.

"Day, Day, Day."

As if he were someone,

A clarion call from the eternal,

A lost protagonist in the night.

"Day, I understand."

"Day, I understand."

And this time?

The repetitiveness of Day, Day, Day—the same way he had thrown out Damn, Damn, Damn—

Had tears behind it.

Each tear was a day in his life without the woman he loved.

Each tear reminded him of the department he had given his soul to.

A department that was immoral.

A department where, more than he cared to admit, more than he would ever let anyone know—

He had done immoral things.

And he had long ago stopped drinking down the lie—

It was okay when he crossed the line because he was doing it for Atlanta.

And when they crossed the line, it was because they hated Atlanta.

That lie didn't hold anymore.

Not here.

Not in this moment, where truth was an ocean, and he drowned in it.

Only Rory's presence kept him from splashing, flailing, and falling under.

And for the first time, he saw it. Saw it.

His shit wasn't right.

And now that Sheena saw him for what he was—

A god who would go there if pushed there.

A god who didn't know how to do manhood any other way.

The irony pressed deep into his bones.

Because the only man who could hold him right now—

The only arms that weren't pushing him away—

It belonged to a man who was sure he only loved men.

And yet—

Rory was the only one who could help him heal the broken little boy inside.

"Okay, I'll hold you as long as you want me to. Shit."

Rory's voice was steady, but a smile was under it—a warmth, a truth.

"I don't usually hold men this long unless they wanna hold me back."

He let the words settle, then sighed dramatically.

"And just like last time you cried over here, you ruined my damn business shirt again."

Rory had a way of being snappy and snapping, crackling, and popping all at once.

The funny that made you catch hold of yourself, even when you weren't ready.

Damien felt the laugh before it came, his head still tucked against Rory's shoulder.

The sound of it cracked through him, small but real. His eyes still had tears, but a smile was finally breaking through.

And then, just like that—he said it.

"Boys to men, nigga."

Rory exhaled slowly, the words sitting between them like something sacred.

"You gonna do exactly what you must do right now for this case."

Damien pulled back, meeting his boy's eyes, reading the weight of what Rory was about to say.

"Because at the end of the day, you got no right to pull Sheena. But I'ma tell you—she ain't got a right to make you anything other than the dude you are."

Rory's voice dropped lower, firm now.

"Yeah, you out here killing niggas."

The words were blunt.

Not approval.

Not judgment.

Just truth.

"And that's right—because if you don't do it, they will do it."

Rory leaned back, rolling his shoulders like he was settling into the weight of what he was about to say.

"I'm a certified lawyer. And I'm telling you—sometimes, Damien, the world needs people who are willing to cross the line to keep the whole goddamn enterprise from going across the line."

And that? That's when Damien saw it.

What he prayed at night that all cisgender, heterosexual, alpha Black men would know.

Rory grabbed his glass of water, sipping at it like a pastor about to deliver a word.

Then—his voice steady, clear, weighty.

"Damien, this is your call back into the game."

"You gonna have to be do or die with this case and with Sheena—"

"You can't hold onto either unless you are willing to be your big dog self and possibly lose both."

"'Cause if you do you and lose—you still win."

"Because you would have gone from a boy to a man—where most men in grown bodies never go. They seem always to fail."

"Besides—" Rory leaned forward, his voice lowering, pressing. "You gotta do this for me."

"The gay community streets are talking."

Damien's body tensed.

"It seems the victims—the ones the Governor don't wanna admit are being slain in association—"

"They're gay men, Damien. And they're being hunted."

"It's serial."

The words landed.

Solid.

Undeniable.

"You were right."

"Damien, you are the only one who believes us."

Rory exhaled, his fingers tightening around the glass.

"This is a turning point for you. For us. For all of us."

"We need you, Day—'cause nighttime is killin' us all."

"Shit, Rory—" Damien ran a hand over his face, shaking his head.

"I came here to have my goddamn tears wiped, and now you tellin' me to keep puttin' my job on the line? Not solve my love life?"

Rory didn't blink.

Didn't flinch.

He leaned forward, smooth as cotton in a hurricane, and plopped the glass on the table simultaneously.

"You damn right to all that selfish, childish shit you just said."

His voice was sharp, cutting, but not unkind.

"And just so you know, I love you, Damien—"

Rory exhaled, shaking his head, his lips twisting between a smirk and a scowl.

"But this here—this thing between me and you? It's quid pro crow."

Damien blinked.

"Quid pro what?"

"Quid pro crow, nigga. I said it right."

Rory squinted, pointing at him like he was calling a bluff that didn't exist.

"I'm squintin' your ass for help."

A pause.

A breath.

"People out here dyin'."

"And you—"

"You ultimately gon' get the girl if you go be a man, boy."

"Be a man, boy."

Damien rolled into the elevator just as the doors eased open into the living room.

He pressed the button down.

Slipped his hands into his pockets.

Not 100%.

But better.

With a note to the world—

From his teacher.

If Damien still had two loves—Sheena, presumed gone, and his career, slipping from his grasp in the city that once belonged to him—then reclaiming them would not come easy. Sheena had survived her night; now, Damien had to confront his day.

The weight of Atlanta bore down on him as he drove, his mind fractured between past and present, between what had been and what still haunted him.

He had just left Rory's, their conversation lingering like smoke, curling around thoughts he couldn't fully grasp. Now, he was headed to Em's—he needed to see his baby play ball, hear her laugh, look prep-school pretty. He had to see himself still alive, even if only in her.

The city blurred past, but he wasn't seeing it. He was seeing Cascade—not the traffic-choked lanes of 285 North but another time, another place. The steam rising from car exhausts threw him into a haze, a flashback—

Moment VII: Flashback Before We Were Brothers

Early 2000s.

"Stay here in the car, man—she ain't gonna know you here. You might learn something from your big brother."

"Aight, cool, but why you flexin'? Leavin' me in the dark with the radio off? Can I put it on?"

"You scared? How will you be a ladies' man when you're scared like it's the '80s? Leave the radio on and leave the car running—I don't want my battery to die. You hear me?"

"But what if—"

"Leave the car running! She hittin' me with the signal."

Here's a refined, immersive version of your scene that keeps your voice intact while improving clarity, pacing, and emotional impact:

Damien jumped out before the car entirely stopped, leaving the door open. Slim cursed, reaching over to pull it shut like a doorman at a rundown restaurant. That Datsun B210 was his whole life—and Slim's only ride past East Point—but Damien had one focus right now.

He was at Sheena's window before they could've even sung the first hook of their song—the one still ringing hot from their talent show performance a few nights ago.

Friday nights in Atlanta were fire. But nothing burned hotter than Sheena at that window.

She saw him and laughed, shaking her head, the glow of her lip gloss catching the streetlight. She was beautiful—chocolate-rich, eyes dancing, the cutest teenage face he could've painted in his wildest dreams.

"My dad's in the other room," she whispered, grinning.

Not that Damien had expected more. He didn't need more. Just a kiss. Just to feel her close, to breathe the same air, to press against the warmth of her body.

He climbed through the window, further than he ever had

before, landing in her bedroom, standing close—too close. Hands on her shoulders. Bodies pressed.

Heat.

The kind that curled at the edges of a moment, making it dangerous. Making it right.

They kissed. Teenage, breathless, laughing into each other. Her lips were softer than he imagined. She hadn't kissed as much as he had, but she could. He could feel her smiling against his mouth, and they both snickered—he was still learning, and she liked knowing it.

Then—

A shadow.

A voice.

Like Darth Vader, loud and booming but full of something worse than menace—hatred.

Steven Colucci.

Standing in the doorway. Steaming. Seething.

"The hell are you doing in my house?" he thundered. "What the hell are you doing with this boy in my house?"

Not even looking at Damien. Only at Sheena.

The blame was hers. The shame was hers. The rage was hers to bear.

Damien moved before his feet registered the floor—vaulting back out the window, hitting the ground hard, sprinting for the car. He was fast. Athletic. But what did that mean when he was running away?

Slim was still inside, none the wiser.

"What happened?"

"Just drive."

The tires screeched, and Damien stared ahead, but he knew what was behind him.

Sheena. Alone. Taking the hit.

Pressed down. Crushed under it. Like a car in the junkyard.

And just like that—he was back.

Back in 285 traffic.

Back in now.

Because 285 wasn't like this back then.

Because everything about back then led to now.

He had run.

But Day had to deal with Day.

Kiss 104.1 played the moment's soundtrack, weaving emotional quicksand through the car speakers.

Atlantic Starr crooned, caressing the night.

"Let's get closer, hey yeah, closer than close…"

And just like that, Damien was back in 2000.

But this time, not at Sheena's window. Not at Cascade. Not on fire with teenage heat.

This time, it was a few days after.

A few days after, she had taken the bruising—the scathing—at the hands of Shim, promoted by her father, Steven Colucci.

A few days after, Damien had screamed out for her in every subtle way he knew how.

But she was gone. She had left.

Howard had taken her away. And Atlanta, for the first time, felt empty.

This night, though—this night was different. This night wasn't about her.

Damien and Slim had driven their Datsun B210 downtown, rolling into the heart of Black Gay Pride—a world they didn't understand, a world they had been taught to mock.

They were young, reckless, stupid.

They had pocket change and ignorance.

And so they did what real men did—or so they thought.

They hurled eggs at Black gay men from the safety of their car, laughing like it was a sport like it meant something.

Because that's what they had been conditioned to do.

But fate—or God, or irony, or whatever ran through the city's veins that night—had a lesson waiting for them.

They pulled into IHOP downtown, their last few dollars pooled together for a meal. IHOP, back when it was more than just a restaurant—back when it was a meeting spot for young folks, for dreamers, for the broke and the bold.

And that's when he met Rory.

Rory Davis.

From Savannah. A Morehouse freshman. A boy from a fine family, brilliant, charming, openly gay.

And the conversation—the chastising, the reckoning, the shift—was so grand, sweet, and unexpected that it stayed with Damien longer than any prayer his mama had ever forced him to say.

He had never considered it before—that someone's sexuality didn't take away their humanity.

That someone's existence wasn't an invitation for ridicule.

That being a man didn't mean stripping manhood from others.

Not every gay man wanted him.

That someone like Rory, so confident in himself, could mentor someone like him—could teach him what it meant to be whole.

That night, their friendship started.

And so did Damien's real growth.

Funny, how the song on the radio—"Let's get closer, hey yeah, closer than close"—didn't just pull him back to Sheena.

Funny how it pulled him back to that night.

To the night, he started to see the world differently.

To the night he met Rory.

In the night, he began to become a man.

A few weeks after the love of his life had left, he had purposefully terrorized Black men.

And not just them—he had terrorized humanity.

Then—a flip of the station.

A break from the monotony of stop-and-go, no-go, now-go traffic barely past 17th Street.

"Damn, Hero be puttin' on a production."

V-103, the soundtrack of middle-aged folks hyping themselves to stay awake in this melee-melee of headlights and horns.

"When you're out in the club and you think I'm a punk—"

Boom.

Rolled up, that's all you heard—

They got my pump—

"I ain't never scared. I ain't never scared."

And just like that—the haze pulled him back.

His pager vibrated against his hip, breaking through the bass.

A number he knew by heart—344.

Beth. Sheena's little sister.

Once upon a time, she had been the tag-along. The one who'd pop in and out of Sheena's room when Damien came by. He'd meet Sheena at the bus stop when Beth was waiting, the three of them walking home together. Beth had a crush on him the way Slim had on Sheena.

Big brother, big sister.

Starting to kiss sometimes.

Holding hands.

Passing notes, writing raps, always an entourage.

And funny enough, the tag-along—Slim and Beth—had also ended up falling for each other.

If only for different reasons.

Beth's 344 flashed again. It wasn't a page you ignored.

Before he knew it, he was at the same damn window.

But this time, it wasn't to dodge Darth Vader.

Maybe it was time to deal with Darth Vader.

"Hey, stay in the car. I gotta check on her. You know how their dad is."

"Oh, nah. Not this time." Slim unbuckled. "You left me in the car before. I missed all the fireworks."

Too late to argue.

Luke Skywalker and his little sidekick were already inside.

Beth. Spoiled as ever. And no Princess Leia.

"I just wanted you to come by 'cause my dad won't let me curl my hair-go to the party a Doug tonight."

Damien exhaled. "I thought something was wrong. You know how he did, Sheena."

Beth rolled her eyes. "That ain't why. You always thinkin' about Sheena."

And then—

A shift.

Beth smirked. "I just wanted you to come by 'cause I need a ride. You jump for her—and your little buddy here."

Beth smirked. "I just wanted you to come by 'cause I need a ride. You jump for her—and your little buddy here."

"I ain't nobody's little brother," Slim shot back, puffing up. "I go to Tri-Cities. I'm from the EPT—Outkast rippin', girl! But you cute, though—just like Day's girl. Yo big sis. So... can I get them digits or nah?"

Beth scoffed. "I am the big sis. And no to the seven. You from the Eee P T? Ask Kandi B, your schoolmate, about No Scrubs."

Before Damien could react, it was already too late.

As if on cue—but this time, slurring, stumbling—

"Goddamn it, you in my house again?"

Steven Colucci.

Darth Vader himself.

Damien could smell the liquor before he saw the rage.

Beth darted past him as her father lunged.

A honk.

Beth—gone.

Fifteen years old, jumping into a car with the very girls she had paged right before paging him.

Damien had no time to react before Colucci swung. A rush. A tussle.

Then—a spark.

A candle was knocked over.

Flames licking the carpet.

Slim grabbed Damien's arm. "We gotta go."

Smoke followed them out the door.

But the neighbor—

She had seen a young Black man running.

And that was all it took.

And that's how Slim was sacrificed.

Not like Trayvon. Not like Mike Brown.

No, Slim was still breathing.

But he was gone all the same.

Steven Colucci died in that fire.

Slim took the charge.

Pled guilty to attempted robbery.

Beth was no good because she wasn't there.

The house was gone.

She went to live with their aunt—until the house was repaired.

Sheena came for the funeral. Never asked who was there—
never cared.

She was just glad she wasn't.

Slim did four years.

Three in juvie. One in mid-level adult detention.

That's where he became Saint Hustler Slim.

Producer. Rapper. Legend.

And Damien—

He owed him.

Even if Slim never lets him forget the debt.

Even if Slim still called him Big Brother.

Damien had trampled on his little brother's innocence—

And set Steven Colucci's world on fire.

A fateful night.

An accident.

But still—

Day had to deal with Day.

But Day couldn't deal with Day unless Day first and last—most
importantly—had to deal with Night.

Sheena had broken up with him at Pascal's almost as quickly as they had found their ultimate union.

She saw him as indecisive.

You killed on my behalf... but you couldn't come get me.

The weight of her—of his love for her, his respect for her stature, her love for their people, her sheer inner and outer beauty—crushed him.

Because deep down, he knew the truth.

If it happens again?

If he was put back in that same situation?

He knew just like the car next to him now, swerving onto the hazard ramp, breaking the law just to get where it needed to go.

He'd do the same damn thing.

And in the last flash of this elaborate traffic, closing in on his final destination, he saw him—

The street hustler cat who owed him a favor.

A favor that had been sitting collecting dust.

"Let me say this to you, Raglan. You owe me, dude. I saved your life, and more importantly—I'm keeping you out of jail."

"Aight, what you want?"

"I got somebody I need you to take care of. His name's Shim. Old dude. And he hurt mine."

"Whoa, whoa, whoa—hold up, Snoop Doggy Dogg. You mean to tell me, you wanna cash in your street favor now? With me?"

Raglan grinned. "What you want, dog? You tryna get me to sling poison again? You know I left that for you. It's filed off. That ain't me no more."

Damien couldn't believe he was this guy.

That he had been this guy.

And in an instant, he was back there again.

Back to the moment that sat like an embargoed secret inside his chest.

Back to when Raglan followed Shim home.

To Southeast Atlanta.

To some corner neighborhood in the Bluff, one of those spaces that was part apartment, part house, all no-way-out.

To when he crept up behind Shim, put the barrel to his temple—

And pulled the trigger.

A clean execution.

They pinned it on gambling debt, drug deal gone wrong. Whatever they needed to believe.

Because Shim was a demon of a man. The worst among us.

Damien had done what he felt he needed to do.

But now?

Now, he had to face himself.

She was evident in his thoughts now, her words stamped in his inner ear—*indecisive, indecisive, indecisive*—the echo tightening in his chest, hardening in his gut.

But the truth was, when Day met Night, he acted decisively.

And now, he had to ask himself:

Am I still that guy? Do I know how to be different?

Was he just a man who hadn't been tested—again?

Damien was dealing with Sheena's Day in his dark places.

As Damien passed through the Ivy League-like gates of The Lovett School just off West Paces Ferry Road and Northside Drive, he eased his car down the hill, the manicured drive offering crystal-clear evidence of the refinement his well-earned tuition dollars had secured for Em.

He needed to see her ball.

He needed this place—her place.

He needed the school's atmosphere—warm and enveloping, like the motto it served: *Omnium Dei Gloriam*—To the Greater Glory of God.

Tonight, the campus wrapped around him like God's glory itself.

Because with everything he had been through—to face Damien's future, to confront the fate of his embattled two loves, uncertain of what was to come—

He would need a now version of the glory of God.

Moment VIII: From My Brother to My Baby Girl

Right after the buzzer went off, the whole gym exploded. Everyone jumped around, pouncing on Em in celebration. She crawled through the crowd, eyes scanning, and jumped straight into Damien's arms.

At that moment, his daughter's love comforted him about his two loves.

He always marveled at her strength—a girly girl on the surface but sharp as a blade underneath. Smooth on the court, stern as a daughter.

Even at 16 years old, she had two things working for her: The upper-crust refinement that came from Tamika's world. And her daddy's street hustle- she used it to run the court like a boss.

She brought him joy- he could hold on to good that, more often than not, seemed to evade him no matter how hard he tried.

Later, in the car, they laughed, talking about how Em had game and Damien had none.

"Dad, you got game. Mama wasn't good enough, and Sheena ain't ready."

"...Em, don't start."

"No, I'm serious. Mama ain't never gonna be good enough, and Sheena better get ready."

"...Girl, watch your mouth."

"In fact, I told that IG hoe she don't need to be playing with me!"

Damien cut his eyes toward her.

"...Em."

"What?"

"Stop calling her that."

Moment IX: Are Gangs Brotherhoods?

The club was loud enough outside, but back here, it was quiet. Too quiet.

Cain sat across from Anthony Dumas, aka Lil G, who ran the underbelly of Atlanta with a code—a street pastor in his own right.

Lil G leaned back, swirling his glass.

"Preacher man got a request? Ain't that something."

Cain smiled. Relaxed. Calculated.

"I do. Two things."

Lil G sipped slowly. Let him talk.

"First, I want access to one of yours. The boy. YD."

"That so?" Lil G studied him. Sizing him up.

"It is."

Cain let the pause sit. Power was in patience.

"And the second thing?"

"A problem. A cop who might be watching. Needs to disappear."

Lil G exhaled a laugh.

"You come to me for that?"

"I come to the best."

A smirk. That preacher knew how to talk.

"And what's that worth to you?"

Cain didn't hesitate.

"Twelve. Six for the boy. Six for the cop."

Lil G set his glass down.

"Man, you don't tell me prices. I tell you prices."

Cain nodded, accepting the correction but not the insult.

"Of course."

Silence.

Lil G let it stretch, watching Cain.

"But you come with the right number."

A slow grin crept across Cain's face.

"I know."

Lil G chuckled, nodding.

"Alright, Preacher Man. We got a deal."

Cain rose. Straightened his cuffs. Walked out knowing the man had no idea he'd just signed his own loss.

Moment X: Cain kills A Young Brother

Both sides had played well.

As Damien ended his night with Em's kiss on the cheek, walking her to the door of the semi-mansion her mother paid for easily—even without his child support—he had to admit: he was glad his daughter was well-kept.

Though he and Tina didn't get along, they agreed: Em deserved the best. And she was a good kid. She had played well. Maybe even played him well.

And just as she walked into the house...

On the other side of town, not as elite, on the outskirts of Old National, just outside of Atlanta in Fulton County, at the Red Roof Inn...

YD was fading.

Woozy. Drowning in lean. Top amphetamines still buzzing through his system. He was slipping in and out, but he figured it was just the drugs.

Just another party.

He most certainly hadn't played well.

He had been played.

In the haze of his vision, a figure hovered over him 30 minutes after his gang members walked out. A voice cut through the fog—calm, deliberate.

"If you thought I was gonna let it go like that..."

YD blinked.

"You made me do it."

The voice was soft. Almost regretful.

"You went out there and told. You told. And I didn't even hurt you that night."

A pause.

"But you didn't know the streets would tell me, my son. How dare you tell people what I would never tell about you?"

YD's sluggish mind tried to process the words. But the weight in the man's hands was heavier than his thoughts.

Before he could speak—before he could beg or fight—the first blow landed.

A fist. Then another.

His vision blurred, then blackened. He couldn't breathe, couldn't see, couldn't scream. The pressure on his throat was cold and absolute. Naked and humiliated.

The darkness wasn't merely the absence of light but a suffocating blend of pain, shame, and enforced silence. Cain ensured it enveloped YD completely.

A faint, metallic click echoed through the thin walls of the seedy motel as a neighboring door's deadbolt slid into place. The sound reverberated, a stark reminder of the lurking dangers that prowled beyond the flimsy barriers.

Methodically, Cain wiped the blood from his gloved hands, his movements deliberate and unhurried. He retrieved a small card from his pocket, its edges crisp and unblemished, and with meticulous care, inserted it between YD's parted lips.

This was his message:

Keep your mouth shut about mine.

Because I may love men.

But men will have to fear me if they ever try to tell me that I love men.

Standing over the lifeless body, Cain whispered, "Quos deus vult perdere, prius dementat." The Latin phrase lingered in the stale air, its ominous weight pressing into the shadows.

Outside, the distant wail of sirens approached, their crescendos slicing through the night. Cain adjusted his coat, casting one last glance at YD's motionless form, then slipped out into obscurity, leaving behind a scene that would haunt anyone who dared to uncover its truth.

YD rested in peace; Cain sought no rest, and for some reason, not knowing what was next, Damien couldn't rest.

CHAPTER 6

THE TRUTH BLEEDS TOO

Moment I: The Black Boy's Body Bleeds

YD fought for his life and lost.
His bloody body screamed, "I ain't no snitch."

His story was told through the lip-glossed mouth of a brown bombshell—an ex-reality TV host turned journalist, style over substance be damned.

"Hey, y'all, I think we got something going on in the A—yep-yep—in the A-T-L. We're gonna go live—and if you miss us here, get me on the Tok! Always remember, get in where you fit in—@ me."

The pulsating voice of the bombshell reporter clashed with the bass booming from passing cars, the irregular rhythm sitting heavy in Damien's chest as he woke the morning after his night away from Sheena.

His thoughts drifted between Kent and YD
Gang life ain't no joke here in the ATL. We might need to combine homicide and this gang-gang business. This gang stuff got nine lives.

The streets were eating their kids up.

Damn Drill Rap. Gang-coded language. These stupid asses admitting to the crimes they did—wow. Really.

A quiet devastation rolled in like a Savannah, Georgia tide—unspoken, unpredictable, but there.

He knew YD wasn't a snitch.

Byron Donaldson had a warrant.

And now? Damien was next.
Fighting for his own.
Because if YD was proof of anything—life is a bitch.

Then, with crystal clarity, the news blared:

"A young gang member, also being claimed as a member of the gay community, was found dead early this morning at a cheap motel on Atlanta's Old National Highway. Representatives from Atlanta's Black gay community and the Make Atlanta Great Again (MAGA) movement have converged on the State Capitol in a combative protest. The Black gay community asserts this is proof of serial murders against their members, while MAGA claims it is a ploy to halt economic progress by the 'woke' gay mob."

The TV split into two screaming sides:
One side protesting—"You will NOT be killing Black bodies!"

The other side is raging in defense. "Man, not again—there's no serial killer! Stop killing Black gay bodies!"

The tension was thick.

Local shopkeepers slammed their doors shut.

Residents screamed—

"Turn up! Turn up! Time to turn up!"

A teen with an iPhone 11 pointed at the camera, grinning.

"Live, local, late-breaking, bitch! They got another one!"

The whole ATL crime scene exploded.

Another young gay man. Found.
This time, just outside the Atlanta city lines—in South Fulton County.

Damien shook his head, a decisive "No" escaping his lips. He yanked his notes from his bag, feeling the oppressive weight of the bullies' barricade pressing against him, his heart pounding.

At that moment, he tore up his theory sheets—emphatically, undeniably.

No more overthinking. Just action.

He scribbled a quick plan, barely thinking—just moving.

The sirens wailed outside, but he had no intention of stopping.

His phone vibrated again. Persistent. Relentless.

A buzz that echoed like a warning bell, demanding his attention.

Drawing a deep breath, Damien steeled himself, ready to confront whatever lay ahead.

Then—his phone pulsed. Urgent.

Damien hadn't checked his texts all night, missing every message—including Sheena's.

Now, the screen demanded his attention.

"10-31, damn, what's up?
Come to Old Nat.
Red Roof.
No lights.
Off the record.
Your boy—Full Blue.
Urgent."

Grabbing his suit jacket, he knocked the stand over with a clang-thud.

Reciting the text as he slid into the car, he muttered, "Damn, why is Carl—Fulton Blue—hitting me? What's at Old Nat worth dragging me out for right now? Urgent and off-the-record?

Shit done, hit the fan."

One hand gripped the wheel, foot hard on the gas, eyes flicking nervously at the phone—hoping for another heads-up before he stepped into hot shit.

Moment II: The Black Boy after Blood Letting

Damien stepped outside.

The white noise supplied by the 18-wheelers rolling through I-285 East pushed him into clarity—pacing back and forth, territorializing the hotel parking lot.

The cool air hit his face, sharp and sobering. But it didn't cut through the weight on his chest.

The smell of blood was still on him.

It wasn't his, but it might as well have been.

He pulled out his phone. Checked the texts. Checked the calls.

Nothing.

Someone let YD walk free.

And whoever cut him loose—that was the key to everything.

He dialed.

Ring.

Ring.

Click.

"Kent."

Damien's voice was sharp.

"Dog, who cut YD loose?"

A pause.

Kent sighed. He already knew why Damien was calling.

"Man, it's crazy, bro."

"Talk."

Kent hesitated, then let out a breath.

"I was asked to do Homie Thugs a favor and give them back their boy."

Silence.

The words settled like concrete dust in a collapsed building.

"You what?"

"Listen, man—it wasn't me. The order came from somebody I don't even normally deal with."

Damien's jaw tightened.

He already felt where this was going.

"Who?"

Another pause. Longer this time. Like Kent was deciding whether the truth was worth it.

Then:

"Morgan Cantor."

Silence.

Damien clenched his teeth—the name shot through his skull like an alarm bell.

"Morgan Cantor? Morgan fucking Cantor?"

Kent kept talking.

But Damien wasn't listening anymore.

He slowed his breath—deliberate now. Strategizing.

Not because he wasn't angry.

But because he was. Too angry.

Morgan Cantor. Clarence Thomas in a badge. Tim Scott with a gun.

Damien already knew—this just became a different kind of war.

Kent's voice broke through.

"Man, I don't think he knew YD was gonna get killed. But somebody with more pull? That's another story. The Blue Wall says political power did the pull and shattered the peace—"

Damien's pulse pounded.

Morgan let that kid out.

To who?

How did YD get to Old Nat?

Kent sighed. "HTs. Gang shit. And from there? That's gonna be your job—catch me if you can."

Damien closed his eyes.

It was all coming together now.

Morgan. HT. A powerful, manipulative puppeteer.

This wasn't just street politics. Somebody up top was pulling the strings—but why?

Why YD?

Shit. YD knew something...

And now?

Damien was in this for real.

The investigation had just flipped.

And he knew exactly who he had to see next.

Connor.

Because if he couldn't get to the truth through the front door?

He'd go through the back.

Moment III: Young Brother's Blood Cries Out

When Damien entered the coroner's office, the lingering scent of Chick-fil-A fries hit him first—a stark contrast to the sharp bite of formaldehyde, which acted like a cocktail chaser. He exhaled, adjusting to the mix of fast food and death, then walked deeper into the room where YD's body waited.

Standing there, waiting for him, was Atlanta's favorite pot-belly—5'8" Connor. A good old boy to the bone, Connor wasn't about to let Atlanta's changes run him off. He was good as long as the city still had chicken wings, lemon pepper seasoning, Chick-fil-A, bourbon, cigars, and hip-hop. That was his kind of living—cheap, available, and damn good—especially on a city coroner's salary.

Most people assumed Connor was MAGA through and through. But what they didn't know? This Georgia boy had married the love of his life—a Black woman. Every now and then, he'd joke with her, "Shoe polish sure does make me feel good."

Connor's motto was simple:
Love everybody. Trust nobody. And when a body lands on my table—tell the truth, no matter who gets caught.

Damien loved him for that.
And Connor loved Damien right back.

Their bond wasn't formal—it was built on the way Damien got a kick out of Connor's corny-ass jokes and how Connor, in turn, constantly tried to one-up him.

Connor smirked before Damien could even speak.

"Well, detective, I wondered when you was gonna come by

and see me. You been working this case, and I got wind I ain't even supposed to tell you what I'm about to tell you."

Then, with a knowing grin, he added, "By the way, you need to marry that fancy girl of yours you invited down here for 'wooork.' She's good for you. 'Cause the way you missed this one? Man… how long you gon' be gone 'til you catch up with me?"

Damien grinned, but the jab barely registered. He was already thinking about how much he had missed Sheena, even if returning her text seemed like a luxury he hadn't yet grown to deserve. He clapped Connor on the back.

"Alright, old boy, tell me the truth."

Connor led him down the corridor to a private wing—where they kept the bodies that were either unidentified or under criminal investigation. He pulled back the sheet covering YD.

Dry blood. Tattoos. A life gone too soon.

Connor folded his arms.
"Detective, this is what I been trying to teach you," Connor said. "You missed things. You don't have to look too hard—I got something for you."

He pointed from YD's neck down to his middle torso.

"Whoever's killing these boys? He's in your community. And yeah, it's all connected."

Connor folded his arms.
"I done took the details, and ain't nobody gonna be able to come against you. I don't care who they is, how much golf they

play with the governor. By the way, I played with the lieutenant governor once. They ain't no good."

He let the words sit, shaking his head like the thought disgusted him.

"Ain't no good," he repeated like he was issuing a personal indictment.

Then he pointed at YD's head.

"See this whack here? He got stuck right up front. But then... then he did other things to him. Almost ritualistic. And he's a smart one."

Ritualistic as in religion. Smart, as in cunning?

Damien took in a deep breath and exhaled trapping the implications of Connor's words.

Damien noticed Connor's voice change—the country twang that rang through the room was now sterile. Clinical. Perspective-rattling. Calculated.

"Most killers get messy. This one? He's careful. And I'm telling you, this old boy doesn't know God."

Look at this body. Mutilated like this?
Nah, this one—he's got access. Influence.
Enough where folks don't run from him right away.
'Cause like I said..."

He let the sentence trail off, but Damien finished it for him.

"There was no struggle."

Connor nodded.

"I got the chem back from tox, but I've dug through enough of these to know he was high as a St. Patrick's Day kite. These boys doin' a lot of 'Lean,' they call it."

Damien eerily mirrored the murkiness.
"Damn. They drugged my son."

Connor nodded.
"As a matter of fact—look closer at the buccal cavity. Postmortem rigidity indicates that something was here post-asphyxia—and it ain't here now. FYI."

Damien nodded—his authority put a period behind his ownership of the moment.

"Well, you look kinda sad, detective. What's up? You told me last time you was gonna bring me some of that tequila you been drinking. When you bringing it by?"

"We'll have that drink, Connor," Damien said.
"But first, I need to ask you something.
Are you willing to go on the record?"

Connor squared his shoulders.

"I ain't scared of them folks you scared of. They might shake you, but they ain't ever gonna shake me."

He smirked.
"Hell, I been here damn near since before Atlanta got burned.
My great-granddaddy probably stood right there when Grant left.

And me? I'll still be right here when this whole mess is over."

His history lesson wasn't accurate.

But Damien got the point.

Connor wasn't scared.
And he wasn't going to be moved.

Governor, mayor, whoever—the truth was the truth.

Damien drove away with the weight of Connor's words settling in his chest.

It was strange—this place was a dead museum, filled with horrors that most people wouldn't dare to face.

And yet, he always left feeling better.

Because the world was a better place with Connor in it.

Scene 4: Damien vs. Morgan – The Final Call

Damien sat in his car, Zaxby's wrapper crumpled on the dash, his lemonade sweating in the cupholder.

The smell of fried chicken still clung to the air, but his appetite was gone.

His phone buzzed. Morgan Cantor.

Damien exhaled slow. He already knew.

Still, he let it ring. Let it breathe. Let Morgan sit in his own impatience.

Then, just before it went to voicemail—he picked up.

"Yeah?"

Morgan's voice came clipped, professional. A snake in a suit.

"Detective DeBerg. This is Morgan Cantor—Senior APD Liaison, Independent Investigator, Staff Reviewer—"

Damien cut him off. "Yeah, yeah. All-but-dissertation. I know who the fuck you are, Morgan. What do you want?"

Silence. A brief flicker of ego bruised. Then—Morgan's voice, sharp as a knife.

"I thought I told you to get off this case."

Damien leaned his head back against the headrest, rolling his jaw. "You did."

"And yet here we are."

Damien didn't answer. He stared at his reflection in the rear-view mirror. He barely recognized the man looking back at him.

"You're done, detective." Morgan's voice was firm now. "Your badge. Your gun. HR has your papers. As of now, you're no longer an officer of the Atlanta Police Department."

Damien flexed his fingers on the wheel. He should've felt something. Rage. Betrayal. Something.

But all he felt was hollow.

"You lucky I don't put your Black ass in jail." Morgan's voice was venom now. "This goddamn affirmative action shit never works. Just hiring people 'cause they Black. We need to be hiring the best officers—the ones that can listen."

There it was. The mask fully off.

Damien exhaled a slow, measured breath. He'd heard men like this before. Different suits, different names, same venom.

Bull Connor. Lester Maddox. One of those old-school segregationist Georgia governors.

Damien didn't say a word-not out loud.

This ain't gonna stop me.

This shit ain't right.

He stared out the windshield like it was a mirror.

You ain't shit, Morgan.

The words thundered in his mind, louder than anything Morgan could've said.

You a houseboy in a custom suit. A badge ain't a backbone. And power without purpose? Ain't nothing but betrayal.

Damien gritted his teeth, jaw tight.

What goes around comes around.

I see you. And I'ma get your ass in check.

He didn't give Morgan the satisfaction.

He just ended the call.

And kept driving.

Eyes steady.

Heart loaded.

Vengeance righteous.

Because now, he had nothing left to lose—

And everything left to prove.

CHAPTER 7

DAY BY DAY

Moment I: Beat's Bed and Day's Pull.

Since Sheena had been home, the ATL in this room pulled the biggest smile from her unmade morning face.

The bed at Steve Colucci's? Too small—eck.

The bed at the Ritz? High-end luxury—yet too damn big when you're alone.

But this bed—Beth's? Beat's? Bethney's? This Buckhead condo? Damn. Just right.

Sheena slipped out from under the covers just as her iPhone popped off—

"Dat chick—Jazmine Sullivan. First thang—dang, V-103. Let's do…"

"I'ma move to Atlanta… I'ma find me a rapper…" Beth's voice rang through the walls- same song to wake her.

Sheena blurted, "Damn, girl, I slept good. I'll be out in a minute." The music swirled through the condo, lyrics stretching in the air.

"God is my witness, I just wanna live on the other side...
I've got dreams"- Sheena to Day as Beth sang backup.

Sheena caught all of Jazmine Sullivan's sexiness but none of the neediness in the song.

She only sang the parts that felt real to her—like Beat in the booth, but with a sparkling aspiration:

"I just wanna be taken care of... I deserve that life... Damien's housewife."

Beth, still in her room—or rather, her room—heard Sheena celebrating the morning, popping bars that leaned more R&B than hip-hop:

"On the other side... on the other side..."

Then, laughter.

Sisterhood stretching back to their Cascade days, where time had rubbered out the edges of their childhood but never erased the foundation.

Sheena and Beth, laughing like girls again.

Jazmine Sullivan— their spiritual producer—giggled through the speakers, blessing their reunion with a soundtrack of survival.

But sisterhood, real sisterhood, was more than just nostalgia. It was becoming—threaded through generations, stitched into whispers between grandmothers and aunties, sealed over sweet potato pies and survival tactics.

"Nah, I don't use nutmeg—never did."

"Girl, yours has always been good—brotha even said so."

"I'll buy it for you—ain't no need to beg them—I got you."

"Soror, it's okay to leave—his cheating ass? He ain't your destiny."

"She'll be calling you soon enough—begging you to take his sorry, pretty-boy ass back—right after he sleeps with his paralegal... again."

Yet, this sisterhood—the one between Beth and Sheena—had been deliberately fractured.

A father who hated himself for hating himself had split them like only a Georgia plantation could do to Coletta's beautiful, differently hued Black girl children.

A wound left to fester. A bond once stretched thin.

But tonight, in this laughter?

It was healing.

"Why Are You Here?"

Beth's voice broke through the morning ease.

"Can I ask you something, Sheena? Why you here?"

Sheena smirked.

"Cause you invited me to stay at your second condo in the same city?"

"No, big sister. Why are you here?"

Beth's voice sharpened, her tone cutting through the air with something deeper.

"You just said 'Damien's housewife.' And I know Jazmine personally. I opened for her ATL show a while back, and she say Day's name nowhere in that song.

"So, no, trick. Why are you here?"

Silence.

Sheena took a deep breath—lemon-infused mist opened her nostrils.

She exhaled, rolling her shoulders.

"That's the question of the day. That's the question about Day. And I'm thinking through it in real-time.

"I need his help with this situation. And he needs me with his. Why did you ask, though?"

Beth slid onto the plush, just-right bed next to Sheena.

Her voice softened, cooing—but all Sheena heard was:

"You love him. Everything else is bullshit, and you know that."

Then Beth hopped up like a client leaving therapy five minutes early, stretching as she walked toward the grand room and into her master bedroom. On the way out, she grabbed Sheena's arm—just a light touch, a reminder.

"If you want this pajama party to continue, girl, I got us some breakfast ordered. It'll be here in a minute."

Then.

Beth turned, locking eyes with her sister.

"Sheena, you fight for everything else."

"Fight for yourself. For Day. Today."

Sheena raised her head, her half-pinned-up hair tickling her face, matching the tickle in her stomach at the mere thought of Beth's proposal.

And just like that, Sheena was alone in the room with the aroma of morning bath oil, pushing her thinking for the day about Day rapidly downhill.

Moment II: Shena Reflects on Day Break

Thinking about Damien—immersed in him—wrestling with the question: what do Day and Sheena even mean?

She had texted.

No word.

She had no idea that Day was fighting for his career, for his case, and yet, longing for her touch—aching for it—but standing in the frost of confusion.

Identity theft.

It's not the kind where someone steals your bank account.

The kind that shifts the very ground you stand on.

Not indecisiveness—not that ugly thing she had accused him of.

No.

This was Blackness in a world that rained shame on men like him.

YD was a symptom.

The problem? Damien cared.

But he had only ever learned one way to fight—to attack the bad and pray that made him sound.

And she—she had called him out on it.

"Damien, I can't have an indecisive man. You didn't come for me."

Her words now haunted her in a cold, unsettling way that hadn't emerged from her memories of him at or since Mays High School, sharing Popeye's Chicken on a $4.75 budget. This wasn't mere second thoughts; it was a deep dive into the conflicting values of a woman both intelligent and in love. The sting of the moment had faded, yet it erected a wall between them.Was she wrong?

Was Beth right? Was Tina?

Damien, now on Old National, tracking his case.

Sheena, here at Beth's.

Tracking them.

Tracking Day.

"Damien, I can't have a man in it just for himself."

Sheena wrapped her robe around herself, a soft, sophisticated gesture that announced to herself, "I'm always in control—of myself, situations, and especially my thinking." She knew the foundation of overconfidence was a facade over the fertile ground of swelling emotions.

Stay entrenched, safe in self? Or fight for Day—for us—for me?

Moment III: Compared to Day

She grabbed the remote and flipped on the TV—too big for this room or any room in a condo.

BREAKING NEWS.

A young gang member, also being claimed as a member of the gay community, was found dead early this morning at a cheap motel on Atlanta's Old National Highway.

Representatives from Atlanta's Black gay community and the Make Atlanta Great Again (MAGA) movement have converged on the State Capitol in combative protest.

The Black gay community asserts this is proof of serial murders against their members, while MAGA claims it is a ploy to halt economic progress by the 'woke' gay mob."

The screen split into two screaming sides.

One side: "You will NOT be killing Black bodies!"

The other: "Man, not again—there's no serial killer! Stop killing Black gay bodies!"

Sheena was drawn in—then, just as quickly, she pulled herself out.

"Damien still didn't text or call. I'm sure there's a lot going on. Has Atlanta changed that much?"

She paused, murmuring to herself.

"I know this church thing is different—way different. And that pastor? He's not just different… he's interesting."

Then, like Tamron Hall introducing the next guest, the TV forced her back into the story.

"Wait—Damien, is that Bishop Cain with the MAGA protesters?"

Her voice came out loud this time, bouncing off the high ceilings of the well-decorated condo.

"Oh my God, this guy is everywhere but where he should be, doing what he should be doing."

She crossed her arms—judge and jury—her forced laugh dripping with righteous indignation.

"I'm gonna get your ass for what you did to God's church and those humble people. I don't care if it was twelve dollars, twelve hundred, or twelve thousand—right is right, and wrong is wrong. Damn, the greed is palpable."

Then—

The phone rang from the other side of the big bed.

In her head, she had already reached for it.

It must be Damien. It has to be—with all this going on.

But then—

"Hey, Sheena."

A voice too smooth, too polished, too professional.

Her stomach dropped.

White men are too professional, even when they're personal.

His voice pierced the helium high of Black girl magic and dragged her down—out of the clouds, back into a world of sterilization and kindness.

The puppy-dog kind that kills big-dog dreams.

She stilled, trying to reorient.

Why now? What does he want? Is everything okay in Chicago? He does know we're done, right? I'm a grown woman. I'm home.

What?

"Sheena? You...?"

"Yeah, hey back, Scott. I'm here. How are you doing? What's up?"

Her own voice felt off-rhythm, choppy, like she wasn't even comfortable with herself in this moment.

Sheena never treated people with less care than her natural love allowed.

And Scott... Scott sighed—long, slow.

She knew that sigh.

Like the one he gave when he lost a chess match.

The lack of eye contact was evident even over the phone.

And the truth? He still loved her.

Sheena sighed. Moments ago, her robe had felt sensual, a garment of intimacy. With Scott Alfred Hogarth IV's unexpected call, it seemed to transform into a judge's robe, heavy with authority. The remote in her hand morphed into a gavel, symbolizing the verdict she would render on their past relationship.

Her ex-boyfriend. Scott's chivalry lapped and slobbered like a Labrador retriever.

Her feelings toward him were like those reserved for the student who couldn't quite keep up on the dance floor—who struggled at the skating rink—who missed the Color Purple's nuances. And now, it was clear for her—in the bedroom, too.

"No, Scott. I'm okay."

She couldn't help but see the contrast now.

White privilege had allowed Scott to move freely, to make life-and-death decisions for others, because his own life had never truly been in danger.

For Damien?

Every day above ground was a fight.

"I'm actually having a pleasant visit."

She paused.

A memory flashed—her kissing Day a few nights before.

Her insides tingled.

"Yeah, a nice time. A few things to work through. I have an interesting group I'll probably help solve a problem with its leadership. Yeah, it's well here in the ATL."

The ATL.

Scott had always called it "Atlanta."

But proximity meant knowing better.

The same man who could pull her hair—"Pull my hair, Day"—Was the same one who knew it was the ATL. The A.

Never just "Atlanta."

Scott said more, but she barely heard him.

Until—

"Sheena, before I go—"

A pause.

"Now that I know you're fine, I didn't call for us. I know you've moved on—grown, as you said. Beyond us."

Sheena swallowed.

"I called to tell you that I want the best for you. I think that gentleman—Damien, Day, as you presented him—is the one for you. You are your own thinking person. But I'm committed to your truth. And I know you."

A longer pause.

"You're in Atlanta on pretense. So stay there in truth—love who you love. Don't put up barriers to real love. Call me when you get back to Chicago. I'm so glad you're well. Bye-bye, dear lady."

The line went dead.

Sheena shook her head slowly, then sighed.

I wish you well, Scott. I'll always be fond of you.

She just sat there.

Painted one index nail a different color.

Blew him away—gently.

She knew she could return-could keep walking that tightrope between code-switching and genuine emotional connection.

But why should she have to?

Scott was decisive.

But he downed in white bread without the ends- the kind that is only good for too-sweet bread pudding.

And yet, his words had landed.

Shocker. Love who you love.

Someone else is telling her to fight for Day.

Today.

This Day

Her Day.

Moment IV: Tamika for Day?

Still processing Scott's unexpected call, Sheena emerged from the spacious bedroom into the expansive grand room of Beth's Buckhead condo.

The oversized television murmured in the background, its

sound a mere whisper against the panoramic view that drew her to the couch.

Downtown Atlanta sprawled before her through the floor-to-ceiling windows—a dynamic tapestry of ambition and energy.

The city's pulse was palpable: skyscrapers reaching skyward, streets teeming with life, and the distant hum of progress resonating. Amidst this urban symphony, patches of dogwood trees punctuated the landscape, their blossoms like nature's confetti celebrating the city's relentless drive.

Settling onto the plush couch, Sheena allowed herself a moment of reflection, absorbing the juxtaposition of her crossroads against the backdrop of a city grappling with rising tension. Deacon McClendon's embrace and hopeful vision for the church echoed in her mind, offering an emotional pat on the back and a gentle reminder of the escalating crime she felt compelled to address.

Yet, as she was drawn into the freshness of the still-emerging day, the serene beauty of the dogwoods stood in contrast to the steel and glass edifices, symbolizing growth and resilience. Unfortunately, the city's challenges were evident, even reaching Scott in Chicago.

Scott still lingered in her thoughts.

Damien.

Church.

Sheena had two loves.

What next?

Sheena stared at the cracked door, watching Beth enter the grand room.

Her presence was comforting and confronting, pressing against the bumper cars of Sheena's swirling thoughts.

"Sis, I know you eat eggs. I got the chef in there whipping it up."

Beth's voice was light, full of that easy, self-assured energy she always carried.

Sheena smirked. "You brought in a chef for a day? You extra."

Beth flipped her curls. "I got to treat myself right. And I got to get Damien's little boo thing Georgia fine."

Sheena raised a brow. "Beth."

Beth shot her a look. Sheena matched it.

"Why everything with you gotta stay straight street with all this? You know you really from Cascade."

The sisters nodded, then laughed in unison.

The condo air was set at 68 degrees—just right.

In the background, the chef worked—bang, slips, snips, slap—the rhythm of a professional at work.

Sheena listened. "She got an assistant."

A voice called out. "Hand me that, please."

Another. "Check the notes, please."

The aroma of crab meat and chives atop a shrimp omelet and the scent of freshly squeezed cucumber juice and warm, freshly baked muffins piqued Sheena's curiosity. Who could be in the kitchen? Names like Chanel Jordan, Bella Jones, Michelle Roberts, Erika Council, or Angella Hall came to mind—a potential starting lineup of culinary talent, with many others who could have been putting the final touches on the bouquet of fruit, especially the pink grapefruit that Sheena favored.

Look at God.

Stephen Colucci's daughters.

Making it big.

Sheena's phone rang.

Was it?

No.

The screen lit up like an Atlanta movie premiere.

Tamika DeBerg.

Sheena's brow creased. "Tamika DeBerg?"

Beth sat up instantly. "Who?"

"Tamika DeBerg."

Beth's smirk was instant. "The DeBerg? The Tamika DeBerg? Damien's ex-wife?"

Sheena exhaled. "Why is she calling me?"

Beth leaned in, wide-eyed with curiosity. "Answer it. I know that trick. I knew that trick in high school. She went to Doug."

Sheena gave her a sideways look—the kind only a Mays girl could give a sister when a Frederick Douglass girl was calling, seemingly ready to call them out.

Beth waved her off, her voice shifting into full-on Atlanta gossip mode.

"Girl, I don't even think about her. But answer it. I know Tamika. She always acts like she is some heavy hitter."

Sheena tilted her head. "What's her deal now?"

Beth scoffed. "That woman is ALL front. She out here giving away her coochie on Snapchat for six tokens a minute, then got the nerve to be talking about she's a real estate mogul."

Sheena choked on laughter but forcefully corrected her. "Seriously?"

Beth shrugged. "I heard she do move some properties, but really?"

Sheena pressed her lips together.

Beth leaned back, arms crossed. "She even tried out for The Real Housewives of Atlanta. But even their raunchy entertainment wouldn't stoop that low."

In moments, turn as if on stage, Beth reverted to her defense mechanism. Now determined no one was ever gonna stunt on her big sister again, she went into complete Beat challenging Lotto mode, now playing Future's Lil Demon-

You movin' wrong, we clutchin' (that's gang). "

We slime, we're sharin' sluts (that's slut)- Lil' demon in the cut...

Then.

"Yeah, hey, um, Sheena—" Tamika's voice came through steady, clear. "It is finally a pleasure to meet you."

Sheena straightened in her seat. "And you as well."

"Meet you, talk to you," Tamika corrected herself. "Look, I'm a straight shooter. Always have been."

Sheena smirked. "Okay, I hear that."

Tamika exhaled. "And listen, I don't pry into Damien's business. He and I are through and through. But there are a couple of things I need to say."

Sheena's stomach tightened. Here we go.

"One—he is an excellent father. Always has been."

"Two—he was an excellent husband. It just wasn't for me."

"Three—he loves you."

Sheena's breath hitched.

Tamika continued firm but kind.

"Girl, I don't do fours. But I want to let you know—"

"I don't know why you came back to Atlanta. But I'm glad you did."

"Because I heard his happiness, his neediness, his decisiveness—through my daughter, Em."

Sheena froze. Through Em?

"I don't want to get in your business," Tamika continued. "But I know from Em, and I believe her, that you're a good person. And I hope you and Damien work it out."

Sheena couldn't even put the phone down.

Beth was damn near slobbering on her like a puppy, straining to hear every word.

Tamika's mature, compassionate plea on Damien's behalf settled over her like a weight she wasn't ready to carry.

The church.

The case.

The feelings she kept swallowing down like bitter medicine.

Now, even the breakfast before her—beautiful, rich, and warm—felt too good to eat.

Overwhelmed.

Not just by the moment.

But by the truth.

Because she knew.

She knew.

This was it.
The final time, she was told to fight for Day.
And before she even realized what she was doing—
She was calling him.
"Hey, Shee- you alright- I'm glad you called. I didn't call you first- it's been a rough day so far".

CHAPTER 8

CAIN ANSWERS QUESTIONS?

.

Moment I: First Questions

After he had been caught- before Chapter 10 of this book-

"I, Emmanuel Cain III, here at the Atlanta Police Department's Public Safety Headquarters, have a right to be heard. I will present the truth as I know it. As it is. This is ridiculous."

The interrogation room had been adjusted for my presence. Not transformed—just... accommodated. A slight upgrade to the standard cell. The same room YD had sat in, but where he had faced cold metal and unrelenting scrutiny, I was afforded small comforts. A softer chair. A warmer light. The influence of a man like me demands such things.

I shifted slightly, the scent of disinfectant and my cologne mingling in the still air. The light above cast harsh shadows, but they didn't faze me. I was used to standing beneath brighter ones, commanding far larger crowds. This? This was just another stage, another sermon—except the pews were empty, save for one man seated across from me.

The interrogator sat with a notepad open, pen poised, eyes

unreadable. His presence was meant to feel imposing, but I had faced far greater adversaries.

I offered him a measured smile. Set the tone and control the moment.

"I'll answer your questions," I began, my voice even, deliberate. "But understand this—I am now under the care of a psychiatric physician. Given my recent breakdown, I cannot be held accountable for anything I may or may not have done."

The detective remained silent, his pen still hovering, waiting. Then, the first question.

"Why did you engage in a heated confrontation with Attorney Rory Davis at the Georgia Capitol during the MAGA versus Black Gay Men protest?"

A pause. The words hung in the air like incense in a sanctuary. My jaw tightened for just a moment. A flicker of something passed over me before I exhaled, settling back.

"You want the story?" I murmured. "Fine."

Morehouse. Early 2000s.

I remember the weight of my name walking those halls. Cain. A legacy. A family with standing. A family of faith. And Rory? He came from a respectable family, too. But the moment he stepped onto that campus, he chose... a different path.

Even then, he emulated Bayard Rustin, wearing that title like a badge. A self-proclaimed revolutionary, but really? A distraction. An obstacle to the movement, if you ask me.

While I was establishing my place and building alliances, Rory was out there disrupting—waving rainbow flags, calling himself a feminist, demanding inclusivity. He was a queen among women, an advocate for their rights to do what men should have done. Contradictory. Confused.

We ran in the same circles, briefly, until he started spreading rumors.

I am a preacher. I have always been a man of God, order, and structure. And yet, Rory told people I was… what? Gay? That we had shared a lover?

Ridiculous.

He was jealous. That's what it was. He had feelings for that boy—what was his name? William? Ready? Reedy? It doesn't matter. I tutored him, guided him, and helped him graduate. And Rory? He twisted it, made it into something else. Because that's what people like him do, they distort the truth. I am not, nor have I ever been, gay. I am a bishop at my church. God, believe me.

Back to the Capitol.

So when I saw him that day—standing there, speaking against the very structure of the Black family, parading his agenda as if it were righteousness—something in me rose.

There is no Wayne Williams 2.0. Our city is safe. But people like Rory—woke activists—they want another handout, another false enemy to fight.

I didn't get violent with him. I… grabbed his arm. A firm hold, a demand for his attention. Like the Patriots on January 6th. We have to take our country back. It is not a crime to fight for what you believe in.

I met the detective's eyes, my breathing steady.

"Now," I said, smoothing my lapel. "Are we done here?"

The detective didn't move. Then—slowly, deliberately—he scribbled something on his notepad.

I exhaled sharply, the weight of my justifications pressing down on the room.

"I need some water," I murmured, shifting in my chair. "And a break."

"And let's get on with this-this 'investigation'-your next 'question'".

He gave a small nod and signaled to the guard. The sound of the door unlocking filled the silence, and as I leaned back, the room seemed smaller than before. The presence of small blue-collar workers can have that effect on a place.

Moment II: Another Question

The water sat in a cheap plastic cup. Chilled. Like this room. Like them. I wrapped my fingers around it and felt it bend beneath my grip, but it didn't break. Not yet. I have done nothing wrong. Ever. That's the part they don't understand.

That twelve thousand dollars? Not stolen. Not taken. Not misappropriated. It wouldn't even be a discussion if that damn Sheena Colucci hadn't decided to play detective with my sheep. Believing an ignorant man. That's how this started.

My armor bearer, OT—Otis Truman— told me Deacon McCleadon has been waiting to take me down since I became pastor. Of course. Of course. I knew that already. These men—they sit in the congregation, judging. Waiting. Like the devil himself lurks in the pews. They watch a man of God rise and instead of reverence, they sharpen their blades. Yes, you should give double tithes. Yes, I should drive a Bentley. Yes, I need the finest suits. Do you think the Lord's anointed should walk barefoot? Huh? Do you think David would have driven a Honda?

Then, the detective had the nerve to interrupt me.

I looked at him, measured him. Weak men interrupt strong men. That's how they convince themselves they have power. But I could see it—he didn't even believe in his authority.

The plastic cup cracked.

Not nerves. No, not that. I don't get nervous. It was frustration. These men, these people—they sit across from me, refusing to believe, no matter how I explain. It's the same when I preach. The truth is right there, but they still sit in defiance, squeaking like neophyte Christians, the ones who need every little thing spelled out like toddlers in the faith.

The last drop of water ran over my fingers. Just a little wet. Like baptism. That's all it is. A little water. A little cleansing.

Then the question came.

"Why Beth Colucci? And all of the details that led to her 'kidnapping' and 'assault?'"

I sighed. Long. Let the words hang. I wanted to see if they would ask it again—if they were so weak in their conviction that they needed to hear it twice. But they didn't.

I smiled. Fine. Let me educate them.

So. I went to her.

I called her up first and got her number from my secretary, who—McCleadon's people would love this—prides herself on keeping me informed. I called her, and I thanked her. That's what this was about. Gratitude.

See, we don't usually take cash. Especially not that much cash. It's a matter of accountability, of stewardship. But I wanted her to know that I appreciated her even though we are used to receiving large donations. And I knew she was having a showcase.

Now, as a man of God, as a shepherd of lost souls, it is my duty to go where they are. Jesus went to places like that, didn't He? Didn't He? So yes, I have gone to places like that—many times.

Her showcase was over behind Piedmont Park. Some little spot called ATL Spit. Not ATL Lick—that'd be too obvious, wouldn't it? No, this place had class. A little storefront club, packed wall-to-wall with maybe 500 people inside. Exclusive. And lucrative because I know money when I see it. Like we stream pay-per-view at my church, they did it here.

I went in. I observed.

And then, at the end, we spoke—Beth and I.

We left together that evening.

I was going to pray for her.

That's what this was about. A prayer. She told me she wanted to pray. That was her choice. I drove her. We left the club. We left willingly. I don't see how that's difficult to understand.

Yes, I took her to my property. A home I own out by Chastain Park. A retreat center, a peaceful place. Many people have been there. Many people have been healed there.

Now, my wife knows I have struggled. The church knows. I am a man. A man who has fallen before but always gotten back up. And yes, Beth and I were there together. And yes, she had been drinking.

I didn't want her.

But she got sick. And things happened.

She—she bound herself.

That is what happened. She was irrational, emotional, and overcome. She was free to go.

She passed out. That was not my doing.

When I left, I went back to the church. I had responsibilities. I had a flock to lead.

And then, of course, they all showed up.

Detective Damien Kirkland DeBurg. Her noisy sister—Sheena Elise Colucci—oh yeah, forgive me—Doctor Sheena Elise Colucci. That ghetto, low-life record producer—who, according to Beth, won't even marry her sinful ass.

Pardon me. I'm hurting. I'm not well. I want to forget.

This—that mess they have caused.

And what happened? Hmm? What happened to me?

I was assaulted. I was hurt.

But I had to hurt them too. Defend me- the way I had to with Beth.

I had to go there.

And that's the whole truth.

There was no kidnapping.

There was no assault.

And yes, she was not well when you found her. But that's what those girls do. Those street urchins. Those rappers, that world. They wind up here, in rooms like this.

And to answer your question—

Why Beth?

Because her nosy sister was in the way.

And I was establishing a good relationship.

That's all.

That is all.

Did that answer your question?

Oh—oh, no, I am not out of hand.

I am very calm.

You better know that.

I am here willingly. My doctor knows that. My psychiatrist knows that.

There's no problem here.

I am simply a man under attack.

Now—oh? Now, you need a break.

Yes.

I think we all do.

Moment III: Yet Another Question

"If I hear 'Sir, we can or we can't' one more time, I swear to God—"

I slammed my palm onto the table. Not out of anger. No, not that. Frustration. This wasn't how men of my status were supposed to be treated.

I turned my head slightly, let my eyes settle on the detective, then leaned forward, voice measured but unyielding.

"I am not used to this treatment. Ask my armor-bearer, OT. I make way more than you do, detective—way more flavor and blessing. God loves Bishop Emanuel Cain III. I do ministry with street urchins. I go to clubs and parties because that's where the sinners are. I do the work of the Lord."

A pause.

"I normally don't deal with people unless they are tithers unless they come on Sunday. And even then—" I exhaled, shaking my head slightly, letting the weight of my words settle. "I require them to be blessed. I require them to have made their confessions before they come near me. I cannot be touched. It is dangerous—you will break my anointing. I am anointed. And if you do not make people see the value in the Lord's work, they will use you. Do you understand?"

I didn't wait for an answer.

"Do you know who eats first? Moses or his people? Joseph or his brothers? Jesus or Peter? Paul or Timothy?" I let the silence fill the space. "You're not feeling my preach because you've already decided I'm guilty of something. But God ain't telling you that."

I watched their faces—flat, unreadable.

"Fine. Let's pray before we go any further."

A cold smirk curled at my lips as I closed my eyes momentarily, letting the room breathe in my power. I wasn't asking. I was leading.

Then—

"YD?"

I laughed, sharp and humorless.

"You're asking me about YD? A known thief? A gang member from HT's? A menace to society?"

I leaned back, adjusting my cuffs.

"Yes, I've done ministry with YD. I minister with many young men like him, both in and out of the church. I am not gay."

I let that linger. Watched them absorb it. Let them question themselves before I continued.

"That night?" I tilted my head slightly, pretending to think. Pretending.

"I arrived at that cheap motel. Red Roof Inn. A sleazy little place. YD called me and said he needed guidance. He said he'd sinned. Said he had talked to that officer, Damien DeBerg—who I now know is part of a whole damn conspiracy to take me down. That's right. A conspiracy. Him, Sheena Colucci—she was his plant, wasn't she? Sent to dig up dirt on me?"

I licked my lips, exhaling through my nose.

"YD was high when I got there. Lusting. Weak. Needing my ministry. He grabbed me, pulling at my shirt—my muscle shirt—and I rebuked him. Hard."

I let my fingers tap against the table in a steady rhythm, mimicking my heartbeat.

"He fell back. But then he got up—stronger like he was on something. He was wild. Unhinged. He started grabbing at me, saying things like, 'I know you're gay. I'm gonna tell what you do to gay people.' And the heat—Lord, the heat was rising in that room—and he just kept grabbing at me, pulling at me, pushing me."

I paused.

"This is a Stand Your Ground state. Just like Florida."

I let those words settle in. Let them marinate.

"And this? This is a lie. Just like they lied on Zimmerman. Trayvon Martin was wrong all day and YD? YD deserved—"

I let my voice drift, then tightened my jaw.

"I'm not perfect. I was assaulted. I didn't want to put myself through this. But look at me now—I am here. Just like Beth—he made me do it."

I leaned forward, voice quiet, intimate, like a confession.

"I told him, 'I gotta hurt you. I gotta hurt you for putting all this on me. Me—the man of God.'"

Silence.

Then I shifted back, straightened my collar, and let my eyes meet the detectives.

"No more questions."

A deep breath. Then—

"I want to see my lawyer. Now. Damn it."

The room was thick with tension. The detective scribbled something. A guard shifted by the door. I was done.

I stood, smoothing out my suit.

"It was self-defense."

The door opened.

I stepped out this time with my lawyer—a man from the same firm that protected MAGA defendants, the same firm that pushed gentrification efforts in Atlanta while claiming to end poverty.

Money well spent.

And now?

Now, I'm in a Georgia psychiatric hospital. Minimum watch. Temporary.

I will be acquitted.

I deserve to be Beloved in the ATL.

Not this.

Not this foolishness.

Damn, Sheena.

Damn Damien.

Damn Beth.

Damn Atlanta.

Moment IV: Next Question, Please

Detective Kent Cantor pushed out of the interrogation room, the heavy door thudding shut behind him. His hand lingered on the knob for a second longer than necessary, fingers twitching. Only then did he notice the tremor.

Easy, Kent.

His pulse pounded in his ears, his shirt clinging damp against his back. The corridor's air-conditioning should have been cooling him down, but it felt thin like he wasn't getting enough of it. He dragged in a long, slow, controlled breath, but it did nothing to steady him. Cain's presence clung to him like a shadow.

Even now, the bastard's voice echoed in his head—calm, measured, like a man with no fear of consequence. That was the worst part. Cain wasn't worried. Not about his freedom. Not about the charges. Not about them.

Kent replayed the scene: every word, every pause, every slow, deliberate smile.

His stomach turned.

"I don't know how Day does this shit."

Talking to evil.

Not just evil—something more profound. Something that wrapped itself around you got under your skin, whispered in your damn ear.

He ran a hand down his face. He was supposed to be the one asking the questions.

So why did he leave with more than he walked in with?

Why did he feel like Cain had been interrogating him?

A shudder ran through him.

Damn confusion.

Strictly. Fucking. Confusion.

He glanced back at the closed door.

Cain was still in there. Still waiting and still knowing.

Kent exhaled hard, then turned and walked.

He needed air. And answers.

Cain lay in that chair like he owned the damn room, the slight curl of a smirk never entirely leaving his lips. There'd been a small, barely noticeable moment when Cain had closed his fist around the flimsy plastic water cup, cracked. The cheap thing had collapsed in his grip, water spilling across the table and ripping down his wrist. But Cain didn't react. No flinch, no irritation—he just watched the droplets run down his skin like it was nothing. Then, with the same eerie calm, he flicked them away and kept talking like he hadn't just crushed something with his bare hand.

Kent swallowed hard-mouth cottony. Had Cain been making a point? A message wrapped in something small, insignificant—a flex of control disguised as nothing. Because that was Cain's power. Not just what he did but how he made people feel. Cornered. Unsteady. Like he had already won.

Kent's palms sweaty patted themselves against his pant leg, realizing too late that it was damp with sweat. Across the hall, two uniformed officers nodded just a little tighter than those bobble head dolls - "We with you steady brother-be strong for the blue".

He straightened his shoulders, gave them a quick nod, then

kept moving. He didn't trust his voice yet. Didn't trust that if he spoke, it wouldn't shake.

He needed a very loud- tick-tick-tick from the government-issued clock.

Kent paced a few steps, rubbing his forehead temple- dragging a hand through his hair, his mind still circling the wreckage of that interrogation. Cain had just proven two things in that room:

First, that he was as dangerous as they feared.

Second, if they didn't keep him locked up, his influence alone would come back to haunt them all.

Anyone listening through the observation window would've felt it, too. The underlying menace in Cain's voice, the chilling confidence with which he spoke. The man acted like he still held all the cards like this was just another sermon, another moment in which he controlled the entire room.

Kent braced a hand against the wall, balling the other into a fist, forcing the tremor away.

We have to make this stick.

This wasn't just about catching Cain. It was about making sure he stayed caught. If this case slipped through the cracks, if one loophole gave Cain a way out, Kent could already see it. That man would be back in his pulpit by Sunday, draped in his preacher's robe, spinning some grand resurrection story to his congregation.

And they'd believe him.

They'd call it a test of faith.

They'd throw more money at him.

They'd let him do it all over again.

Kent bit down on his cheek, anger cutting through the fear. He wouldn't let that happen. Not on his watch. Not after what Cain had done.

What he did to YD...

Kent's stomach twisted. The damage Cain had inflicted on that kid was irreversible. YD would never be the same after what he'd been put through. And Beth Colucci—Kent shuddered, picturing her that night. Her face, the raw fear in her eyes. She was lucky to be alive after Cain's so-called counseling session that "just got out of hand because she wanted to hurt him and take advantage of him"- he had actually said.

And God only knew who else had been Cain's victim.

Damien DeBerg suspected there were more. That what they knew was just the tip of the iceberg.

Kent clenched his jaw. Cain's reach was long. Even with him in custody, his influence seeped beyond these walls like smoke through cracks.

Kent shook his head repeatedly, pushing back the thought gnawing at him. How the hell was he supposed to help Damien get his job back?

A whisper of guilt coiled in his chest. His voice barely broke the silence as he muttered, "If I hadn't cut YD loose— I had to cut YD loose. I was doing what I was told."

Cain's reach didn't stop at the walls of this station.

It stretched through the pews of his church.

Through the mighty men who protected him.

Through the ones too afraid to speak.

Even locked up, Cain wasn't contained.

And then there was Dr. Sheena Colucci.

Kent let out a slow breath. She'd figured this out before any of them.

Sheena had been putting the pieces together while the rest were still stumbling in the dark. She'd seen Cain for what he was. And she'd been right—every step of the way.

Kent knew he needed to talk to her. He needed to understand how she'd connected the dots so fast, what she saw he hadn't. Maybe she could help him make sense of the tangled mess in his own head.

Because right now, none of it made sense.

His heartbeat had finally begun to settle, but his body still carried the aftershock. He flexed his fingers, trying to shake the last of it off, but the residue of Cain's voice, his presence, was still there. Like a stain on the air.

Kent prided himself on being calm under pressure. Unshaken. But in this session?

This session, he'd been rattled.

And he hated that Cain had seen it.

Inside that room, Kent had felt his poise slipping and pulled into the dark gravity of Cain's words. For a second—just a second—he'd found himself praying.

Is this evil?

Kent Cantor opened his eyes. The hum of the fluorescent lights above him was deafening. The hallway stretched out ahead, empty, sterile, and yet he felt Cain's presence still there, pressing against him like a cold hand on his chest.

He exhaled, tugging at his tie as if it had suddenly grown too tight. His throat was dry. The taste of the interrogation still lingered, bitter on his tongue.

Then, Cain's voice slithered back into his mind.

"This isn't over, Detective."

Soft. Calm. Absolute.

Kent shivered. It wasn't just the words—the way Cain had said them, the slight upturn at the corner of his mouth, that eerie stillness in his eyes. The kind of confidence that belonged to men who already knew the ending before the story was finished.

Kent could still hear it.

Feel it.

Like a weight pressing down on his ribs, like something whispering beneath his skin.

And then—another voice.

"I gotta hurt you."

It struck through his memory like a cold knife. That wasn't a threat. That was a promise. A ritual. Cain had whispered it like a holy vow. Like scripture.

Kent exhaled sharply and shook his head, trying to shake off the feeling. But it clung to him. Damn, that was chilling. Horrid even.

His footsteps echoed as he started walking, slow, deliberate. A gnawing uncertainty fueled each step.

He was off balance now.

Kent looked back over his shoulder.

The interrogation room sat behind him, but the weight of it still pressed against his chest. The air felt thick, suffocating.

Then—

The snake charmer moved. Waving his hand—

Now, like a beauty pageant queen.

Now, like a CEO.

Now, like a preacher at the pulpit, he pulls Kent back and drags him into the principal's office.

Cain smiled.

"Son. Let me say this."

"I have been thinking—about you—this inconvenience you have put me in. Wasting both of our time."

"But I don't hold you accountable."

"You have been led astray. Just like so many in this city—this worldly, godless place called Atlanta."

Cain tilted his head, eyes slow and studying.

"Although you've given me nothing—

I must do my job.

I mean—my calling.

And pray for your soul."

Kent's stomach flipped. He saw the hand coming before he felt it—

Cain, reaching.

Gripping.

Kent ripped away.

"Take your goddamn hands off me—I'll put your ass in cuffs, tie you to that motherfucking table—sit. your. Ass. Down".

Cain didn't flinch. Didn't blink.

Instead—he laughed.

"Oh, I see it now."

"You don't know who I am. The anointing on my life. Look at you, boy."

Cain's smile widened.

"You're shaking. Just like YD before he attacked me. I see into you. Well. Deep."

"I am a general in God's army. I can take the needless persecution."

Then, soft—whispered like a prophecy:

"Quos Deus vult perdere, prius dementat."

The door slammed open.

A rush of blue. A black hand.

"Detective Kent—are you okay in here?"

Kent exhaled. Shook his head.

"Yeah, yeah—damn right we good."

But he didn't look back.

Cain is still in there.

Still waiting.

Still certain.

And for the first time, Kent wondered—

How did we get here?

CHAPTER 9

TURN OUT THE LIGHTS

Moment I: First, Sweet Shit

The rapid licking of his fingers—Polynesian sauce-sweet, clinging to his skin—competed with the sharp beep-beep of his phone vibrating against the dashboard.

Sheena Colucci calling.

A small smile crept across Damien's lips, the first in eight hours. Cool, subdued—even as a storm brewed inside.

I know these killings are all connected.
Damn, Morgan and APD—wow. Kent really cut me loose?
She called me indecisive? After all these years? After everything?
And now—now—she was calling?

He swallowed hard, clearing his throat of the thick mix of Polynesian sauce and hot chicken spice. Reaching for the best version of his voice—steady, present, composed—he answered.

"Hey, Shee... you alright?"

His hand hovered near his drink.

"I'm glad you called. I didn't call you first—it's been a rough day so far."

There was a pause. And then—

"Hey, Damien."

The way she said his name caught him off guard.

Not like before.

Not the teasing "Day" from Mays High.

Not the breathy whisper from late-night calls.

Not the sly greeting after dinner.

This was formal. Careful. Intentional. Weighty.

And that's when he knew—this was bigger than he expected.

Especially after how they'd left things. The breakup. The sting. The silence.

He stumbled a bit inside himself, caught in that space where pain meets nostalgia—but still, he felt it. That tug. That pull. That *her*. That *Shee*.

Even through the distance, her voice felt like warmth. A giggle—not quite laughter, more a memory—slipped through the line like sun cracking through closed blinds.

"No, I texted you earlier... yesterday, I think."

"Yeah, I know. I'm sorry. I just—I had a lot going on. And to be honest, I didn't want to explain what I hadn't even processed yet."

He exhaled slowly, fingers tightening around the steering wheel.

"Besides... if it ain't good with you, then—"

"I love you, Day."

The words hit him like breath after nearly drowning.

"Wow," he said, voice catching in the back of his throat. "I needed this—shit, Sheena, I—I—"

"No," she said, her voice low and sure. "I've been thinking, and I need to apologize. Can we talk? In person?"

The distance between them collapsed.

The car, the case, the city—all faded into the background.

His breath caught—not from hesitation, but from knowing.

Knowing her voice.

Knowing what it meant.

Knowing what it still did to him.

Even through the speaker, her tone slid over his skin like heat, like memory. Like a promise.

Everything in him leaned toward her—not out of habit, not out of hunger, but out of something more permanent. More dangerous.

Damien swallowed, his pulse uneven and unsteady. The car felt less like a vehicle and more like an intimate room. The moment pressed them close—closer than words could manage.

The years of need in him didn't dissolve all at once. But they began to ease, as only spiritual connection could.

And as he listened—truly listened—to her inviting him back into her life, into that sacred space where love and memory lived together, Damien accepted.

Softly. Completely.

Damien swallowed, his pulse uneven and unsteady. The room and the moment pressed against them like conjoined twins.

"Yeah," he murmured, feeling it in his chest. "I'd like that. I need that. How about dinner tonight? Say the place. Do I need to pick you up?"

"No. I am here at Beth's condo- she has a 'set' tonight- it is pay-per-view- a pretty big deal- but the venue is small- just need to be somewhere where I can watch after dinner even if we are still together?-Day-did you hear me right this time-Day".

"Yeah, so- I have a call coming in, and I have to take this-I will 'decisively' hit you where to be at 7:30ish- it will be a place we can talk business and business- you will be able to speak to Damien and Day depending on how you come."

"Bye, Day—but know this, I'll actually respond to your text."

Before the click, he could hear her smile through the phone.

Then—before he could enjoy the sweetness of it, the next call came in.

"Hey, this is Detective Deburg—Damien Deburg."

Moment II: Now Street Shit

The phone vibrated in Damien's hand.

He had just left Connor behind, his mind still caught in Sheena's voice.

Sweet shit. That's where his head had been.

But this?

This was about to be something else.

He answered. "Yeah."

"Hey, man. You already know. Slim and some folks say you can be talked to."

Damien frowned. "Who is this?"

"Gee, man. Lil G. Rep'n the A—real H.T."

Not a name he expected.

Damien sat up, rolling his shoulders.

"Okay. Say less. I know this is a phone. What can I do for you?"

"I'ma be real wit' you, Day. We got all the pieces to the puzzle."

Lil G's voice cut through the static—low, deliberate. Then, like a verse already loaded:

"Playboi nigga—
I'm on Deebo lit.
I'm on Migo lit.
On Kilo lit.
I go psycho, bitch."

He let it hang in the air, like a signal.

Damien clocked it. That wasn't just a random flex. That was Playboi Carti's R.I.P.—quoted word-for-word. Not Drill Rap gospel, but lit- spit like scripture in the street.

Damien's thoughts went corrective-

Damn, these you Cats caught up-no where near as creative as the artist they quoting- coreny as hell-

He leaned back for a second, let it wash over him.

This wasn't the same Atlanta he grew up in.

Gang life had always been there—but back then, it was whispered. Hidden in hand signs and hood legends.

Now?

Now it had a beat.

A bassline.

A Billboard chart.

A mixtape—and crazy shit chopped and mixed with fentanyl for lethal profit.

Atlanta didn't just hustle anymore. It broadcasted. It streamed. IG thugs were harder to run down—not because they were slick, but because their feet weren't even on real ground.

Get at me—what did that even mean?

Where? How?

But the money—the reason—still moving.

D.A. Fonni Wilson wasn't wrong.

But good can't get done when there's inherent freedom of speech trapped in structural bondage.

Dark lines etched deep—shackling Black girls' and boys' minds for all their short time on earth.

This whole gang shit?

Nowhere.

Fast.

But not slow.
And somewhere in all that noise, the bodies were still dropping.
And the kids? They were listening.

Drill rap wasn't just music anymore. It was mapping the violence. Coding confessions. Singing war.

But Lil G dropped back into his own voice, this time less performative. More pointed.

"But nah, bruh.
It ain't just flexin'. We really got love for the A.
And for real ones like you.
Niggas that put they thang in—for the clay. Pullin' out the mud.
Not just the government check. Not just for show. For real."

Damien exhaled, rubbing his temple.
"That right?"

Lil G chuckled.
"Yeah. But look, I ain't tryna do all this on the drop. Come by."
A pause. "Say lunchtime."

Damien squinted, listening.
"Sounds like you smacking on something."

"You setting the time and reading my mind now?"

"Nah. Just making sure you don't come thirsty."

Another pause.

"You know the name. You know where we at. Just ask for Gee."

Damien's jaw tightened.
"Alright."

Then Lil G's voice dropped again. Lower. Heavier.

"Detective DeBerg.
Slim says you a Snoop Doggy, man. Real Crime Gruff. You solid—
Built from the A-Town streets.
We got trust for him.
But you?"

A stretch of silence crackled between them.

"You sound like Snoop Doggy."

Damien leaned back. Stared through the windshield.

He could play along.
Or he could remind them who the hell he was.

His voice came out steady.
"I am who I say I am. But let me be clear, bro—whether it's Detective or Damien, I don't play games.
"And I expect you don't either. Nigga, this ain't no play against you—this about us getting caught lacking. We ain't scheming, ain't setting shit up. We fixing what got fucked up."
A silence.
Then, Lil G exhaled slowly. Real slow.
"Then we one hunnit."
A pause.
"I'm going to be honest with you, man. I think we can help each other. But now? It's gon' be on some real street shit.

Don't bring any heat.

We can't let you get down like that.

Let us know who your second is.

We gotta know you legit.

You good?"

Damien didn't hesitate.

"I rock with Rory Davis."

"I'll hit him. Certified legal of the court?"

"I can rock with you. He's got my back. This the hit back for confirmation."

Lil G grinned through the line.

"I'm on Deebo lit—

I'm on Migo lit—"

He was clear—

He knew.

He heard it loud.

Sheena wasn't Polynesian sauce.

She was built for this.

Custom-built. Built for him.

Able to hold two halves of a man with two loves.

Damien. The mission.

Then Day.

Neither had to cancel the other out.

"Get 'em, Day—I'm in. I trust you. Like I said, I love you."

Like Beat always said—

"Hartsfield-Jackson. Jet fuel."

Click. The line went dead.

Damien stared at the phone.

Clear.

His smirk was slow. Controlled.

Everything was set now.

"Playboi Carti, huh?"

A slow nod. Then—

"Yeah, Come fuck with the boss."

He tossed the phone onto the passenger seat.

Sweet shit was over.

It was time for the street shit.

Moment III: A Cut Above Street Shit

Damien stepped into Leron's Barbershop, just past the airport in Riverdale, where the air was thick with the smell of clippers, cocoa butter, and deep conversation. This wasn't just a barbershop—this was a boardroom, where men didn't just get cuts, they got clarity.

Fresh from a manicure and pedicure—a reminder that no matter what happened outside, he had himself on the inside—Damien knew the truth. This was self-care, sure. But deep down? He was preparing himself to be given away—to Sheena, to the city, to whatever was left of his purpose.

He made his way to Kim's chair, the lady barber with hands steady as wisdom. She was more than a stylist—she was a seer. The kind of Black woman who cut beyond the grain, seeing not just who you were but who you could be. She chopped away doubts like dead ends, sharpening his look like she sharpened his spirit.

"You stay running, Detective," Kim murmured, shaping his line with surgical precision.

"Gotta stay ready," Damien replied, voice low.

"Mm-hmm. And for what, exactly?"

She knew. They always knew.

This wasn't your average shop talk. No tired debates over LeBron vs. Jordan. No empty chatter about who was next up in the rap game. Leron didn't allow foolishness in his house.

You had to bring some to get some.

And Leron had brought plenty. His story was currency.

Once caught up in the system, he had loved a woman who loved him back, even through prison walls. And when he got out—pardoned under Obama, freed by more than law—he moved different.

Not for the money, not for the suits he now flew to Italy to buy, or the trips he spoiled his wife with—but for what he could build.

At Christmas, he gave out toys.

For the boys without fathers, he gave out game.

And for the men who came in tired, beat down by the weight of this world, he gave them room to breathe.

That's why Damien chose this shop. That's why he trusted Kim with the clippers.

She knew who he was, not just what he did.

The Gospel of Growth

The shop hummed with conversation, but when Leron spoke, the room listened.

"They been talking," he said, his voice smooth a as a razor in warm cream- like he had the keys to something ancient. "Preachers gone astray. Men of other faiths, other walks, just standing by, watching it happen."

Leron let the words settle, the weight of them pressing into the air like a hush before the choir comes in. Then, he shook his head, sweeping up the loose hair—not because the younger barbers couldn't, but because Leron was a servant before he was a boss.

"It ain't about religion," he said, the broom gliding smooth against the floor. "People get caught up in the preacher. Think because somebody got a billboard, that mean they got a calling."

He tapped the broom once—a gavel, a verdict.

"But a billboard don't make a preacher either."

The congregation of the shop, usually full of side comments and laughter, sat still. Listening. Absorbing.

"What makes a real preacher? A real Christian?" Leron's voice dipped lower, pulling the room in. "They build others up, even as they continue to decrease."

And that's when it hit.

Through the shop speakers, Elder William Murphy poured through with a baptism deep enough to drown in—

"This is my season for grace, for favor…

This is my season to reap what I have sown."

The barbershop shifted.

Somebody closed their eyes.

Somebody tapped their foot against the tile.

Somebody gripped the arms of the chair, not ready to testify out loud, but feeling it deep all the same.

And then, a voice from the back, gravelly but clear—

"Man, that's my frat brother singin'—Be out, Doggie!"

And that was it.

Omega Psi Phi in the building.

The brother wore his gold and purple every Saturday, but especially when he was standing beside Leron, handing out school supplies to kids or making sure another young Black man left with a fresh cut and a fresh perspective.

Damien let the moment breathe. He knew exactly what was pulsing through the shop. That mix of faith and fire, the tension of belief and reality, the balance of knowing that church is real—but so are the ones who've perverted it.

Then, soft, to Kim—

"I gave my life to Jesus Christ in this shop because of y'all. Before? No way."

Kim, still lining his hair with steady hands, didn't even pause.

She already knew.

She already felt it.

"Keep going, Damien," she murmured.

Because everybody knew.

This city, this ATL—it had a sickness.

Somebody was using the pulpit to prey instead of pray.

But the Spirit?

The Spirit loved her.

Had always loved her.

And never stopped flowing.

And Damien knew, deep in his gut, that Leron had just put words to something the city had been whispering all along.

Because if a billboard preacher was hiding behind the good book—who the hell had been haunting Atlanta all this time?

Moment IV: Smarter than the Shit

No badge. Rory had his back—always had, always would. Brotherhood wasn't built on credentials, sexuality, or fake religion. It was built on standing in the fire with somebody, knowing they'd stand in it for you.

Just like the day they met.

Freshman year. IHOP parking lot. Rory, sharp-tongued, fearless, eyes locked on some drunk frat boy twice his size. Damien, still young, still learning, still thinking masculinity was something you had to prove, had a rock in his hand before he even knew why.

"Don't," Rory had said, voice calm. "Not because you can't. Because you don't have to."

He exhaled, shaking his head. "You hating a Black man—a Black gay man, a Black straight man—how is that different than the Klan? Than Reagan? Than some New York businessman like Donald Trump, who took out a whole ad calling for five Black boys to die over some white girl in Central Park?

"Trump threw out accusations. Called for their deaths.

And when he found out he was wrong? He ain't even apologize. Ain't make it right again.

"I guess bullies gotta stay great—even if it's just in their own mind."

That was Rory. He talked. He translated humanity. He made Damien listen. Made him think.

And from that day, Damien wasn't just strong. He was aware.

And that's why, years later, badge or no badge, this bond didn't waver.

Rory's voice snapped him back.

"Damien, I'm in your kitchen—I know you got help, 'cause it's double spotless."

Rory's head bent around the wall, eyes up, face flushed against the gray.

Damien smirked. "I see, and it stays clean even when my people don't come. Em deserves it." He shrugged. "And really? I eat out a lot. Like them fries that go cold 'cause I'm talkin' too much—one fry, conversation, another fry, conversation."

Rory exhaled. "Every other fry."

"Every other fry."

Damien leaned against the counter, wiping his hands—now cold. He pressed the refrigerator faucet, let a stream of water fill the glass, then pushed it into Rory's hand. A small gesture. Enough to re-center him.

Rory exhaled, head shaking slow.

Damien caught it. Something was on him.

"But what's up, brother? You don't need no invitation—but I'm on a tight."

This room had spun clockwise with Sheena right on time.

Now, counter-clockwise—an ass-kicking waiting to happen.

Rory settled into the chair, exhaling as he finally let his body relax. His eyes flickered over Damien's hands—fresh cuticles, clean polish, not a single rough edge. He smirked.

"Self-care season?"

Damien barely glanced up from his drink. "Gotta stay sharp. Moving forward requires maintenance."

Rory nodded, but his face held something heavier.

"Look, man. I gotta tell you what happened."

Damien's brow lifted. "I saw you on TV. Capitol steps, right?"

"Yeah. I was called down there by my organization—the association of gay Black men I'm with. Of course, me being the lawyer, I'm the spokesman." Rory shook his head, frustration creeping into his voice. "And we get out there, Day, and all I see? MAGA signs.

'Make Atlanta Great Again.' Like they some damn local yokel talking big. Which, really? They just yokel."

Damien sat forward, eyes narrowing. "What happened?"

Rory inhaled sharply. "Man, I had to speak out. Forget the rhetoric, the sycophants, the 'woke this, woke that'—Black gay men are being murdered, and nobody is saying a damn thing."

He hesitated. Then—he let it slip.

"And then it got worse."

Damien's jaw tensed. "Worse?"

Rory exhaled sharply. "Guess who the hell showed up out there? Emmanuel Cain."

Damien's face stilled. "Come again?"

"You heard me. Bishop Emmanuel Cain III was out there." Rory sat back, disgust clear on his face. "You know I went to Morehouse with him, right? Knew him before the robes, the billboards, and all this mess."

Damien's fingers drummed against the arm of his chair. "Yeah."

"Day—Cain's been moving foul for years. Comes from a preacher family, always had that voice, that image. But I checked him back then, because I'm somebody too."

Damien's grip tightened around his glass. "You saying—?"

Rory held his gaze, unblinking. "Are you sure?"

Rory didn't waver. "I'm saying he's gay."

Blunt. Flat. A gavel to the table.

"Preaching about gay people, making it worse. Closeted and complicit."

Damien exhaled, fingers still wrapped around his drink. "How do you know?"

Rory leaned forward, voice cooling like a blade sliding into place.

"Because we shared a lover."

Silence.

Damien's eyes sharpened. Rory didn't flinch.

"Cain was sprung. I was one and done." His voice was

smooth, but the edge was unmistakable. "And our guy? He told me everything."

The air between them thickened.

"Said Emmanuel was new. But eager. And constant." Rory exhaled sharply. "And always saying 'no'—while never really meaning it."

Damien let the words sit.

Let them sink.

Because that? That wasn't just a scandal. That was a pattern. A truth Cain buried so deep he built a damn pulpit over it.

And if Cain was desperate enough to swing on Rory in public?

He wasn't just hiding.

"He is running, Damien—my goddamn nerves—with his hypocritical, closeted, hot-collar-wearing ass."

Running.

From himself. From exposure.

But Damien felt it now, something shifting in his gut.

What if Cain wasn't just running from his secrets?

What if he was running from something worse?

Damien exhaled sharply, his focus sharpening. "And you confronted him?"

"Damn right, I did. Right there, in his face, on those Capitol steps."

A smirk flickered at the corner of Rory's lips, but his eyes were deadly serious.

"I wish they had got it on camera, because baby—he almost hit me."

Damien sat back, expression unreadable. "Cain tried to put hands on you?"

"Damn near." Rory's voice was low, dangerous. "You know how he is—over-masculine as hell, hyper as a toddler on Red Bull. Got too close, eyes bulging, voice shaking. Tried to bark on me like I wasn't ready to knock that bitch out his ass."

A slow smirk crept onto Damien's face. "What happened?"

Rory leaned in, voice thick with heat. "Day, had that man put his hands on me? I'd have beat his ass clean off that damn billboard."

Silence.

Then Damien exhaled, rubbing his temples. "Billboard?"

Rory's grin widened. "Yes, Day. Yes. Bishop Emmanuel Cain III. The one all up on these damn billboards—the same ones rappers buy on I-75/85 by Boulevard. You've seen it. 'Welcome to the ATL. Our pastor is here for you.'"

Flying by, had Damien misread it?

Rory let the ink settle into the page with a low voice.

"But what it really should say? Welcome to the ATL. Our pastor is in the dark—hiding in the closet. Somebody knows. And they're finally gonna tell it."

Damien's stomach turned—that damn billboard.

He had seen it a hundred times. Just passed it with Sheena. Laughed about it. Dismissed it.

But now? Now that billboard felt like a warning. A dangling carrot. A damn confession in plain sight.

And if Cain was desperate enough to swing on Rory in public?

He wasn't just hiding.

He was running.

From what?

From who?

The city hummed outside.

The storm was coming.

And Damien was already too deep to turn back now.

But if he was being real?

He didn't want to turn back.

With all the bullshit—and being the man Sheena would have to love—

He couldn't go back.

Bullshit was heavy.

But it would be handled.

Moment V: Dealing Directly with Bullshit

Damien ran his finger, connected to soft hands, over his fresh cut. Sharp lines, smooth fade—the shape-up that said he was ready for business. Or war.

Roaring Damien's playlist—"I'm here."

Jeezy, his corner man, set the tempo.

Look at my watch, look at my wrist

Nuthin' like yo man, he ain't shinin' like this

Nuthin' like yo man, he ain't grindin' like this..

He thought about all that had led to the club to meet with a gang member-

Straight bullshit.

Jeezy answered back.

I'm a good God-fearin' man with a criminal mind state

Now—it was time to move. Street Shit.

The club was nameless for now. I just bought it with cash— probably was gonna buy, probably never get a name, let alone sprout a business license on the wall.

But its location was prime—a short walk from The Tabernacle, smack in the pulse of Atlanta's music scene.

HT had influence here.

Hell, they even signed one of their artists to Slim Thug Records. A favor for a favor.

Back when Slim was locked up, HT took care of him.

When he came home, he took care of them.

The system fed itself.

Inside, it was all at once suffocating.

Blunt smoke. Vape clouds. Stale liquor sweating in plastic cups.

Damien scanned the room, eyes cutting through the haze. There was money—but no wealth.

This life? It pulled you in like quicksand. Fast, intoxicating, then suddenly—gone.

It was a mix of skateboarders and scapegoats, kids trying to dodge a system that didn't give a damn.

And it wasn't like these cats moved like the mafia.

They weren't organized crime. They were just the mob.

Atlanta drill music pumped through the walls, basslines thick enough to shake the floorboards. Names he recognized, lyrics he barely caught.

Then—

Like his voice was part of the track itself—

"Yo, it's me."

Lil G.

He didn't push through the crowd.

Didn't need to.

No bodyguards. No showmanship. He was just there. And people moved around him naturally, like water breaking for a stone.

A voice from the side checked Damien before he even got close.

"Aye, my nigga, you got that stizzy?"

Damien barely looked at him. Just lifted his chin toward the sign on the wall.

"Check your boy."

The man sized him up—then looked to Lil G.

Lil G nodded once.

That was enough.

"It's good."

That was the thing about this world.

No need for extra tech-tech-techie.

When men kept their word, that was the weapon.

Lil G grinned as a light-brown, jewelry-bedecked woman floated up beside him.

She looked like a long-lost cousin of Beyoncé—if she had never made it, if the money never came.

She leaned in, overseeing Damien.

"What you want, Lil G?"

Lil G nodded toward Damien.

"Get my boy a water. That's right, Nig, yeah?"

Damien smirked. Like an attendant in first class, she disappeared and returned with the bottle already cracked open.

She set it down. He didn't touch it.

Lil G caught it but didn't say anything.

"You see that?" he asked.

Damien shook his head. "I'm good, man."

Lil G's grin widened. "Nigga, they say you like that."

A slow sip of his drink.

"You like that?"

Then—like it was written into the beat—

Lil G started talking.

Fast. Hard. Unapologetic.

He laid it all out with the game, the betrayal, the setup- in his language-street shit ATL Drill language:

"YD was supposed to go can, then plug in.
He ain't pay. He was patty. We put a pattern on him.
We wasn't gonna let him legging.
The civilian was supposed to draw YD out for the P.S.
He owed HT slime.
But we wasn't even gonna punish him for fake snitching—civilians
ain't stepping. Ain't snitching
Ain't in it".

The problem? The civilian went mince on YD.

Started giving stacks. Fucking up future stacks.

Civilian my nigga moist.

Lil G shook his head, eyes gleaming in the low light.

"This HT slime. This HT slime. Ain't no way we partner with the po-po, but to you? Proper. Big proper. OG Slim, he with you."

A smirk. A knowing look.

"So proper D-E-T Day. That's who you is now. Beyond the police. Snooping Day."

Damien said nothing.

Let him talk.

Let the truth spill out.

Lil G leaned in.

"Nigga, he hurt bad like he had to do it. We not trading racks for this. We giving a scoreboard. You know who's on it."

Damien's eyes narrowed.

Lil G's grin stretched wider.

"It's the preacher on the billboard."

"The one who used to be BMF back in the day."

Damn. The lights in the room blinked off and on.

"We gotta even the score."

"The preacher's on the scoreboard."

Lil G leaned back, watching Damien.

"No racks. We wash our hands."

"You take care of ours—but, for this one, we don't get no blood on it."

A check-in.

A smile that wasn't a smile.

"And you always get what you need from us."

Damien's eyes grew hot—but he smoothed it over, passing the calm to Lil G, who needed it more.

Lil G let it hang between them.

"This ain't no partnership. It's just proper to Slim and proper to you."

Another pause.

Then—casual, but laced with warning.

"What you thinking, my nigga?"

The deal was on the table.

The question wasn't whether Damien was ready for this.

The question wasn't just whether he had a choice.

It was whether he ever did.

What a move it had been.

Sweet shit.

Bullshit.

Street shit.

Everything in between.
This had been informative—but dark.
He needed light.
And the only place left to find it?
Out in the Light.

CHAPTER 10

OUT IN THE LIGHT

Moment I: Out Light Before Business

Damien slipped onto the narrow curb outside Pricci, just north of Peachtree—off Pharr Road, where the money moved differently.

Chris Standring's "Liquid Soul" oozed from the Platinum Poshue, parked illegally but strategically—propped up like it had every right to be.

And then? Sheena.

Oiled-brown legs slid out in time with the beat, pearl-white toes catching the streetlights just right. The day's heat had lifted, replaced by the calm hum of an April Atlanta night.

The Pricci stage was perfect. A place to test their light.
They were here.

With Beth and Randall. With Darius and Nina. Quincy and

Monica. Melanie and Derwin. Janie and Tea Cake. Sydney and Dre. Jason and Lyric. Sheila and Troy.

They weren't just at the table.
They were the table.

But could Shee and Day hold theirs? Could Sheena and Damien get down to business and remain Shee and Day?

"Damien, that was sweet, sending the car for me. Really, though, I could have—"

Damien cut her off. Not rudely, but decisively. Maybe with a look. Maybe with a simple:

"I know. But I wanted to."

He let it sit. Let her feel it. Then, steady—

"But you've got to know I've grown."

He exhaled, gaze locked. "You've got to know I've grown."

Pause. A shift. His body language smelled of strength. The kind that didn't need proving. The kind that just was.

"Some things, though?" He let the words settle. "They don't change."

"Damien—Day."

His arms relaxed, not interrupting, just listening. A warm, sensual glance.

"Oh, I'm Day again?"

"You never stopped being Day. There are just some things we —Shee and Day—have to get together so we can—"

Before she could finish, a smooth voice slid between them.

"Good evening, ma'am. You must be Ms. Sheena Colucci. And sir, you must be Mr. Damien DeBerg. I was told this is a special occasion—ah, a reunion of sorts. I'm Kevin, your server and personal conduit for what Mr. DeBerg has described as, and I quote, his attempt to 'Make it last forever.'"

Kevin placed a bottle on the table with practiced ease, a knowing smile in his delivery.

"With that—a bottle of Méthode Traditionelle Sparkling Chardonnay from a single vineyard in Santa Lucia Highlands. Barrel-fermented cuvée and tirage-aged for twenty months in the bottle prior to disgorging."

Sheena raised an eyebrow, lips curving.

"Damien, how did you know I rock with the McBride Sisters?"

His smirk was barely contained.

"I know the sister I love."

Then, a playful shrug.

"But a little bird told me—Beth. She said you only drink wine made by Black women. And McBride Sisters? That's your favorite. Along with—"

He met her gaze, savoring the moment.

One of the greats must have a bottle close by, close-Ntsiki Biyela. Darjean Jones. Theodora Lee.

Sheena exhaled, shaking her head, that undeniable smile breaking through wine by black people's excellence.

The wine played in the glass like a slow, knowing hum.
A tining—lalallah, tinaling.

Then, the appetizer called low and slow, "Relax, you're in a safe place."

Sheena purred, "Mmm. Taste that."

Damien eyed her, skeptical. "Ooooh, no. You gon' learn—I don't go that deep with oysters."

Sheena's brow lifted. "Oh really? That could be a problem. No—gon' be a problem."

Damien's head tilted back, laughing before it dropped suddenly. "Oh really?" He leaned in, low and teasing. "Then hand me the oyster—but it better always be kosher."

"Sllluurrrp."
"Shlllrrrkk."
"Hhlrrrppp."

Sheena smirked—a knowing smile tugging at the corner of her lips. "Ooooh, detective. You've done that before."

Kevin, unfazed, stepped in just in time—rooting for them, like he knew how this dance always ended.

"Sir, your main course will be arriving shortly. Could I interest Ms. Sheena or yourself in a cocktail?"

Damien smirked. "Yes—before I get in too deep." He turned to her. "Shee?"

Sheena met Kevin's gaze with ease. "Kevin—Sheena is fine if you bring two tequilas. Neat."

Then, before dessert—

"Damien, I owe you an apology."

"No—you don't owe—"

"But, She—"

"No. Please."

Her voice was soft. Steady.

"I've loved you since we were sixteen because I knew who you were.
A Black boy, determined to be a man.
A man determined to see me become a woman."

Damien's breath caught.

"Sheena—Shee—"

"Day… it's time," she whispered.

"I love you- forever baby-for better or
worse."

For years, she'd held him at arm's length.
A shield.
A habit.
A fear.

But tonight, the shield fell.

A pause.
Deep.
Heavy.

"You are all I have ever loved.
And I know I'm a worthy man...
because I get to love you—
and be loved by you.
I love you, Sheena."

They   stayed.
They   settled.
They confirmed the freedom in his heart.

Damien leaned back in his chair, watching Sheena with a quiet
intensity, the kind that said more than a thousand compliments
ever could. Their flirtation had mellowed into something richer—
like good jazz simmering low beneath conversation.

Just then, an older couple at the next table took notice.

Sheena hadn't seen them at first, but the woman—regal in her
pearls, hair silver but flawless, and wrapped in a Chanel shawl
that whispered *old Atlanta money*—had been watching them with

a glint in her eye. Her husband, all salt-and-pepper refinement in a tailored tan blazer, sat beside her like a content secret.

The woman leaned in.

"Sweetheart," she said to Sheena, "he looks at you the way George looked at me in '63."

Sheena turned, startled but instantly intrigued.

The woman smiled—bright, bold, and still beautiful.

"I'm Mattie. And this here's my George. Fifty-five years, three kids, too many grandbabies to count, and a whole life of choosing each other. We were just saying how… refreshing it is. To see something that feels like love."

George nodded, eyes kind. "Real love. The kind that don't let go."

Mattie winked. "That's how you last."

She leaned forward, her voice lowering like a preacher about to speak plain.

"You didn't ask—"

George sighed, already knowing. "Ah, dear, you're still doing it."

Mattie brushed him off with a laugh. "No, George. Marriage is important. You and I made it—because we were poured into. Hugh and Kathy—our mentors—taught us early, and I'll be damned if I don't pass it on when I see love taking root."

She turned to Sheena and Damien.

"So I have to pass it on to Ms. Sheena… and this handsome young man—Denzel—" she grinned, "I mean, Damien."

Damien let out a slow laugh. "Close enough, Ms. Mattie."

Mattie smiled but her tone shifted, settling into wisdom's register.

"Time will come when you two may not even like each other."

Her eyes gleamed with a knowing light.

"But don't worry—I can tell he doesn't like me right now."

Sheena burst out laughing. "Mattie!"

"No, listen." Mattie raised her glass, her voice unwavering. "All that 'I'm in love' stuff? It's beautiful—but it's fluff. The truth is in how you *treat* the relationship. The real you. The intimacy. The respect. That's what you invest in."

George gave a small nod, encouraging her like he had for decades.

"Treat the love like a child—then a teenager—then an elder," Mattie continued. "You grow it. You protect it. You don't walk away when it gets cranky or fragile."

She tapped her wrist, steady and clear.

"You treat each other like arteries. You might clog, you might ache—but you cannot live without each other."

She looked at both of them now. Firm. Clear. Warm.

"One day, you'll wake up—25, 30, 50 years in—still choosing each other. Not just lovers, but partners. Not just fire, but faithfulness."

A hush settled around the table.

"And, finally-"

George stepped in like a referee waving his white table cloth like a infraction flag at the Superbowl, "Ah, Mattie, it should have never gotten to 'finally'".

"George, please so we can get to 51- remember precious couple-sex is doing, love is being and marriage is choosing-George put the cloth down I'm paying tonight and I chose 51 and 52".

The unified laughter was just dignified enough to alert others in the room.

Kevin, standing off to the side with his towel folded just so, gave a subtle nod—like even he'd been caught in the gospel of it.

Sheena exhaled. Her fingers traced the wine glass stem, slowly, thoughtfully.

Damien's hand found hers under the table. He didn't speak. He didn't need to.

Kevin stepped forward. "He asks if you could defer all business until tomorrow... and I am now adding this—" he glanced at Damien, who smirked behind his glass— "to make this night last forever."

The air changed.

The laughter quieted.

Everything softened, ripened.

Sheena's eyes locked with Damien's.

And she knew. She *knew*.

There was only one answer.

She turned to Kevin, the server.

"I'll take my tiramisu to go," she said with a smile, then glanced at Damien. "And he'll have the crème brûlée…"

A pause.

"To go. But no spoon."

Damien's lips parted.

One slow exhale.

One simple, knowing smirk.
A single night about to stretch into forever.

Moment II: Lights Down Before Business

Damien's car waved goodbye as the limousine oozed down Peachtree, stretching dessert across Atlanta in ways only he could. But tonight, all the city had to offer was neon—orange, blue, green, red—flashing past in a silent blessing.

This brother tips well, and she is fine. Let me help him out.

Then Teddy Pendergrass was allowed to shake deep black sensuality:

Turn off the lights and light a candle...

Let's take a shower, said a shower together...

Inside, butter-rum coconut scented the air, heady and thick. It clung to Sheena's skin, inviting Damien's hand to settle on her thigh. The attendant adjusted the lane, just enough to press her body into his touch. The signal was clear.

The driver, sensing the shift, let the partition close. Alexa dimmed the world, letting Luther lay the moment bare.

I used to be afraid that you would never love me this way...

Luther, honey-glazed and sweet, crooned through the dim light—

No one could ever say to me,

And in that moment, in that warmth, in that certainty— nothing had ever been more authentic.

Molten, honey-glazed lips met peppermint-chili nostalgia—grown.

By the time Damien's hand found the limousine door seamlessly opening onto his master bedroom, the baton had passed. The attendant of the house stepped in where the driver left off.

Damien thinking:

To me, it's just a shame you're a lonely guy... But I feel better now.

Sheena peeled back Damien's Brooks Brothers collar. Then, his pants.

Sheena took him in.

Damn, she thought, *you've been fine since I bumped into you at Mays—*

but this? This is a man now. And he's mine if I'm brave enough to stay.

Candles flickered around the garden tub, light dancing over steam, water, heat.

And then—Maxwell.

Oooohhh...

I've never seen sunshine like this.

Her thigh tingled, warm and damp beneath his touch.

I never dug anyone like this.

His hands roamed, firm but reverent.

Damien, fully undressed, lifted Sheena into the water, her body arching into his.

Her panties fluttered to the marble floor, landing in a shallow puddle—an offering.

Damien exhaled, low. "Fortunate to have you," he murmured to himself.

He stiffened, noticing the soft-pruned black curls barely veiling a thin, puckered pink—

and just above it, the familiar whisper of ink.

Day.

That same tattoo—still there.

His eyes lingered.

Not out of shock.

But reverence.

It whispered into the mood:

I'm still here. And it's still yours.

It hit differently now—because he remembered the first time.

And now, back in that sacred place?
The altar of memory and meaning?

It smiled at him—slow, red, and knowing.

Her oiled fingers tugged his ear.
Her other hand jabbed him in the back, nails slipping down the small of his spine.

A bloom of jasmine and amber—warm, intoxicating—rose from her skin.

And Damien?

He indulged.

Sheena indulged.

Again.

Again.

Again.
A roasted marshmallow haze.
A loofah. A cloth. Peeling oil.
Cottony soft.
Bodies together. The water, at times, is a hurricane. At times, still as a tide on the beach.
A horseback ride.
Again- piggyback,
Then mission-then-bobbing-then-riding with her surfboard.
Cooing to herself-*Surfboard, surfboard, Damien, surfboard baby.*
Sheena's hips grinding on the wood, all of Damien's-good-good.
Laughter. Then talk. Not conversation—talk.

"Stop, please."

"Sheena".

"Day."

"She."

"Pull it, Day."

Sheena didn't whisper this time.

She looked him dead in the eyes, complete and present, her voice low but deliberate.

"Day..." she breathed, her lips grazing his cheek. "I want you to pull it."

A pause. Her fingers tightened around the back of his neck.

"Then I want you to kiss it."

He replied to her interdependence- her grown-his grown-their grown.

"Yeah, yeah- kiss it -yeah, baby, right there."

The air between them didn't move.

And neither did he—

Not until he understood.

Not until he heard her.

Not just the words.

But the permission. The invitation. The fire.Jasmine. Perfume. Candles flickered, casting shadows that swayed like dancers in the low light.

The IBest Red wine—Ingrid Best's legacy in a bottle—forced them to sip slower and breathe deeper. Tasting each other - black currant. Black cherry. Red rose tea. Jasmine. Peppercorn. Cumin. Clove- black excellence reserved for this communion.

She finally understood.

It wasn't just the way he held her after.

It was the way he moved.

The way he touched her—like a prayer.

Soft. Intentional. Present.

He stayed in the moment because what else could he give her,

except himself—fully.
His presence was his offering.
His presence was her peace.

It was how he'd permanently moved for her—since Mays.
Since they were young, in love, and still believed the world
could be kind.
Even then, he had shown up when his pockets were light but
his loyalty was heavy.

And now, with his fingers tracing the lines of her spine,
it hit her—deep, steady, and inevitable.

This man?

It was a message to her soul.
Someone you could trust.
Someone trustworthy.

Who didn't need lies—because he was who he said he was,
did what he said he would do,
and was where he said he was.
Had been where he said he had been.

He never had to say, "She's just a friend."
Because he wanted you to know all of his friends—
since you were his best friend.

No second-guessing. No side-stepping.
Just grown-man honesty.
That deep, God-kissed kind of love.
The kind that lets you exhale.
Because he hadn't just fought for her.
He had fought in ways she couldn't accept.

Had acted decisively in ways that scared her.

Had killed—or let a man be killed—in the name of love.

She had pushed him away for it.

And now?

She was pulling him closer.

Because she finally knew.

His decisiveness wasn't just in battle.

It wasn't just in war.

It was here. At this moment. In this love.

And she wanted it.

Her fingers curled into his skin, nails pressing into the small of his back. Her lips found his ear, breathless, surrendering.

"Decisive."

She whispered it this time, softer.

"Show me, baby. Again."

"Right there, yes, right there-please Day".

And Damien continued.

Because what else could he do but continue to walk into love?

The only time their bodies separated was when the Sunday sun insisted.

And as it stretched through the windows, warming their still-damp skin, they realized—

The sunrise had finally found them.

Together.

Forever.

Fortunate—because it was love.

Drunk in love, now sobered by the morning light—ready for business.

Ready for whatever came next.

Moment III: Business After Day's Light

Sheena stirred first. The ATL was kind and cool, blending well with the airconditioner's light hum.

That hazy, love-drunk moment still clung to her, the way heat lingers after a storm.

"I got the sweetest hangover... I don't want to get over."

The lyrics floated through her head, warm and syrupy, as she hovered over Damien, her breath ghosting over his skin. He was still asleep, his face at ease, peaceful in a way she rarely saw.

She inhaled deeply, letting her lips brush against his temple.

Then, without thinking, she whispered a prayer. Not for them—just for him.

"God, keep him. No matter what we face.Thank you for putting me here with Day-this Day"

Damien stirred, a slow grin creeping onto his lips.

"Oh, I'm decisive again now, huh?" he murmured, eyes still closed- reflecting on last night.

She smirked, voice teasing. "Always have been."

With one smooth motion, she grabbed the tie from his bathrobe, looped it around her neck in a mock-business fashion, and let the sheet drape over her shoulders like a blazer.

The contrast—brown skin glowing under white linen, a warrior waking from rest—made her look more like a doctor about to deliver a hard truth than the businesswoman she was about to become.

She perched on the bed, eyes sharp.

"Damien, can we?"

He yawned, stretching. "Can we what?"

"I mean it. It's time to get down to business."

She exhaled.

"I need your help."

Damien sat up, rubbing his hands down his face, still processing the weight of last night, of all the things he'd left unsaid.

"I know things are tough for you at work right now," Sheena started carefully.

He scoffed. "Do I even have a job?"

She frowned. "What?"

"This case, Sheena. They told me to stay away from it."

She blinked. "Who's they?"

"The GBI."

Her stomach dropped.

"Damien—"

"They investigated me. And let's say—" he sighed, "—my badge isn't exactly mine anymore."

Sheena's heart clenched. "Baby... I had no idea."

"I kept going anyway." His voice was low now. Heavy. "Between Rory and what I've seen—what I know—I couldn't let this go. The ATL needs me. These victims need me. And now, I—" he shook his head. "I don't wanna get into it, but my so-called boss is a maggot. A whole MAGA-maggot of a man. He arranged all this and made sure they took my badge. But even without it?" He exhaled. "I still gotta see this through."

Sheena nodded, biting her lip. "I'm so sorry, Day. But—" she inhaled, "—if you can't help me, I still need your advice."

His eyes softened. "What's going on?"

Sheena shifted, grounding herself.

"When I was at the conference," she started, "I met this deacon. He's part of a big church here."

Damien smirked. "We got a lot of those in The A."

"No, listen," she pressed. "This pastor? He's dangerous. The more I hear and observe, the more I realize he's stealing from the church and taking advantage of people. And I don't know, Damien—" she paused, voice tightening, "—it could be more than that. Sexual abuse. Fraud. But I know for a fact he's stealing money. I saw the receipts. Beth and I were there."

Damien's expression darkened. "What church?"

Sheena hesitated.

"You know that pastor on the billboard?" she said slowly. "The one we saw on the billboard the group BMF used to have coming down 175-85 South by University Avenue while headed to 166 towards East Point? Bishop Cain."

Damien's body went rigid.

His entire body.

He blinked. Once. Twice.

Then—

"Wait. Hold the fuck up. The billboard preacher?"

Sheena nodded, lips pressing into a thin line.

Damien sat forward, hands gripping his knees.

"Sheena… tell me you are not talking about Emmanuel Cain III."

"Oh my God. You can't make this shit up."

Sheena swallowed. "Yeah. Bishop Cain."

Damien exhaled. Hard. His whole chest expanded like he was trying to keep something caged inside.

Sheena's brows furrowed. "What? What does that mean to you?"

He ran his hands down his face again.

"Oh my God. Sheena—" he looked at her, eyes wide, mind racing—"You just put the fucking pieces together."

Sheena's breath caught. "Damien—what do you know?"

Her face froze—still, screen-active.

And then?

The world shifted.

"Sheena," Damien started, voice raw, "this kid I just found—he's tied to this."

Her stomach clenched. "What do you mean?"

"I mean, he escaped. The boy was almost one of Cain's victims."

Sheena sucked in a sharp breath. "Oh my God, Damien."

"I asked him who—who tried to come on to him. Who scared him? He didn't know the name but said he was a pastor."

His chest filled with air, and he paused. "Joseph teased Cain that he was going to out him as a gay pastor, and YD said Cain went straight off."

Sheena's whole body tensed.

"This makes sense." She clenched her fists. "It makes perfect sense."

Damien frowned. "How?"

Sheena's forensic psychology mind was already ten steps ahead.

"Closeted behavior leads to self-loathing," she murmured. "When a person refuses to own their identity—especially in an environment where their livelihood depends on it—it festers. It warps. It turns into violence. A criminal profile on someone like Cain?"

Damien's heart slammed against his ribs.

"Damn, Sheena. The kid I just found told me about the kid in the file I gave you—YD. I mean, I have to say his name now. Cain finished him off in that cheap Old National hotel."

Sheena sucked in a sharp breath. "Oh my God, Damien."

"Yeah—it gets deeper. Cain sent me a message."

Sheena stiffened. "A message? What in the world?"

"Yeah, when I interviewed YD, courtesy of Kent—my old junior partner who's now in the gang unit—YD was affiliated with a group whose name you do not need to know. I gave him my card to keep in touch if he needed anything. You don't know this, but I did what was right. I took my card out of YD's dead body's mouth."

Sheena gasped. "Your fucking card? I mean—Damien—no, really?"

"Yeah. But it was during the interview that I got the real information."

A knock at the door.

"Knock. Knock. Mr. DeBerg. Oye I will have you and Ms. Sheena's breakfast ready in dos momentos."

"Sure, but a little more time."

Damien looked at Sheena, his voice lower. "First, are you okay?"

"Please finish," she urged.

" Yeah, like I said. I asked YD, who tried to come on to him. Who scared him? He didn't know the name but said he was a pastor."

Sheena's whole body tensed.

"I saw it- I just didn't have the context to place the anger- the manipulation." She clenched her fists. "It makes perfect sense."

Damien frowned. "How?"

Sheena's forensic psychology mind was already ten steps ahead- now doing her and his second reason for her coming home from Chicago.

"He is the killer."

Damien's breath slowed.

Her analysis was so crisp, so flawless, that for a split second, all he could think was—

"My God. This woman is brilliant."

Sheena saw the way his chest rose. The way his jaw tensed.

"Oh, I'm wifey now?" she teased, eyes flickering with both challenge and amusement.

But then, her voice steadied.

"Day—Cain is dangerous. And like all trapped predators, he will be even more dangerous when confronted. You—we—have to proceed with caution."

Damien's voice dropped, low and firm.

"You been wifey." A pause. "But know this—hubby is built for this. Always have been." His jaw flexed, the weight of what was coming sitting heavy between them. "And just so we clear—I ain't apologizing again for doing what I have to do to keep us safe. Shit—all of the ATL safe."

Sheena exhaled, steadying herself.

How were they going to get Cain out of the closet—from behind the pulpit—out in the light?

Moment IV: Darkness Comes to Show Business

Later that night, at the site of Beth's concert.

ZZZZZooooooooommmmm—whoooooshiissssss—

The pink lights melted into the shimmer of a purple-sparkled dress, flashing across the stage like liquid fire.

The closed-captioned audience watching from their screens saw the bold message flare across the bottom:

"This a $$$lim Think Entertainment Sole Production.

Pirate this bitch at your own risk—just kidding.

Press 'Accept'—$49.00."

10,000 people in the ATL. Another 100,000 streaming nationwide.

The live chat on the pay-per-view was already flooded:

"Nigga, get your popcorn."

"Damn, Beat is sexy as fuck."

"She shouldn't be no rapper—she need to be a damn movie star."

"Wait... ain't she connected to the game?"

"Lotto and Monaleo standing right off stage—bout to watch Beat pop off."

The bass rumbled.

And just like that—Beat stepped into the light.

The bass boomed, the crowd erupted, and the mic was hers.

"I got the ATL pregnant—

I'm you niggas' dream.

I stay rap'n, I'm still saved—

Cuz it ain't all what this shit seems.

I'm beloved in the ATL—

you know my method, it can't fail.

My pee stay drippin'—I'm cat pimpin',

got big money in this world.

My Peachtree cat—look at that.My Peachtree cat P-cat you it's fat

It's Hartsfield Jackson, Jet fuel bitch I said, Hartfiedl Jackson, Jet fuel bitch Jet fuel bith! Jet fuel-yep jet fuel, take a lick Jet fuel."

BOOM. The lights cut—

Then, BLINK-BLINK-BLINK— strobes fired in sync with the 808s pounding through the speakers.

The crowd lost their minds.

Phones shot into the air flashes exploding like fireworks, the chat feeds damn near crashing from the speed of messages scrolling past.

"She talkin' crazy! "

"ATL STAND UP!"

"Yo, this Beat's best track yet—NIGGA, SHE SPITTIN'!"

"Wait... Peachtree cat?? "

"Slim about to have this shit trending."

Backstage, Lotto and Monaleo stood with their arms crossed, smirking, nodding along.

Beat owned the night.

But in the middle of the pulsing crowd, in the shadows of the flashing stage lights—Emanuel Cain watched.

And when he saw Beth?

He smiled.

And just like that—he made his move.

"Beat, this O.G. wanna holla at you."

Cain maneuvered through the crowd, a mix of elbows, liquor glasses, and camera flashes pressing around him. A few shoulders brushed against his Gucci leisure suit, but he held his position, finally planting himself in front of Beth.

His voice was smooth and familiar, making danger feel safe.

"This O.G. is certified—he got money, even if he ain't in the culture."

Beth squinted through the club haze, the flashing lights catching the sharp glint of his Rolex.

"Ms. Beat Colucci," Cain said, slow and deliberate. "I had to come and holla at you—your show was enjoyable."

Beth tilted her head, still catching her breath from the set. "Thank you—uh, ah?"

A bass drop rumbled through the speakers as Monaleo's verse snaked through the after-party air.

"Pulling cards, bitch, this ain't no Yu-Gi-Oh! (Yeah)."

The crowd pulsed around them, bodies moving in waves of heat and liquor, the sweat of 10,000 voices chanting her name still clinging to Beth's skin.

Cain leaned in slightly, his voice cutting through the noise.

"I—I am Bishop Cain. And I am a fan."

Beth's brow arched. "Cain? Bishop Cain?"

His smile widened. "You gave a nice offering to my church the other day."

"Oh, shit—it's you! My spiritual father!" Beth grinned, her energy shifting. "I just got saved at your church! Oh my God—literally—I so wanted to meet you. I should've come and seen you sooner."

Cain chuckled, deep and rich. "Oh no, no—I'm a rap fan. Been wanting to get a gospel rapper at my church." He nodded toward the stage. "I stay rappin', I'm still saved... Jet fuel, jet fuel..."

Beth threw her head back, laughing, her sound swallowed by the music. Her mouth moved without sound.

Cain touched her elbow lightly.

"Let's go somewhere we can hear."

Beth nodded, still giggling.

"I'm up for an after-party counseling session," he mused, his tone warm, coaxing. "Maybe some late-night food? I know you got your entourage—they can come too. I'm—no, the Lord—will provide."

His Rolex gleamed under the club lights, and the way he stood—confident, polished, smiling—he could have been an angel in the garden or a serpent among the trees.

A voice buzzed in Beth's ear.

"Beat—Slim say he can catch you later tonight. He just left for a promo party up by Cobb Galleria—HT prep'n some stuff. He says take the baby home. Don't be out late. He hit you."

Beth waved the message off. "Well, it seems like I've just been chosen."

Cain smirked. "Yep—only if you let me buy the Man of God this evening." His tone dipped, teasing, as he gestured toward the bar. "I can pop bottles for my paassstaaah."

The Bentley convertible slid into the night, the departure barely noticed by the hyped-up after-party crowd.

And just like that—the stage lights dimmed, and the streetlights flickering up Peachtree turned into a moving parade.

Beth Colucci. Atlanta's new hip-hop darling.

Emanuel Cain. Atlanta's most famous billboard pastor.

Side by side.

The further they got from the club, the darker the streets became.

The only question now was—

Where would they "pop bottles"?

Moment V: Pastor's Real Dark Business

Cain's mint-green convertible Bentley slid off Roswell Road onto a cobblestone street, the wheels humming a soft rhythm as the car glided past wrought-iron gates and gaslit lanterns.

The breeze rolled over Beth like a silk scarf, smoothing her out the way sweet Golden Jamaican Kush used to—back when ATL nights meant something soft, not sinister.

Pup-pup-pup-pup.

The subtle jolt of the cobblestones sent a ripple up her spine, making her sink deeper into the plush seat. Her head tilted back instinctively, curls cascading as she closed her eyes briefly—and smiled.

It felt like a dream.

A good one.

"Ms. Colucci," Cain said, his voice dipped in charm, "this can be your community. A place where your neighbors are... of your status."

Beth laughed so suddenly she snorted, her hand flying to her forehead as if to check herself. "Boy, stop!" she said, patting herself as her giggles stretched into a full-on laugh. "If the pastor thing doesn't work out, you might have a real future in real estate. No—scratch that, reality TV. Pastor Cain Sell the ALT."

She turned toward him with a wide grin. "You're handsome enough. You got that smooth tone. Let me do the soundtrack. We'll blow up—again."

Cain chuckled, glancing at her with a flash of perfectly timed humility. "Now you're just gassing me."

"And you're just driving me into a daydream," she said, her tone playful, open. Her posture loose now. Shoulders down. Legs tucked slightly toward him.

He pressed a button on the console, and just like that—

"Driftin' on a memory..."

The Isley Brothers bloomed through the car like incense.

"Ain't no place I'd rather be, than with you..."

Beth melted further into her seat, her fingers lightly tracing the seam of the leather door panel. "Oh, now you are showing off," she whispered. "This? This song right here? Yeah, I'm officially not mad at you."

Cain turned down the volume just a touch. "Thought you might appreciate it."

She nodded, still swaying gently, her eyes fluttering shut for a moment, caught between groove and memory. "My mama used to play this on Sundays, after church. When she was feeling good, this whole thing felt like her living room right now... candles lit, fried, whiting on the stove, phone off the hook. Damn."

She glanced over at him, her voice softer now. "You know exactly what you were doing, didn't you?"

Cain didn't answer. Just offered a smooth, knowing smile.

The stars above shimmered over the tree-lined street. The Bentley coasted effortlessly, the city behind them, the illusion in full bloom.

And Beth?

She wasn't watching the road.

She was floating.

Off-guard. Open.

Just the way he needed her to be.
"Well, Ms. Beat."
Beth smirked. "Oh no, pastor, you not about to keep me in the streets. I was gonna tell you before we left—" she exhaled, then looked over at him. "I know now that what I do is an act, a role I will continue to play. I am Beat, but I am Beth. I'm pregnant—about to be a mother and a wife."

Cain's eyebrows lifted slightly. "So, you're pregnant... not married?"

"That's right," she nodded firmly. "We've been together since we were teens. Built a successful entertainment company. We've done it all—except get married. And, yeah—I'm pregnant."

Cain turned the wheel with controlled ease, his gaze unreadable. "Is the child his?"

Beth let out a small laugh. "Oh, absolutely. He's the only person I've ever been with. I don't sleep around—that's probably the only good idea I got from my father."

The Isley Brothers lingered, their voices stretching through the silence.

Day will make way for night,
All we'll need is candlelight,

Cain hummed in acknowledgment. "Your father was a good man?"

Beth scoffed. "Funny you should ask. I used to think so— wanted to think so- so I could get what I wanted. But I know now... Steven Colucci was a bad man. A divisive man who hurt the one woman on this planet I love more than anyone else—my sister, Sheena."

Cain let out a slow chuckle. "Oh my... Dr. Sheena Colucci is your sister?" He shook his head. "My, my, my..."

Beth giggled. "You said my, my, my like you have been listening to Johnny Gill, preacher."

"I met her the other day," Cain said smoothly. "At the Concerned Black Clergy Crime Symposium. Excellent work she does."

Beth tilted her head, intrigued. "Well, that's how I got to your church. She came to do some research—an investigation, really— and I tagged along. That was a blessing from the Lord because, lo and behold—I was changed. That's why I gave the offering. I don't do church or believe in men, but I believe in that ministry."

Cain nodded, listening.

"You gave your power to Deacon," Beth continued, "and he gave it to me. So I gave back. And there's more where that came from. Speaking of that... this gospel rap group—what's your vision?"

Cain smiled, pulling the Bentley into a secluded driveway.

"This is my close-in-the-city hideaway. I have two homes in Atlanta—the one I live in with my family across from Rick Ross... and this one."

Beth blinked, glancing around. "Oh... I thought we were going to another club or a restaurant or something."

"No, my daughter," Cain said, his voice even. "Preachers go out into the limelight—but we need a quiet, not-lit place to commune. You're okay coming in, aren't you? We can talk about the work—the Lord's work." He reached for the door handle. "I have snacks, wine... or just cold water, whatever you like. I'll probably call a car for you when we're done. I'll get some rest and be up for the second service in the morning."

Beth hesitated for half a second.

Then, she nodded.

Inside, the recessed lights flickered out as Cain flipped a switch.

For the first time, Beth felt the shift.

They went back and forth, Cain pushing, Beth holding firm.

"Can you get your sister to—"

Beth's eyes narrowed, "I thought you said you didn't know my sister?"

Cain leaned back, crossing one leg over the other, his tone deliberate, every word carefully measured.

"Did you know," he began smoothly, "that my deacon, McClendon, is conspiring with your sister to have me investigated?"

Beth frowned.

"See, I'm dealing with the lie, pastor- can we talk about that?"

Cain continued, his voice calm, controlled. "Twelve thousand dollars, Beth. That's the number they're throwing around—saying I stole from the church. And McClendon? Lying through his teeth, claiming I've abused teenage boys in my congregation."

Beth's fingers flexed in her lap.

Cain pressed on. "Your sister wasn't doing 'research.' She's been participating in a gossiping rumor mill that threatens to harm my ministry—confuse the sheep. And you? You bailed them out. McClendon mismanaged the Master's Twelve fund, and instead of holding himself accountable, he blamed me."

Beth exhaled sharply.

Cain's voice softened, taking on that preacher's cadence—half fatherly, half manipulative. "But as my new spiritual daughter, you can help me. Could you help them? Tell Sheena to back down. Stay a sheep."

Beth tilted her head, looking him dead in the eyes. "I hear you… but that ain't happening."

Cain's jaw tensed.

Beth folded her arms. "You gonna find out about me real quick. I stay in my lane. If Sheena thinks something's off with you, then maybe. And I'm not getting involved."

Cain studied her, his expression unreadable.

Beth shrugged. "If you did it—do the time, pay it back, or whatever. That doesn't make you less of a spiritual leader, right?"

Cain's lips tightened. "So you're saying you won't talk to Sheena?"

Beth leaned back, arms crossed. "That's exactly what I'm saying. I don't do messy in church. I do messy with people who pay me for messy."

Cain exhaled through his nose, slow and deliberate. "That's… disappointing."

Then he leaned forward, voice lowered, words weighted.

"She could be in trouble, you know."

Beth's fingers curled into fists.

Cascade—the end closer to John A. White Park, not far from the Beauty Exchange, Clutch Bicycle Shop, and Mustard Seed BBQ—that end of Cascade folks on the other end pretended didn't exist once the sun went down—that part of Beth was rising now. Fully.

"With all due respect, sir," she said, voice steady but sharp, "you are way out of line. And be clear—I walk in love, but—"

Cain clapped his hands once.

The sudden sound cracked through the air like a shot. Beth jolted back.

Then, before she could even react—

He grabbed her arm.

Cain's mask cracked. His desperation—his unraveling—took control.

The first blow landed. Then another. Hard. Unrelenting.

Beth tensed, then crumpled—arms raised, trying to shield herself from the next strike. It came anyway.

Then—restraints.

The extension cord burned as it wrapped around her wrists.

Tighter. Then tighter again.

A cloth shoved over her mouth.

The sharp sting of chloroform invaded her lungs.

Beth's vision blurred, the world spinning, breath shallow. Her limbs grew heavy.

The last thing she saw before the darkness swallowed her whole—

Cain's eyes, wide and wild, inches from her face.

He whispered, barely audible:

"Quos deus vult perdere, prius dementat."

Those whom God wishes to destroy, He first makes mad.

His breathing steadied.

"This… wasn't supposed to happen like this," he muttered. "Goddamn hood rat. Just do as you're told."

And then—

Silence.

The spotlight was gone.

He looked down at Beth Colucci, unconscious at his feet.

Not even he had planned for this darkness.

He stood in it now.

Wrestling with what he'd done.

Realizing he couldn't let them pull him out into the light.

Not now.
Not ever.

Moment VI: Dark Business Out in the Light

If Saturday night had been hot, Sunday morning—already pressing into 11 o'clock—was a slow, rolling comfort. The air in the condo carried the scent of last night's candles, and the warmth of a summer morning in Atlanta cut through the blinds. Sheena woke up first, stretching and peering at Damien. She prayed for him, for them. A quiet celebration. She offered him some yum-yum, and just before they peeled out of bed—

Ring.

Damien groaned, reaching for his phone, but Sheena grabbed hers. Slim.

"Hey, Slim."

"Hey, Slim, what's up?" Damien added, voice heavy with sleep.

Slim's voice came through, clipped, buzzing with something off. "How was last night?"

"She killed it," Slim said. "Yo girl was off the chain." A pause. "But that's just it. She killed it so bad… she done got ghost."

Sheena sat up. "What you mean?"

"She must be with you."

"Nah."

"She at Cascade?"

"No."

"She at the condo?"

"No."

"Sheen, you back in Chicago?"

"I'm here with Damien."

Slim exhaled. "Oh, you there with Big Brother. What's up, Big Brother? I know you hear me, man." His laugh was forced. "Nigga, y'all layin' to death. Y'all didn't come?"

"I was gon' come," Sheena said, heartbeat picking up. "I told her I was. I was just about to text her, but..."

"But you didn't," Slim finished.

Silence.

"So she ain't with you?"

"No."

Slim's tone dropped. "That's a problem then. I don't know where my girl is... or my baby."

Sheena's stomach turned.

"She didn't come home?"

"Nah. I didn't come to my spot last night either, but I assumed—" Slim stopped. "I assumed she went home. You know how she is, Sheen. She grown, she got that expensive condo, she redid Cascade—"

"But she ain't there," Damien said, voice sharp now.

"Nah. And I don't know where she at."

Something cold slipped into Sheena's spine. "Where's her phone pinging?"

Slim exhaled hard. "Shit. Lemme check... She told me not to, but—" Silence. Then: "Her location's at Lenox Mall. But she ain't answering."

Sheena's hands curled into fists. "Try again."

Slim's voice clipped. "Lemme three-way her now."

The call rang. A voicemail clicked in.

"Yo fam, this is your girl, B. But if you are really fam and you got this number, Beth is good. What's up? Leave a message."

A beep.

Slim blew out a breath. "Yeah... yeah, nah. I gotta get off and find my baby."

Sheena and Damien sat in thick silence, the dial tone ringing in their ears.

"Sheena?" Damien's voice was careful.

She rubbed at her temple. "I don't know, Day. I don't know. One thing about Beth—she never just goes off. And I'll be real with you... in the middle of the night, while you were sleep, I woke up with a bad feeling about her."

Damien studied her.

Sheena swallowed. "I thought it was just guilt. Like, I should've gone to her show. But now..."

Damien shook his head. "Girl, your sister knows you're not shallow like that."

Sheena exhaled slow. "Yeah. I know."

Then Damien's phone rang.

Slim.

Damien put it on speaker. "What's up?"

Slim's voice was tight. "Nigga, I gotta be straight up with you. Y'all know I got artists still in the underground, real deep in this drill shit. That's how I get info. That's how I get down."

"Talk to me," Damien said.

Slim hesitated. Then: "One of my H.T. niggas saw Beth last night. She was in a mint green Bentley. With some nigga postin' up like he tryna be hip-hop. But..." A pause. "He knew the dude. The preacher."

Silence.

Sheena went cold.

Damien sat up. "What?"

"She left with him, nigga."

Slim's breathing was sharp, ragged. "Tell me you lyin'."

"Sheena," Damien said low. "Say something."

Sheena's hands tense. "That nigga foul."

Slim's voice was shaking. "I'm finna kill this nigga."

"Where you at?" Damien barked.

Slim's voice flattened. "I know his church."

Damien was already moving. "Say less."

Slim's voice crackled through the speaker. "Nigga, I'm popping body."

"No." Damien's voice sliced through the room. "You get here. Now. We move together."

Silence.

Then Slim: "Nigga, say less."

Before they could process it, the hum of Slim's engine filled the driveway.

Sheena was already grabbing her bag. Damien threw on his blazer, showing no hesitation—only the weight of his resolve.

They rolled out.

To the church.

To him.

It was sunny outside. Bright. Unforgiving. Almost mocking.

But inside the car, inside them, it was dark.

Heavy. Thick. Shadowed.

Slim gripped the wheel, his hands stone, his knuckles tight. Dark was the rage sitting in his chest.

Damien sat stiff beside him, his face unreadable, but Sheena knew better—dark was the storm behind his silence.

And Sheena? She clenched her fists in her lap, her breath coming sharp. Dark was the fear creeping up her spine, the knot in her stomach, the scream she swallowed.

Beth was missing.

The sun was shining.

But they carried night with them.

And the church—the place meant for light—was waiting.

So was he.

The Last Lead.

When Damien, Sheena, and Slim pulled up to the church, Slim agreed to stay in the car.

Luckily.

Because at 12 noon on a Sunday, the lot was still dotted with luxury rides—Bentleys, Benzes, the kind that said status and salvation went hand in hand. Slim's car blended right in.

Damien and Sheena stepped out, moving with purpose.

Inside, the sanctuary was still warm with leftover praise, the lingering hum of the choir barely fading.

As they stepped into the aisle, Deacon McClendon was already moving toward them, his posture stiff, his face set.

And just behind him, Deacon Cain followed, shaking his head.

Cain reached them first. "I'm glad y'all are here. He need to be—" He exhaled sharply. "Y'all men ain't got enough to arrest him. But as bad as he preached today? The lies he told? He should have been arrested for that alone."

McClendon scoffed. "Got up in the pulpit talking about how a preacher can do things and can't nobody touch him."

Sheena's stomach turned.

"He said he was untouchable."

McClendon's voice dropped lower. "And I'll make a direct quote—'There are certain things that you wouldn't want in your life to come out in the light.'"

Damien's jaw locked.

Out in the light.

McClendon nodded grimly. "And he the same way."

Deacon Cain spat. "He even had the nerve to twist scripture— 'He who is without sin, cast the first stone.'"

Sheena crossed her arms. "And the congregation bought it?"

Cain shook his head. "Worse. He made them part of it."

McClendon's voice was edged with disgust. "Poured rocks out of bags, right up in the pulpit. Told people to take one—said if they really believed in grace, they wouldn't throw it."

Damien exhaled slowly.

A show. A spectacle. A distraction.

McClendon sighed. "I had never seen such stuff. But y'all need more than a bad sermon to take him down."

Sheena met his gaze. "We're not here for his sermon."

McClendon studied her.

She let the words land.

"We're looking for them."

A silence stretched.

McClendon and Cain exchanged a glance—brief, knowing.

McClendon nodded. "Chastain."

Damien's pulse jumped.

McClendon's voice dropped lower. "The house he cools out in. That's where the rumors always start."

Sheena leaned in. "What rumors?"

The deacon's jaw clenched. "That he takes young boys there. From the congregation. Throws out Atlanta—muscle shirts and all."

The words hit like lead.

McClendon exhaled. "It's a rich community. But don't let that fool you. It's dark."

Damien nodded.

Sheena, barely breathing, nodded too.

McClendon held their gaze. "If you're looking for Beth... start there."

Then, quieter: "If you hear anything... start looking for his death there."

And then, even softer: "If I hear anything... you'll know."

The message was clear.

This was where it ended.

Damien turned on his heel. Sheena right beside him.

Time to move.

Out in the Light

Damien's car swerved to a stop.

Before the tires even settled, Sheena was out.

Behind them, Slim's car rocked hard, brakes slamming, metal groaning.

Damien, full police mode, threw a hand up, waving them back. His voice rang out, sharp, commanding, desperate.

"Beth—Pastor! It's Detective Damien DeBerg!"

The air was thick, buzzing—the kind of silence that comes before a storm.

Slim was already moving, gun drawn, charging the door.

"Slim!" Sheena called. "Let Day—"

But the door swung wide open.

And suddenly, Cain and Slim were face to face.

No words. No hesitation.

They hit the floor—hard.

An unorganized panic—recover, recover—panic.

Then—a gunshot.

Damien was still in the doorway when it rang out, the sound splitting the air like a crack in time.

And just like that—he wasn't here anymore. He flashed back to the first time they came to Beth's rescue years before in Sheena's bedroom after Sheena had gone off to school.

Moment VII: Important History Long in the Dark

They had been here before.

He and Slim.

Younger. Reckless. Fists swinging.

Steve Colucci.

The fight. The flames. The moment that changed everything.

Then: Sneaking In

Beth was already waiting when Damien and Slim climbed through the window.

The same window he'd kissed Sheena in once—before Steven Colucci had caught them.

Beth smirked, arms crossed. "Ooh, yeah. I'ma tell. Sneakin' in the house—Sheena gone. What y'all want?"

Slim brushed off his jeans. "We ain't the ones who called. You paged us like it was urgent."

Damien eyed her. "We were downtown."

Beth raised a brow. "Downtown? What y'all doing down there? That's a gay vibe."

Slim scoffed. "Throwing rocks."

Beth rolled her eyes. "Throwing rocks?"

Damien smirked. "Yeah, until some young cat from Morehouse stopped us. Rory."

Beth's expression shifted, unimpressed. "What's that mean to you?"

Slim sighed. "Man, what do you want, Beth?"

Beth's eyes gleamed with mischief. "I want y'all to take me to this party."

Damien shook his head. "Hell no. I'm not taking you to no party."

Beth leaned in, taunting. "I hope my friends don't come then. You better take me to my party."

The Breaking Point

Then—BOOM.

The bedroom door flew open, rattling against the wall.

Steven Colucci stood there, rage vibrating off his skin, his eyes locked on Damien.

"What the hell are you doing with my daughter?"

Beth froze.

"You got nothing to do with my damn daughter! The same thing you did to that other one—she's at Howard now, with her uppity ass!"

Beth bolted, slipping past him and running down the hall. Fear in her bones.

And then—the honk.

Outside, their friends pulled up. A horn splitting through the tension like a bell ringing for war.

Then Steven Colucci attacked.

The Fire

They crashed out of the bedroom.

Down the hall.

Into the foyer.

Slim and Damien weren't even trying to fight. They just wanted to get out.

But Steven wasn't letting them go.

Damien slipped, hitting the hardwood, the wind knocked out of him.

Steven lunged.

And Slim snapped.

Big brother down? Ain't nobody touching his big brother.

Slim swung hard—fist cracking against Steven's jaw.

A stumble. A crash. A candle tipping over.

More Fire.

Liquor bottles shattering, flames crawling fast.

The blaze swallowed the room before they could even process it.

They had to go.

They had to run.

Smoke. Flames. Screaming.

They were out the door before it was over.

Steven Colucci never made it out.

Slim took the hit. I did 10 months in Juvie, and months in Big Boy lock- gotta high school diploma, had much street respect, and learned how to work the rap hustle.

Moment VIII: Choose Light

Cain's hideaway mansion—where power had been perverted, truth manipulated, and pain passed off as prophecy—now echoed with reckoning.

Slim groaned in the corner, clutching his bleeding arm. The moment's chaos hung heavy, thick with smoke, sweat, and silence.

Cain dropped his weapon somewhere in the scuffle—or maybe the weapon dropped him. Either way, he was exposed now. Frantic. Flailing. A wolf without cover.

He had cast himself as a pure white lamb, cloaked in counterfeit innocence. But he was never beautiful enough in soul to be truly Black. Never righteous enough in deed to be truly right.

Not a lamb.

Not a shepherd.

A deceiver.

Wounded. Cornered. And ready to be unmasked.

Damien moved before his mind caught up—lurching forward, fists flying, heart thundering. It was no longer about the badge or the case. This was about everything that had been stolen. From Beth. From the city. From faith.

Cain grunted, buckled, then sagged.

But Damien stood tall. Breath heaving. Pulse pounding.

Ready to end it.

A weapon in his hand.

The weight of voices echoed in his head:

"You ain't no damn good." — *Steve Colucci.*

"Here's the baby you wanted." — *Tamika.*

"Surrender your badge. We need officers who follow— I'll put your Black ass in jail." — *Morgan Cantor.*

"Do your job! Save us from the Woke Mob!" — *A city filled with noise and hatred.*

One man. One weapon. One moment.

Damien stood over Cain, weapon raised, his knuckles white with decision.

Slim watched, silent. Bleeding. Waiting.

And then—

Sheena.

Her voice broke through the haze, soft and trembling—but steady like a drumbeat under the chaos.

"Damien," she said, stepping closer. "Please. Baby, please."

He didn't turn, but she knew he was listening.

"Atlanta needs you. *I* need you. We need you."

She swallowed, breath catching.

"I love you, Day. I love you."

The words landed like balm on a burn.

She kept going, heart full.

"Don't let him steal what we've built. Don't let him stain our story. Remember us. We made it, baby."

Her voice cracked, but her spirit didn't.

"We *are* BeLoved in the ATL. We always have been. And we always will be."

She reached for his hand.

"We got him. You did it. We're out in the light now."

And Damien?

He exhaled.

Long. Slow. Full.

He lowered the weapon.

Cain collapsed fully, defeated, exposed by something greater than fists or firepower—

The truth.

Damien turned to Sheena.

Eyes locked.

His breathing steadied.

He chose her.

He chose Atlanta.

He chose love.

He chose light.

And in that moment, Damien Kirkland DeBerg had two great loves—still:

Sheena Elise Colucci.

And the city that made them—the ATL.

They were:

Beloved in the ATL: Out in the Light.

EPILOGUE

Moment I: Beth Wakes Up in the Hospital

In this hospital room, Damien Kirkland DeBurg sat between two loves—one beside him, breathing, healing; the other just beyond these walls, the ATL, steady—for now.

But then, his phone buzzed.

A text .
Nigga. Really? You didn't take the shot—your only shot.
You not the folk no more. What you got to offer?
Nigga, yo opp for real. We gotta get at you.
HT / Lil G. No cap. Drill-drill.

Damien exhaled, his head rolling back, then down.
He glanced at the screen once more, then typed.
Shit, nigga. Then get at me.
You won't win.
He hit send, then dragged a hand down his face. This wasn't over. Not by a long shot.
Then—movement.
A shift in the bed beside him. A slight sound, barely audible, but enough to pull him back.
Beth.
Beth drifted into consciousness slowly, as if rising from deep

water. The weight of her body held her down—her head a leaden anchor, her limbs sluggish, uncooperative. Even the air pressing against her skin felt thick, suffocating.

Somewhere inside the haze, pain pulsed—a dull, relentless ache at the back of her skull, throbbing in time with her heartbeat. When she shifted, a sharper pain knifed through her ribs, ripping a soft groan from her lips.

Voices stirred around her. Low murmurs. A sniffle. Someone exhaled sharply, the sound fragile, hesitant.

Light bled through her closed eyelids—too bright, too intrusive. She forced them open, blinking hard against the sterile glow. The world swam before settling: white walls, the soft hum of machines, familiar faces hovering over her like ghosts.

Her throat burned, dry as dust, lips cracked like desert ground. She tried to speak, but the words rasped, barely a whisper.

"Did I…" A swallow, rough and painful. "Did I lose the baby?"

Silence.

The energy in the room shifted, tightened, her question sinking like a stone into deep, still water. Someone sucked in a breath—sharp, uneven.

Then, warmth. A familiar hand slid into hers, fingers wrapping around her own. A squeeze.

"No," Sheena said softly. "We still have our baby."

Relief flooded through Beth, even as pain pulsed through her skull. Slowly, she adjusted her gaze. Sheena stood beside her—eyes tired but steady. Slim was on the other side—his broad frame tense, his usual bravado stripped away.

The bullet had missed anything vital, but the wound carried its own kind of weight.

Her voice wavered. "Slim? That you… or Sheena?"

Slim chuckled, then winced. His hand twitched toward his

side, instinctively protective. The street cred would come, but the pain was real.

"Whew… yeah, Beth. It's both of us." His voice was rough, but his smirk tried to soften the moment.

Sheena brushed a hand across Beth's forehead. "We're here."

Beth squinted at Slim. There was something different in the way he held himself now.

"What—what's wrong with you, Slim?"

He hesitated, then shot a glance at Sheena.

Sheena's voice was firm, but gentle. "Later. Slim's fine. And so are you."

Beth tried to nod but thought better of it. Just then, a high-pitched squeal filled the room, followed by rapid footsteps.

"Oh my God, oh my God, oh my God!"

Beth frowned slightly, her foggy mind trying to place the voice. A younger girl bounced on her toes, practically vibrating with excitement.

"I am in the room with Beat!"

Beth arched an eyebrow—at least, she tried to. Her face felt stiff, sluggish. "You called me Beat?"

The Em grinned. "Yeah! That's who you are - right? You hot in the game."

Sheena chuckled. "She is a fan."

Beth smirked, a weak but genuine curve of her lips. Before she could respond, Rory scoffed from the corner of the room, arms crossed, unimpressed.

"Yeah, yeah," he said. "But let's be real—she ain't about to be no rapper."

Em's smile faltered like she had been called out and back into her alter ego, Emily. "Huh? Excuse you."

going to Spellman on scholarship. SAT scores already through the roof, and you still in the tenth grade."

The girl crossed her arms, "I'm a baller and a rapper."

Damien chuckled. "Yeah, well, I thought you were a baller."

"I am a baller! But I'm gonna be a rapper too."

Rory rolled his eyes. "Yeah, yeah—but you're still going to Spelman on scholarship. All that other stuff? Whatever."

Beth let out a weak chuckle, wincing slightly. Her gaze shifted to Rory. "Well, whatever she does-I hope you're a better attorney for her than you were for me—'cause you got me up here suing my own man."

Laughter erupted in the room. Even Slim, despite the pain meds wearing off, cracked a smile, rubbing his chin as he shook his head.

Rory threw up his hands. "Hey! You did get the bag, though."

Beth let out a breath, sinking deeper into the pillows. The laughter softened the edges of the moment, letting warmth seep into spaces where fear and pain had lived too long.

Sheena smirked. "Beth, I'll come back in a few days. We can stay at your condo or Cascade."

Beth shook her head. "We are not staying at Cascade. I want to sell it or rent it out—but I'm not doing this—us—there. We've had enough of that place."

Sheena opened her mouth to respond, but before she could, Damien placed a hand on Em's shoulder, rubbing it absentmindedly.

He hadn't been sure if Sheena was ever coming back. Not really.

But now, hearing her say it—to Beth, not to him—something settled in his chest. Maybe she was only coming back for her sister. Maybe that's all it was.

But maybe—just maybe—she was coming back for him, too.

Sheena nodded. "I agree. Us is better together—somewhere else."

Beth met her gaze, the unspoken understanding settling between them.

Sheena smiled. For the first time in a long time, she felt something close to peace.

But not everyone in the hospital was okay.

As the laughter faded, the weight of what had happened still lingered.

And down the hall, in another room, Emanuel Cain lay motionless.

Moment II: The Fall of Cain

The room smelled of antiseptic and stale air, the quiet punctuated only by the steady beeping of a heart monitor and the faint hum of the overhead lights. Emanuel Cain stirred, his body wrecked with pain, every breath a struggle. His swollen eyes barely opened, the world around him blurred by trauma and sedation.

Metal clinked against the hospital bed. A handcuff.

Cain turned his head slightly, wincing as fire shot through his jaw. He had been hit hard—repeatedly. The weight of his injuries pressed down on him, a reminder of how far he had fallen.

Through cracked lips, his voice rasped out, barely more than a whisper. "Nurse… come in here."

The words drained him, but they were all he could manage. He wasn't used to asking. He was used to commanding.

Footsteps approached. A woman, dressed in soft blue scrubs, entered. Her eyes were warm, the kind that had seen pain before, the kind that tried to soothe it.

Cain struggled to focus on her face but noticed the hesitation in her posture. She recognized him.

He still had believers.

"I demand answers." The metallic jingle of the cuff against the bedframe echoed in the small room. "Why do you have a God damned pastor in handcuffs?"

The nurse patted the cuffs, landing on his arm, smoothing the tension. "Sir… you were brought here from county jail -You were taken to processing, then transferred here under medical custody. And in county, you were attacked. Beaten. It was bad."

Cain let the words settle in the sterile air.

What she didn't know, what he didn't know, was that this wasn't random. H.T. had moved in silence. Maybe Slim, too.

Damien refused to pull the trigger.

So the streets had pulled it for him.

The word had gone out. The debts had been called in. And Cain had barely escaped being beaten to death in custody.

The nurse gently dabbed his swollen face with a towel, her touch careful but firm. Beneath the bruises and contusions, he was barely recognizable. To the world outside, he was just another broken man, stripped of power, his reign reduced to whispers and scars.

But she knew him. She had once thought highly of his ministry. She had believed in him.

"Sir," shaking her head, "A lot has happened to you."

Cain exhaled. "Yeah," he murmured, his cracked lips twisting into something almost resembling a smile. "A lot's happened to me. People trying to ruin me. Hurt me. Wanting me to be something I'm not. Getting mad—" He paused, a flicker of something unreadable in his eyes. "An eye for an eye… gonna be my answer."

His fingers twitched against the bedsheet, a faint tremor rippling through him. His voice had dropped to a whisper now, but something dark was in it. Something unbroken.

"I'm out in the light," he rasped, each syllable slow, deliberate. "But... Cain will rise again."

"Pray for me."

"I will, Pastor," the nurse said softly. "But you heal up and pray for me, too—because we all in the ATL need prayer."

Cain exhaled, a breath that barely stirred the air.

And then, in a whisper only he understood, he muttered the Latin phrase.

Beep. Frussssh. Beep. Frusssh.

A drowning whisper: "I will rise again."

A sharper gasp of breath.

"Quos deus vult perdere prius dementat."

The monitors screamed.

"Thank you for praying for me, Bishop—Bishop—Bishop— I need a cardiac emergency team, stat!"

"I will rise again."

"Mr. Cain—this is Dr. Marshall and Dr. Horvitz—can you hear me? Mr. Cain!"

The beeping turned frantic in the too-bright hospital room.

Down the hall, in another hospital room, Beth Colucci stirred.

The city paid no attention.

The light, indifferent, poured in through every window.

Moment III: Love and Leaving: Beloved in the ATL: The Departure

Damien Kirkland DeBurg pulled up to the curb, his Escalade sliding into place with the quiet authority of a man who never had to force anything. He glanced over his shoulder at the flow of traffic like a matador eyeing a charging bull. His body language said it all—Not now. Not today.

From the back seat, Em screeched, "Oh, I got something for y'all two old folks!"

Before either of them could react, her iPhone hijacked the Bluetooth. The opening chords of If You Leave by Musiq Soulchild and Mary J. Blige poured through the speakers.

And just like that, the mirror reflected Sheena and Damien—the She and the Day—framed in the harmonies of love, loss, and the possibility of something more.

"If you believe you'll do best without me
I'll let it go, girl, it's over...
But before we say goodbye,
Let's give it a try..."

Sheena, forever in Em's graces, played along to Mary's part, her voice sultry with a teasing smirk.

"I think you're so full of it, full of it
You just don't know when to let up, baby
I think you're so arrogant, arrogant
Do you think you're so much better, baby?"

She leaned into the moment, caught in the rhythm of the song and the energy between them—until Em cut her off, stretching the last line off-key for maximum dramatics.

"To focus on you and IiiiiiiiiiiiiiIIIIII!"

Sheena burst into laughter, shaking her head as she stepped out of the SUV. The rush of Hartsfield-Jackson Airport hit her—jet fuel and fresh coffee, the hum of rolling luggage, the controlled chaos of travelers on the move.

The rear door popped open. Em jumped out, still buzzing.

"Weeeeee can work it ouuuuutttttt!" she sang at the top of her lungs.

She clung to Sheena like a little sister who wasn't ready to say goodbye, like letting go would break the magic of the last few days.

Sheena pulled her close, warm and protective. Em inhaled deeply, imprinting the scent of her perfume—the rich, soft kind that would stay in her memory long after Sheena was gone.

Damien stepped up behind them, resting a firm but gentle hand on Em's back. "Alright, shorty, get back in the car."

His voice was steady, but something about it was different today—less guarded, more certain.

Em hesitated.

Sheena met her eyes and gave her a slight nod.

Reluctantly, Em climbed back into the SUV. The door shut with a quiet finality.

Damien didn't stop there. He walked Sheena inside, past the crowds, the security lines, the voices calling out destinations. He waited for her when she stopped at a small newsstand, flipping through a magazine and always waiting for her.

She turned back, and when their eyes met, he spoke before he could stop himself.

"The other day... you told me you loved me, Sheena."

She barely let him finish.

"I'm coming back, Damien."

He exhaled, slow. Steady. The weight of uncertainty lifting off his chest.

Then his eyes dropped to the magazine in her hands.

Not just any magazine.

A bridal magazine.

His heart kicked up in his chest.

Sheena smiled—that smile. The one that haunted him healed him, changed him. And then, with a confidence only she could pull off, she asked:

"Will you marry me?"

Damien blinked. Once. Twice.

"Damn, Sheena," he muttered, shaking his head with a slow grin. "That how they do it in Chicago? We in the A. I'm supposed to ask you."

She tilted her head, considering, then shrugged.

"I'm coming back, Damien. Because you don't have to tell me you love me. You love me. I know that."

And then she kissed him.

Soft. Slow. Final, yet full of promise.

"I love you, Damien-Day Deburg." Her voice was steady, full of knowing. "I'm always beloved with my Day."

She stepped back, her eyes locking onto his for a moment longer.

"And when I'm here in Atlanta, I'm always beloved in the ATL."

And just like that, she was gone.

But this time, Damien didn't call after her. This time, he believed her.

She was it—Beloved in the ATL.

This time, he knew she was coming back.

But there was a problem.

When she got back—to him, to them—to Us, She and Day—HT and Lil Gee would know he hadn't taken the shot.

And what was coming back at him, at them—at *Us*—in their ATL?

For now, though, Damien Kirkland DeBerg had two loves.

AFTERWORD

From Truth to Thriller: The Real Story Behind Beloved in the ATL
Told to Shaun Heckstall by Akeem, A neighbor
(This interview is transcribed as it was told to me. Akeem granted full permission for his story to be included in this book.)

Akeem: You ever hear about Teddy Smith?

Shaun: No, I don't think so.

Akeem: That's the thing—most people haven't. But he was one of the first. This was before Wayne Williams, before they even called it the Atlanta Child Murders. He was just... gone.

I knew him. We grew up together. We used to walk to the Jell-O Bean Skating Rink all the time. That was our spot. Just two kids, man. Ain't nobody worried about nothing back then. But one night, I was supposed to go with him, and my mama wouldn't let me.

I still don't know why. She didn't have no real reason—just a feeling.

Teddy told me, "Man, I'ma just go up there by myself." And I watched him walk off. That was the last time I saw him.

His sister came to my house later that night, looking for him. "Where's Teddy?" she asked me.

"I didn't go," I said. "He should be back in a minute."

But he never came back.

They found him a month later. Melvin Drive. Kimberly Road. Just left out there like... like he didn't matter.

And after that? Everything changed.

There was a curfew. The whole city felt different. Kids stopped playing outside. Parents stopped trusting the streets.

You ever had your whole childhood stolen from you? Because that's what it felt like.

One week after Teddy disappeared, another kid went missing. Then another. And another.

Then they put Wayne Williams' name on it. But see, I know somebody—somebody real close to him—and they say Wayne ain't do all that.

Some folks think it was the Klan. Some think it was the police. Me? I think they were working together.

And man, let me tell you something—how those cops started patrolling our neighborhood after that? They weren't looking for nobody to save. They were hunting.

Shaun- Brother Akeem, thank you for sharing your story.

FROM FACTS TO FICTION-THE AUTHOR'S END NOTES

Like Akeem, I , Shaun Heckstall was a kid when the Missing and Murdered cases were happening. I remember being driven to school by my mother or father listening to WAOK the prominate black AM radio station as Hal Lamer reported the lastest occurrence related to the case. I remember being all at once transfixed to the story and desiring the radio be turned off. I was the same age as those children going missing and with every announcement a part of my childhood went missing-lost forever. It altered me in such as way that my love for basketball was prematurely thawted. I remember it clear as day—my father told me I had to take the bus home by myself in the evenings, and I was scared.

I was a good football and basketball player, but I quit basketball because of the Atlanta Missing and Murdered Children cases.

Here's why: During football season, my dad could pick me up. But during basketball season? His work prohibited him from picking me up late. I lived in East Point, Georgia, but I went to St. Anthony's Catholic School in the West End of Atlanta. Playing basketball meant I couldn't take the after-school bus home—the P-82, the school bus that got me home safely. Instead, I'd have to walk from St. Anthony's about half a mile to the bus stop and then wait alone in the dark for nearly twenty minutes.

That's an eternity when you're eleven years old and convinced there's a monster hunting you.

I wasn't about to be the next name on that list.

Monsters, predators, and bullies in our communities can reshape a child's life in twisted, life-staining ways.

That kind of fear stays with you.

That fear shaped this book.

Atlanta is beautiful, but it has ghosts.

There are things that happen in this city that can rewrite your whole life story.

This book isn't just fiction—it's born out of that reality. The murders in Beloved in the ATL? They aren't just random crimes. They're echoes. They're history. They're Atlanta whispering, reminding us that it never forgets.

I thank you for reading this book, for feeling it. Because it's more than just a novel.

This is real.

And this is only the beginning.

More stories—born from the real Atlanta—are on the way.

So grab your wine. Get your popcorn. Call your girls. Call your guys.

Oh, the stories we have to journey through together.

Stay tuned—there's more to come.

Until next time—no matter where you are—endeavor to live in the spirit of

Beloved in the ATL.

ACKNOWLEDGMENTS

To Atlanta—for being more than a backdrop, but a heartbeat—I'm grateful for the rhythm you gave me.

To my brother Andre, whose pride and talent once won the Mays High Talent Show—you showed me what was possible on a stage.

To my sister-in-law Kim, a Mays graduate who lives its godly tenacity with every breath—and whose quiet strength has held Sharon and me through it all.

To Reverend Albert E. Love, my pastor, my forever friend—still reading me from the other side. I've been too busy to miss you, besides... I carry you inside. Every day I still hear you:

"Preacher, you going to a Black restaurant, doc?"

And finally—and never least—Mom and Dad.

Joe and Tina.

Who came down from New York City in the early '70s, locked out of the Black elite but carrying excellence in their bones.

That excellence propelled your children from poverty to wealth in half a generation.

You really are—though few may ever notice—some of the builders of the modern Black Mecca.

Keep going, Joe and Tina.

ABOUT THE AUTHOR

Shaun Damien Heckstall, Ph.D., is a writer, speaker, social justice theologian and creative force born in New York City and raised in East Point, Georgia—just outside Atlanta. With roots in both the sanctuary and the streets, Shaun weaves stories that reflect the beauty, struggle, and soul of Black life.

He credits his love for storytelling and culture to his time at The Lovett School—where, ironically, he laughs about failing every language arts class—and to Howard University, where he took just one drama course but never quite had the courage (back then) to chase his dream of a theater career.

Now, he's telling the stories he was born to write.

Shaun is known for blending truth, tension, romance, and spiritual depth into narratives that linger long after the last page. His debut novel, *Beloved in the ATL: Out in the Light*, is a romantic thriller rooted in identity, justice, faith, and home.

He writes to reveal what lives in both the shadows and the light—because both are real.

Follow his journey and future releases at www.beloved-atl.com.

COMING SOON

BeLoved in the ATL:
ATL Refugees

The saga continues...

www.ingramcontent.com/pod-product-compliance
Lightning Source LLC
Chambersburg PA
CBHW030348120726
47901CB00007B/1962